# GREAT

# GREAT

SARA BENINCASA

HARPER TEEN

An Imprint of HarperCollinsPublishers

HarperTeen is an imprint of HarperCollins Publishers.

Great

Library of Congress Cataloging-in-Publication Data
Benincasa, Sara.
    Great / Sara Benincasa. — First edition.
       pages   cm
    Summary: In this contemporary retelling of *The Great Gatsby*, seventeen-year-old Naomi Rye becomes entangled in the drama of a Hamptons social circle and a tragedy that shakes the summer community.
    ISBN 978-0-06-222269-5 (hardcover bdg.)
    [1. Wealth—Fiction.  2. Conduct of life—Fiction.  3. Celebrities—Fiction.
4. Fashion—Fiction.  5. Blogs—Fiction.  6. Lesbians—Fiction.
7. Hamptons (N.Y.)—Fiction.]  I. Fitzgerald, F. Scott (Francis Scott), 1896–1940.
Great Gatsby.  II. Title.
PZ7.B4339Gre  2014                        2013008047
[Fic]—dc23                                 CIP
                                              AC

Typography by Ellice M. Lee
14 15 16 17 18  LP/RRDH   10 9 8 7 6 5 4 3 2 1
❖
First Edition

FOR BRIAN GLENNON
of the Hunterdon Central Regional High School
English Department

His lessons inspired this book.
Also, he made high school way better.

# CHAPTER ONE

My dad, who did all the heavy lifting when it came to child rearing and was far better suited to the job than my mother, gave me some good wisdom after my first summer away in East Hampton. I was twelve, and my mother had her personal aesthetician and stylist, Jonathan, put some blond highlights in my mousy brown hair when he came to the house for her weekly appointment. When I flew back home to Chicago before school started, I brought my blond highlights with me. Dad stared at me like I was an alien when he opened the triple-locked apartment door to let me in. When I was unpacking in my tiny pink bedroom (this was before I painted it brown and covered it in vintage posters of Jeff Buckley and the Afghan Whigs and Liz Phair), he came into the room and gave me a little speech.

"That place at the beach with all your mother's fancy friends—it's another world. I'm not saying it's a bad one. It's just different. But whether you're in this world or that one, you still have to live with yourself. Remember that you can't be one person in one place and a totally different person in another place. Right is right and wrong is wrong, no matter where you are."

I wonder what he would've said if he'd met Jacinta Trimalchio.

What I remember the most about Jacinta is her eyes—those enormous green orbs flashing joy and pain and longing from that impossibly delicate face. They were always so full of hope—irrational, astonishing, sometimes even irritating hope. Hope that it would all work out, somehow, even when it was plain to see her dream messily slipping away like wet sand through a child's fingers. But to understand her, and what she hoped for, and what she got, and how she almost, *almost* managed to hang on to it, you've got to understand where it all happened.

East Hampton, that storied playground of the extremely rich, and those who work for them, is a town of traditions—whether those traditions are new or old, once something is declared "traditional," no variation can be tolerated. My mother *loves* traditions. And she's made a mint convincing women that she's the arbiter of all things domestic. My mother, the Queen of All Cupcakes, spends most of her waking hours figuring out how to conquer television, radio, publishing, and the Internet with her sugary signature confections. She convinced millions of America's mothers that they needed to make their own organic sprinkles from scratch, or risk a lifetime of scorn from better, more evolved female specimens. She started out as a cocktail waitress in Chicago, worked her way up to the kitchen, started her own catering business, acquired some celebrity clients, and *bang!*—she was off to a life of glitz and glamour and fondant in New York City, leaving my father and me behind in the Second City.

My dad didn't take it so hard because, as he told me the day Mom left, "She's not the person I married, anyway. I don't even know who she is now." Since he's a good guy, he added, "She does love you, you know. And you love her, too." But she never stops buzzing around long enough for me to get a good look at who she really is, so I can't decide if I love her or just feel like I ought to. She imprisons me in East Hampton each summer, because the court says she can and because I don't have any real reason to refuse, except that I really, really don't like her.

Anyway, traditions.

In East Hampton, houses should *always* be clad in cedar shingles—possibly the most boring building material available to modern man. Cars should have dark tinted windows to cloak the celebrities or (more likely) wannabes who sit inside. Bathing suits should be completely covered—preferably, by couture—on village streets. Children should be seen and not heard. And you never ever talk about money.

When I came back from the Hamptons after the summer I met Jacinta Trimalchio, Chicago felt like the biggest relief in the world. Watching the grid of lights unfurl before me as the plane drew down lower to O'Hare, I felt my whole body relax.

My shoulders dropped. And then I started to cry—real, gulping sobs, the kind my mother would never have approved of, the kind I don't think Jacinta Trimalchio ever let herself shed, even when she should have, especially when she should have. Even though we were pretty close to landing, a flight attendant came by and gave me a bunch of tissues.

"Here you go," she said, leaning down to my aisle seat. "It's going to be all right. It's almost over." She patted me on the shoulder and walked back to the galley. She was right. But she was wrong, too. I don't know if it's ever really going to be over. Not for me, anyway.

That my summer had been overrun by fakes and liars was no surprise. That's how fancy people stay fancy—not usually through outright lies, but through selective omission, partial revelation, and what they might, on the SATs maybe, call "delicate subterfuge." The Hamptons is full of fancy people who spend their days pretending, and their nights dreaming, that their pretense is real. But the biggest, fakest liar of them all, Jacinta Trimalchio, was also the best person among them.

She stands alone among everyone in my life as the only person who truly believed in the power of love to overcome everything—*everything*. That she was wrong in the end doesn't diminish in any way my respect for her. You could call her a lot of things—delusional, obsessed, a fraud—but you couldn't say Jacinta was without passion. She did everything bigger than everybody else, including falling in love—or whatever it was she fell into with Delilah Fairweather. Maybe it was an obsession.

Or maybe it was just an innocent hope, pure and true, that she could regain the life that had been stolen from her.

You might argue that she did herself in, that she deserved everything that came her way, ultimately, but I'd be willing to fight you on that point—physically, if necessary. I should've fought harder for Jacinta when I had the chance. But I didn't, and that's why I came home from Chicago like a raw-nosed girl crawls sickly and gratefully to her bed at 7:00 a.m. after a night-long coke and booze bender, wiping snot off her face and bile off a pair of lips she can't feel. And if you think I'm too young to know what that looks like, you've probably never been seventeen years old and spent a summer in the Estate Section in the Hamptons.

# CHAPTER TWO

That summer began differently from all other summers in East Hampton. Usually I take a coach flight from Chicago sometime in mid-June (Dad pays for it, because he doesn't want me to get a big head from flying around on Mom's first-class dime), and Mom sends a giant black SUV with tinted windows to pick me up at JFK Airport. (Because, you know, a five-foot-tall girl with two suitcases really requires a ginormous sports utility vehicle and a uniformed, obsequious driver to get out to the East End of Long Island.) Then he drives me the two hours out to the fancy house my mom bought when I was eleven, less than a year after she divorced my dad and moved to New York to open her own cupcake bakery and begin shooting her TV show, *Bake Like Anne Rye!* (You have to add the exclamation point at the end. It's part of the trademarked name. They can seriously, like, sue you or something if you don't.)

I got to the usual spot at JFK, and there was a driver

holding up a big embarrassing placard with NAOMI RYE written on it. For as much as my mother loves being the center of attention, I hate it with a huge passion. Even my dad, who is about the least show-offy guy you'll ever meet, is better in front of a crowd than I am—he teaches gym and coaches basketball at my high school, so he's always in front of lots of people. He's really good at it, too, and yet his yearly salary is equivalent to about two weeks' pay for my mom. I'm not even kidding—I did the numbers. I'm not supposed to know what they make, but Mom always has lawyers or assistants around talking facts and figures, and last year they published all the Chicago public high school basketball coaches' salaries in the *Tribune*. My dad's was near the bottom, although his win-loss record was almost the best in town. A bunch of parents got together and said he should get a raise, but the board wouldn't give him one. Some people probably think he gets a lot of money from my mom, but the truth is, he refuses to take any of it. The child support goes instead into a trust, which I can't touch until I'm thirty-five, or sooner if I get married, or unless the trustee agrees I can use it to pay for college. I think my dad hates that even more—whenever I cop an attitude, he says, "I'm not raising some trust-fund brat!" which kind of hurts, but I always forgive him. He only says it when he's really, really mad. He knows I'm going to use the money for college, anyway.

I said hello to the driver and followed him out to the car that was, as usual, some kind of armored tank. He lifted my bags as if they were peanuts, popped them into the back of the car, and held the door open for me, and soon we were off and rolling. Only this time, instead of heading out toward Long Island, he started driving toward Manhattan.

"Um," I said. "Um." I'm not good at public speaking, even when the "public" consists of only one stranger. My mom could do it with two hands tied behind her back, blindfolded, and probably gagged, to boot, but not me.

"Um," I tried again. "Isn't—I mean—we usually go the other way. To East Hampton. When we drive there. I don't mean you and me, because this is the first time I've met you. I just mean, you know, me and whoever is driving me. Which is usually someone I've never met before." I shut up then, because I'd come down with what my friend Skags calls "a case of the Nervous Naomi Babbles." Skags and I have been best friends since we were in kindergarten. She's this boyish lesbian (she says she rocks the "boi" look, but that spelling annoys me), and she looks like a ten-year-old kid. She's hilarious. My dad used to be kind of afraid that I was going to turn out gay, too, I think—he never said it, but I could tell. But he chilled out once he found me sobbing in my bedroom over yet another boy who didn't want me. He softened toward Skags even more when she yelled at him from the bleachers to run some specific offensive play I don't know the name of. I'm a coach's kid, but I can't tell you a damn thing about how the game is played. Maybe it was actually something about dribbling? I don't know.

The driver said, "Oh, miss, we're not going to the Hamptons. We're going to the Downtown Manhattan heliport."

"Why are we going there?" I asked, alarmed. Before he could answer, my cell phone rang. I checked the incoming number.

"Mom?" I nearly shouted into the phone. "Why am I going to the Downtown Manhattan heliport?"

"Hi, darling!" she trilled in the fake-happy voice she only uses when people she wants to impress are listening. Her vowels soften, her pronunciation becomes more clipped, and she sounds like she's trying to fake a posh English accent. If you could hear Skags do an impression of it, you'd die laughing. It is seriously dead-on.

"Isn't it a wonderful surprise, dear?" Mom continued, letting out a peal of fake laughter. "And I had absolutely nothing to do with it! You know Senator and Mrs. Fairweather—I'm sitting with Merilee right now at Baxley's—have their own helicopter. Well, Delilah happens to be taking it from town to East Hampton today, and Merilee was kind enough to suggest that you take the trip with her! Isn't that generous of her, darling?"

Okay, a few things: My mother had absolutely everything to do with me being offered a chance to catch a ride with a Republican senator's ridiculously beautiful (but, I'll admit, shockingly nice) fledgling model daughter. She'd been hammering away at Merilee Fairweather for years, trying to lock down something she could actually call a friendship, and it seemed she'd finally done it. The helicopter offer alone wasn't evidence that Mrs. Fairweather had succumbed to my mother's relentless hounding, but the "sitting with Merilee right now at Baxley's" was.

Baxley's Restaurant and Ocean Golf Club is this aggressively charming restaurant in a weather-beaten clapboard Victorian home right on its own private little stretch of beach in East Hampton, with a members-only golf course and palatial club next door. It's kind of an East Hampton institution, and the fact that my mother had wrangled herself a seat at the Fairweathers' reserved table was for her, I knew, a dream come true.

"Hey, Mom," I said halfheartedly, because I felt like I should acknowledge her victory, "it's really nice that you're having lunch with Mrs. Fairweather."

"I know," she whispered. "She just got up to use the bathroom. I am just—delighted is not even the word, Naomi. Between this and getting ready for the IPO . . ." You'd think a self-made millionaire Food Network host/cookbook author/cupcake bakery owner about to launch her own branded line of kitchen supplies and food products—not to mention a magazine—wouldn't need the approval of some anorexic socialite, but you don't know my mom. Being accepted by Merilee Fairweather was way more important to her than Bake Like Anne Rye!, Inc.'s initial public offering of stock, an upcoming event that she'd been trumpeting all over the cable news networks in recent days.

Skags, who loves sports and financial news like she's some old 1 percent-y rich dude instead of a middle-class teen with a lesbian faux-hawk, tried to explain to me what an IPO is when my mom texted me about it, but I didn't care enough to listen too closely. The gist is that an initial public offering means you think your company is so badass that you're willing to sell little tiny pieces of it off to the general public, and if the stock price goes up, everybody gets rich and happy.

"And," Mom added, "the senator is apparently considering buying some stock when we go public at the end of the summer!" She tried to maintain a whisper, but her voice kind of squeaked with joy at the end.

"So I guess I can't get out of this helicopter thing, can I?" I said, not in a mean way. I just sort of resigned myself to it at that point.

"Darling," Mom said, sounding surprised. "Why would you want to?" I heard a rustling in the background, and my mother saying to Merilee Fairweather, "Naomi is *so* excited! This will be her first trip in a helicopter. And you know she adores Delilah." That wasn't strictly true—I *adored* Skags. I don't know what the word was for how I regarded Delilah—admiration? Awe? We were definitely from different tribes that spoke different languages and had different customs, and I couldn't imagine us ever being close in the way that Skags and I were. What would we ever talk about? She could tell me about Fashion Week, and I could, like, explain how I'd gotten an A+ in Honors US History II after collaborating with Skags on a comic book version of the first chapter of Howard Zinn's *A People's History of the United States* (Skags did the pencils, I inked and colored, and we both worked on lettering).

In the background, I heard Mrs. Fairweather say, "Oh, well, Delilah thinks Naomi is just lovely." Even though I knew she was pulling that one out of her ass, I actually blushed a tiny bit. Different tribe or not, Delilah Fairweather was exactly the sort of person you want to think you're "just lovely"—not that I'd ever admit that to any of my friends back home, where we called the popular, beautiful girls the Beasts. Skags swore that one of the Beasts, Jenny Carpenter, was completely in love with her, but I was pretty sure that was a delusion.

"Mom," I said, "helicopters kind of freak me out a little." I did not add, "And so do you, and I wish I were back home drinking mint chocolate milk shakes with Skags and making fun of the Beasts and those giant summertime sunglasses that make them look like overgrown flies." I don't think she would've understood a single word I said.

She unleashed another laugh. "Oh, darling. The Fairweathers fly the same helicopter as the president! A Sikorsky—what's it called again, Merilee?" She rattled off model numbers and some facts and figures, which I ignored. Clearly, I was going to lose my copter V-card whether I wanted to or not. "Naomi, I really have to hang up—Merilee reminded me of the strict no-phones policy in the club, and people are starting to notice. I'll see you soon."

I got off the phone and stared out the window for the rest of the ride to the heliport. I was just clambering out of the huge SUV while the driver got my suitcases when I heard an unmistakable sweet voice (the kind of high-pitched but whispery girly tone Skags calls Marilyn Voice) call, "Naooooomi Ry-yyyyyyye!"

I looked up, and there was Delilah Fairweather, slowly walking off the tarmac to where I stood. She seemed to float above the ground like Glinda the Good Witch when she makes her appearance in Oz. I guess that would make me Dorothy, but I usually feel more like a Munchkin when I'm standing near Delilah Fairweather. For one thing, Delilah's around five foot ten in flats. She's also gorgeous, with perfect tanned skin and abnormally huge blue eyes. She has one of those cutesy Cupid's-bow mouths, and when she smiles, her teeth gleam bright enough to blind passersby. For real, she should hand out those Beast-approved giant sunglasses as a precautionary measure before she grins. And of course she's got long blond hair. Of *course*. And somehow—and I'm not saying they're fake—she ended up with a pair of D cups on that super-slim body. She is a walking, talking, living, sexy Barbie doll, if Barbie enjoyed skiing in Aspen, shopping in Paris, and smoking copious amounts of marijuana.

"Naooooomi Rye," Delilah said again in her breathy little-girl way, stretching out the syllables as if it were a novel experience for her tongue. She delicately stepped over to me on those impossibly long legs and bent down to give me the world's best-smelling hug, which immediately sent tingles up and down my spine as if Delilah were actually electric. Delilah always smelled like some combination of movie popcorn and cotton candy and caramel and other foods she has never allowed past her full, bee-stung lips. I'd known her since we were kids, and I'd never seen her eat more than a teensy portion of anything. Still, I found it impossible to hate her—she treated me kindly, for one thing, and for another, she had this way of training her eyes on you and making you feel like you were the only important person in her entire life. She always seemed to have one foot in this world and one foot in some other, rarified realm where magical elves twirl inside sparkling soap bubbles that float on the surface of an enchanted sea.

She lifted a handful of my hair and breathed into my ear, "Your hair looks *stunning* this summer." Her eyes met mine, and she shook her head in wonder. The compliment briefly made me feel as if I had won the lottery.

I have to give Delilah credit for never being mean to me, through all the years my mother tried to force me on her— and, what's more, for making a real effort to be welcoming and kind, in her own flighty way. When the adults had clam-bakes at Baxley's and the kids ran down to the ocean to play, Delilah complimented me on my bathing suit or made sure I had a pail in which to collect shells. When we got older (like, seventh grade) and my mother finagled invitations to various house parties, Delilah invited me to hang out with the other kids at the far edge of the property. I always followed her and her friends at a safe, respectful distance down to the pond or past the pool house or whatever, and she oversaw the passing of the joint or flask. On the frequent occasion that the kids tried to skip over me, she scolded them sweetly and made sure I got my chance. If I took a drag, it was always quick—I don't like pot, and anyway, I don't know how to inhale. I do better with booze, because it's hard to mess up an action as simple as swallowing liquid. Pot smoking, though—there's some kind of weird art I haven't figured out. Probably I never will.

Delilah introduced me to her companions as if I were her real friend and not just the daughter of her mother's ex-caterer. But she was much in demand and couldn't sit around and babysit me the entire night, of course. Consequently, it was up to me to fend for myself at these outings, which inevitably ended the same way. I'm not much of a conversationalist, which makes a handful of people back home (the Beasts included) think I'm a snob. I'd much prefer that reputation to the one most people ascribe to me: "Naomi Rye? Oh, she's such a good listener." *That* was what always ended up happening at these Hamptons parties: everyone else would get wasted while I'd stay sober, and before you knew it, one girl or another would corner me and start pouring out a sob story about how her boyfriend was off in the bushes, having sex with another girl, or how her parents didn't really love each other and everyone knew, or how her brother had tried to commit suicide but failed because the chauffeur had found him in the garage before he could finish hanging himself, or any one of the usual awful things that happen to very rich people. I didn't want to know this stuff, because proud people who confide in you in their weakest moments inevitably end up resenting you, but I managed to collect an arsenal of wealthy teenagers' tales. When those kids become governors and CEOs, which they will, I could make a fortune selling their darkest secrets off to gossip columnists. Of course, I would never actually do that (even though Skags says I should).

Looking past Delilah, I saw two handsome guys on the heliport, waiting for her. One I recognized as Delilah's long-time boyfriend, the ex–child actor Teddy Barrington. I could lie and say I didn't have a poster of him on my closet door when I was ten, but would you really believe me? *Every* girl I knew loved Teddy back then, when *Oh, Those Masons!* was the number one show on television. Even Skags was into him, before she realized she was way more into the girl who played his hot older sister. Not only had Teddy once fueled many a young girl's tween fantasies, he was also an heir to the Barrington Oil fortune. I'd gone with my mother when she catered his tenth, eleventh, and twelfth birthday parties, and they were the most insanely lavish events, each one featuring a private performance by Cirque du Soleil as well as appearances by all his famous costars and a bunch of his favorite sports heroes.

But *Oh, Those Masons!* was canceled when we were thirteen, and Teddy's family announced that he was retiring from acting to focus on his education. (There were rumors that he couldn't get hired for any other roles, but he was so adorable that you just knew those rumors were invented by jealous, mean people.) The over-the-top birthday parties continued each summer, but by then my mother was too busy taking over the world to cater, so I only saw him now and then at a clambake or a pool party—and he never remembered me. Now, six feet tall with light brown hair, broad shoulders, and one of those heroic square jaws, Teddy was the kind of thick-necked handsome that starts to get paunchy in college unless it is continually worked out by university-level athletic competition.

Delilah offered, "You remember Teddy Barrington, my boyfriend. He's a *foot*ball hero and legend of the small screen." Inexplicably, she broke into giggles, and Teddy rolled his eyes.

"Nice to meet you," he grunted, even though we'd been introduced at least once every summer for the previous several years. "Nellie, right?"

Delilah let out an exasperated sigh. "Naomi, you jerk!" she corrected him, hitting him in his meaty upper arm with her delicate little fist. She tried to do it again, but he caught her wrist in his hand and smiled devilishly, bending her arm toward her face as she squealed in protest.

"Why do you keep hitting yourself, Delilah?" he teased as he gently tapped her in the face with her own fist.

"Stop it, you ass!" she protested, laughing.

"No, seriously, why do you keep hitting yourself?" He pushed her fist into her face again, and she whacked his shoulder with her free hand. He caught that wrist, too, and soon he was making Delilah faux-punch herself with both arms.

It was sort of charming and sort of horrifying, but it didn't distract me from noticing that the handsome, dark-haired boy standing beside Teddy was studying me.

"Jeff Byron," he said, holding out a hand. I shook it, which seemed kind of weird and formal, but I liked the way his hand felt, warm and big.

"Naomi Rye," I said.

Jeff cocked a thumb at Delilah and Teddy, who were still play fighting. "This will last another five minutes, until she admits he's bigger and stronger than she is," he explained in a low voice.

"Never!" Delilah shrieked, trying to kick Teddy with the pointy little sandals on the ends of her perfectly sculpted legs. "I never lose, Jeffrey!"

Jeff sighed and shook his head. "We know, Delilah. We know."

"Jeffrey usually summers on the Vineyard," Delilah said by way of explanation. "But he goes to school with us at Trumbo and— Ouch, Teddy!" She whacked him with her tiny, shiny purse.

"So you don't usually *summer* in the Hamptons?" I said awkwardly as we watched the lovebirds fight. It was the first time I'd ever used *summer* as a verb. Only really rich people do that. My mother does it, and it drives me nuts.

Jeff rolled his eyes, not in a mean way. "Usually," he said. "My parents just got divorced, and my mom decided there was no way we were sharing the Vineyard house with my dad and his new girlfriend. So we're renting a place on Georgica Pond."

"I love that you're *renting*," Teddy piped in. "It makes me feel like you're from New Jersey."

"Teddy!" Delilah said. "I love you, but you are a snob with a capital S."

"You're damned right I am," he said, grinning, and began tickling her.

Jeff leaned down and whispered in my ear, "If you need to puke, I carry a bag for that purpose any time I'm with them. All you have to do is ask." I stifled a giggle while I enjoyed the warmth of his breath on my ear. I wasn't used to such a good-looking guy speaking to me at all, unless you counted Taylor Cryan (boyfriend of Queen Beast Jenny Carpenter) asking to cheat off me in science class.

"Hey!" a man from the tarmac called. "Miss Fairweather! Your mother called my cell—she wants us to get a move on!"

Teddy dropped Delilah's wrists, and she landed one good kick to his shin. He yowled, and she said, "Oh, don't be a wuss, Theodore." This set her off into another fit of giggles, which sounded like wind chimes tinkling in the breeze. It was like they were acting out a play for us—this "I love you/I hate you" thing. "If your mother's calling the pilot, we'd better get going," Jeff said. "Come along, children." He began walking slowly in the direction of the pilot, beckoning me to come with him. Uncertainly, I followed him, and Delilah and Teddy followed us.

"Ever been in a helicopter before, Naomi?" Jeff asked. I guess he noticed how big my eyes got when he led me to the Fairweathers' sleek helicopter. "N-no," I said. "Never really wanted to be in one, either."

"So why are you here?" he asked curiously.

"I honestly don't know," I said, which was easier and more polite than saying, "Because my mother is a huge suck-up, and she'd rather risk my life in this airborne death trap than miss a chance to bond with Merilee Fairweather."

The pilot helped all of us inside, and I realized that while the helicopter looked big and impressive, its interior was not nearly large enough for my comfort. We were going to be whirling around the sky in a box, essentially. Like Charlie in the glass elevator with Willy Wonka.

I was squished between Jeff and the happy couple, who commenced bickering over something as soon as the enormous door slammed shut. We buckled ourselves in, and the pilot passed out noise-canceling headphones.

"Do I really need these?" I asked Jeff. I hate feeling like my ears are clamped in.

"You'll have a much better time with them than without them," he said, chuckling. He reached over, and I flinched.

"It's okay," he said, and for some reason his voice actually made me relax a little. He put the headphones on me and adjusted them as I tried to stop blushing. It felt like a weirdly intimate gesture.

"Smooth, buddy," Teddy said, winking at Jeff. "That's your patented move—put on the lady's headphones for her. It's a panty-melter."

"Theodore," Delilah said, "that is disgusting." She took out a one-hitter and lit it, inhaling sharply. I wondered what her staunchly antidrug father, the Republican senator, would have to say about his darling dearest getting high on his helicopter.

"You know when I first heard that term, 'panty-melter'?" Teddy asked us. He looked at us all expectantly, and I felt obligated to shake my head.

"It was at a table read for *Oh, Those Masons!*," he began.

"Oh Lord," Delilah said. "Here we go." She pretended to fall asleep on Teddy's shoulder.

"Season two. I guess I was ten," Teddy continued, as if he hadn't heard her. "I interrupted Danielson"—this was a reference to Drake Danielson, who'd played his older brother and, unlike Teddy, had broken out of the child star mode and graduated to a successful film career—"after he read the line, 'Playing guitar is a surefire panty-melter.' I said, 'Drake, that doesn't make sense. Underpants can't melt.' And the whole table just busted up laughing." He gazed into the distance and smiled wistfully.

"Thank you, Teddy," Delilah said. "We are all happier for having heard that story."

And then it was time for takeoff, which was way smoother than I anticipated. I guess being super-rich really does buy a better everything, because soon we were in the air, with a gorgeous view of the city below. Everything was closer and bigger and brighter. It was so exciting that I forgot to be scared. The sun was on the verge of starting to set when we took off, and as we flew, the sky changed colors. Long Island was below us, first ugly and sprawling, then lush and green, with wide swaths of lawn between homes that seemed to grow bigger and splashier as we went farther east. And to both the north and south, you could see the open water—the words "Long Island" took on new meaning. I felt a poke in my side, and turned to see Jeff grinning at me and giving me a thumbs-up. He pointed to my face, and I realized with a start that I'd unconsciously been wearing a huge smile. I blushed again and instinctively put my hand over my mouth, which made him laugh, which made me blush harder.

I looked away and caught Delilah and Teddy exchanging a knowing glance, and then Delilah smiled right at me like she had a plan. I know it's stupid, but it made me feel kind of glowy and special.

And before I knew it, we were over the East Hampton Airport, which is basically a holding pen for famous people's private jets and other sky vehicles. I guess there's a private little airline that runs flights back and forth from different places, but it had never before occurred to me that some people never drive from the city to the sea, that they always arrive by air. As we gently swiveled west and descended and I caught a full view of the peachy-pink sunset, I finally understood why some people preferred to make their entrance from the sky.

# CHAPTER THREE

As soon as we landed, I saw our mothers—mine and Delilah's—waiting for us on the tarmac. They looked nearly identical, so it was anyone's guess which comely, middle-aged blonde had birthed the comely, teenage blonde. No stranger would've ever guessed the flat-chested, skinny little string bean with the dull brown hair was a product of the lovely lady in lavender.

My mother loves lavender. It's a trademark for her. She never appears on television or at a public function without something lavender, even if it's just a raw silk scarf draped around her perfectly toned, tanned shoulders, while the rest of her body luxuriates in a white silk shirtdress that shows off her beautiful ballerina legs. She danced professionally in Chicago for a few years but never broke out of the corps de ballet, so she quit. When my father met her, she was a cocktail waitress in a not-so-fancy restaurant. She still takes ballet classes (in a lavender leotard, natch), and my father says the reason Mom is so effortlessly elegant and graceful is "all those years of ballet. They taught her to sit up straight, walk like a princess, and never eat a goddamned thing, not even the stuff she bakes." And while it's true that my mother was unnaturally skinny by Chicago standards, where we eat a lot of bratwurst without shame, she fits right in with the rail-thin priestesses of New York high society.

"Darling!" Mom cried out in a voice so embarrassingly sweet I thought everyone else *had* to know it was bullshit. "You look so thin! God, to be seventeen again." She quickly looked at Merilee Fairweather for approval, and when Merilee laughed and nodded her agreement, my mother perked up even further. She rushed forward to envelop me in a Chanel No. 5–scented hug, and I patted her awkwardly on the back. My mom was wearing a silk scarf and silk dress, and she also had on these fancy, white open-toe high heels from Ferragamo (I only know this because she never shuts up about Ferragamo) and a string of pearls, and her fingernails and toenails were done in this kind of off-white champagney color.

I was dressed in maybe a *slightly* dissimilar fashion. I'd made a dress out of this old long black T-shirt with the lead singer of the Cure on the front, and I wore a black camisole underneath (no bra, I don't need one) because the T-shirt falls off one shoulder, and I cinched the whole thing around the waist with one of my dad's old black belts. My hair was up in a ponytail, and I wore a jet-black pair of vintage Doc Martens with slouchy black socks.

I realize from this description I sound like some weird Goth kid, but I'm not Goth in the least. I like the Cure, and the Docs are comfortable. But did I wear all that black because I was kind of hoping it'd freak my mother out a little? You're damn right I did. And it worked, too. I could tell she was a little embarrassed when she said, "Darling, you remember Mrs. Fairweather, of course. Merilee, I'm afraid it looks as though Naomi is going through a bit of a phase." I caught Jeff's eye then, and he looked as if he were about to crack up. I tried hard not to laugh as I greeted Mrs. Fairweather.

"I think you look lovely, Naomi," she said, looking me up and down with the kind of blankly cheerful expression that meant she either liked my outfit or was on benzos. "Very creative. You and your mother should come with Delilah and me to some of the Fashion Week shows this September."

Mom just about died at that one. "We are coming!" she said immediately, before Mrs. Fairweather even had a chance to shut her mouth. "Naomi, I don't care if you have school—I'm flying you out here, and we're going to go. Delilah, will you be walking in any shows again this year?" All I had heard about from my mother the previous summer was how Delilah was going to make her runway debut walking around in clothes designed by a close personal friend of her mother's. It was no one I'd ever heard of, but being around my mother for many years has forced me to learn a few things about fashion, if only through osmosis. Delilah looks like a skinny, gorgeous high school cheerleader, so I never imagined those high-fashion people could make her look bad. But my mother emailed me a link to photos of Delilah walking in that designer's show, and they had managed to make her look like a freaky ghost. Who puts white powder on a blond girl's eyebrows, anyway?

"Yeah, I'm gonna walk again this year," Delilah said politely, her hand intertwined with Teddy's. "In a couple of shows. Maybe three."

"And we just shot a mother/daughter feature that will be in the September issue of *Vogue*," Mrs. Fairweather said proudly. "It was about models and their mothers." My mother gasped with joy.

Teddy spoke for the first time, letting out a snort of laughter. "Yes," he said, putting one arm around Mrs. Fairweather and the other around Delilah. "She's walked in one runway show and done one Gap ad, and that makes her a big supermodel." Delilah poked him in the side and he jumped, laughing again.

"Oh, Teddy." Mrs. Fairweather sighed with an indulgent smile. "You always tease."

"We haven't really spoken since you were a little boy," my mother said, smiling at Teddy. "I'm Anne Rye. I catered a few of your birthday parties when you were small, darling." She widened her eyes and her smile. I was instantly repulsed. She was *flirting* with some teenage football douche. Ew.

"Of course I know who you are, Anne," Teddy said smoothly, reaching out to shake her hand. "I don't just want a handshake—I want an autograph!" They shook hands as Mom let out a happy squeak of laughter. Being completely obsessed with her career doesn't give my mom much time to date, so I'm sure pressing the flesh with Teddy Barrington was her thrill of the month.

"You're the famous actor," she purred. "I want an autograph, too!"

"Only if I get a chocolate cake," he teased. Ugh, I hate when guys work older women like that. It's so obvious to everyone else. It's embarrassing. Some guys do it at school with this one teacher, Mrs. Grey, and she always falls for it.

They all went on chattering among themselves, and at some point Jeff inserted himself into the conversation and was introduced to my mother, who thankfully didn't try to pull a Mrs. Robinson with him. I had enough issues with my mom without her trying to hook up with an underage hottie. (He *was* kind of hot, I had to admit.)

We got into Mrs. Fairweather's huge SUV, and Teddy insisted on getting behind the wheel, which I guess was standard operating procedure when he was around. I can just imagine what my mom would say if I had some boyfriend and he tried to pull that move. Anne Rye is not a woman who knows how to give up control.

"Baxley's for dinner? Or the Living Room?" Teddy asked casually, steering out of the airport parking lot.

"Well, yes to Baxley's," Mrs. Fairweather said. "You know what Senator Fairweather says about the Living Room."

"Well, lucky for us, he isn't here to have heard me suggest it! Or, really, anything else I might suggest later," Teddy said, winking at Mrs. Fairweather. My mother tittered. I looked at Jeff, who rolled his eyes back at me. Jesus, Teddy knew how to play women.

Delilah, meanwhile, seemed oblivious to the interplay between her mother and her boyfriend. She sat with her head against the window.

On the way to Baxley's, we drove past the creepy new version of the notorious billboard advertising Dr. Zazzle, New York's most famous plastic surgeon. It was the only billboard in town and was the source of some controversy—apparently, the local guardians of tradition felt it didn't fit with the community's "character." It showed a cartoon version of a smiling Dr. Zazzle standing beside a buxom blonde in a bikini. She was holding a sagging, gray pile of flesh—presumably, her own old skin. I saw it approaching and blanched.

"Ew!" I exclaimed, surprising myself and everyone else in the car with the first word I'd spoken since we started driving. "What the hell is *that*?"

"Naomi!" my mother said in the voice she uses when I've embarrassed her. "Where did that tone come from?"

"Mom, that billboard is even grosser than last summer's version. She's holding her skin."

"Well, it isn't her *real* skin, obviously."

"Hello? I know that? But it's a totally disturbing image."

"It is pretty weird," Jeff said mildly, and I knew for sure I liked him.

"I can name two people who've spent some time with Dr.

Zazzle," Teddy said playfully, looking at Mrs. Fairweather.

"Don't you start, Teddy!" Mrs. Fairweather nearly squealed. "You are *bad*."

"One of them," Teddy said meaningfully, glancing in the rearview mirror at Delilah, "really *nose* a lot about him. She really *nose* what it's like to go into his office one way and come out another."

"Teddy," Delilah said without taking her gaze from the window, "I will beat you." He erupted into laughter, even though she didn't sound like she was kidding.

"See, Naomi," my mother said. "I told you blondes can be tough."

"You never told me that, Mom," I said wearily, closing my eyes.

"I did, dear. You just don't remember." Her voice had a tiny edge.

"Okay. I don't remember." *Die die die die die.*

"I'm always trying to get Naomi to go blond," Mom said. "You should've seen her when she was twelve, and Jonathan Astoriano did her highlights. She looked *so* much better."

"Did you?" Jeff asked in an urgent tone of voice, grabbing my arm. "Did you *really*? Tell me the truth, Naomi!"

"I really did," I said dramatically. "I really, really did." We both laughed, and my mother looked at us in confusion, not sure what the joke was. Jeff's hand was gone, but I had liked the warmth and the pressure of his touch.

Before long, we pulled up to Baxley's. Teddy flipped the keys to a valet he greeted by name, and we all filed into the restaurant.

Teddy marched a bit ahead of us, and when he approached the thirtysomething hostess, he asked her a question in a low voice the rest of us couldn't hear.

"Folding napkins," the hostess responded loudly, and Teddy winced.

"Folding napkins what?" Delilah asked sharply, her seemingly permanent languid attitude momentarily gone.

"They were just folding napkins at our table, and now it's ready for us!" Teddy answered without missing a beat.

Delilah nodded coolly.

On the way to the table, we passed the bar, behind which stood a good-looking Italian kid. He had what they call a Roman nose, and it stood out from his face like a giant sail.

"Giovanni!" Teddy said, reaching out for a fist bump. Giovanni obliged and grinned. He wore the regulation Baxley's white button-down shirt and tie, but he seemed as if he were wearing a costume. I got the feeling this was a guy more accustomed to sleeveless cotton T-shirts and spotless sneakers.

"Best bartender on the island, this guy," Teddy said with hearty enthusiasm. Giovanni smiled and replied, "Naw, man, just doing my job. Go have a nice dinner."

"You know, we've got a great deal to celebrate," Mrs. Fairweather said once we were all seated. "The *Vogue* photo shoot this past week; Teddy, Delilah, and Jeff finishing up their junior year at Trumbo; Naomi visiting; and of course, the good news from Bake Like Anne Rye!, Inc." Mom blushed with happiness and was momentarily at a loss for words.

"Yes, Mrs. Rye," Teddy said. "I follow the financial news pretty closely to keep an eye on our stock price, and I've heard so many reports recently that you're basically taking over the world."

"Our stock price" meant the price of Barrington Oil, Teddy's family's little global multinational mega-corporation.

"You may all call me Anne," she said. "I haven't been a 'Mrs.' in years, and I only kept the Rye so that Naomi and I would have the same last name."

"Although you can still change it back to Gryzkowski," I offered dryly. My mother looked fleetingly as if she wouldn't mind if the Hellmouth were to open beneath me and swallow me whole. I smiled sweetly.

"Well, Anne," said Teddy, "tell us about what's happening with the business."

Mom launched into a recitation of all the exciting things happening in her sugar-and-cinnamon-sprinkled world: an end-of-summer celebrity photo shoot for *Bake Like Anne Rye!* magazine's inaugural issue; planning the next season of her award-winning Food Network TV show; being a guest judge on a very special dessert episode of *Top Chef.*

"And of course," she added, "launching our very own line of branded food products. Cake mixes, baking tools, and my favorite, *Bake Like Anne Rye!* Secret Recipe Perfect Frosting."

"What's in this 'secret recipe'? What exactly makes your frosting so irresistible?" Teddy asked, wiggling an eyebrow and leaning forward.

"Oh, Teddy!" Mrs. Fairweather giggled. "You make me glad I never had sons! I couldn't have handled it!"

"Well, you might have to handle it, if this one plays her cards right," Teddy said, putting his arm around Delilah. She seemed entranced by her napkin and gave no sign of affection in return.

"You're too young to talk about getting married," my mother chided him.

"We Barringtons marry young and mate for life," he said, and Mrs. Fairweather smiled adoringly.

"Yes, he did actually just say that," Jeff whispered in my ear. I gave him a look that expressed everything I wanted to say but couldn't, and he nodded in agreement.

Our waitress approached the table. She had dyed blond hair pulled into a high ponytail. Her skin was tan in that orange way, and her French manicure was studded with tiny rhinestones. She was prettyish, with a big chest and a perfect body. Skags, who is more judgmental than I am when it comes to women's looks, would've said she had a major case of butter face. (Everything is pretty . . . but her face.)

"Hi," she said, clasping her hands in front of her ample chest. "I'm Misti, and I'll be your server tonight." Her Long Island accent was pretty thick, and I thought I saw Jeff's mouth twitch at the way she pronounced "SIR-vah."

"Hello, Misti," Mrs. Fairweather said with a warm smile.

"Hi, Misti," said my mother.

"Misti," Delilah piped up. "Is that with a 'y'?"

"I'm sure it doesn't matter," Teddy said heartily. "Let's order!"

Delilah looked at him, and there was a steeliness in her gaze that I'd never seen before. He seemed to shrink into himself.

"It's an 'i,'" Misti said nervously, twisting her hands together.

"Of course it is," Delilah said, smiling very slowly.

"That's lovely," Mrs. Fairweather said with the same expression she'd worn when assessing my clothing.

"Anyone in the mood for some drinks?" Misti asked quickly.

"God, yes," said Teddy.

"Now, Theodore," Mrs. Fairweather said mock-sternly, "you know that I cannot in good conscience allow you to order a drink."

"I'm more interested in your bad conscience," he said, winking.

I looked at Jeff. He mouthed, *I know.*

We ordered drinks (wine for the mothers, soda for us), and my mother demonstrated some actual social niceties by drawing Jeff into the conversation. I learned that he was on Trumbo Academy's golf team and was, according to Teddy, good enough to make Stanford's team.

"That's where Tiger Woods played, Naomi," Teddy said, addressing me directly for the first time since we'd been introduced.

"Ah," I said. "Well."

I learned that Teddy was on Manhattan's only private school football team and would be the captain heading into his senior year, just as Jeff would be the captain of the golf team.

"What about you, Naomi?" Mrs. Fairweather asked. "What do you like to do at school?"

"Naomi gets straight A's," my mother interjected with what I think was pride, or maybe she'd already had too much wine. ("Your mother's always been a lightweight," my dad would say. "I mean that literally, and with the booze.")

"Whoa," Jeff said. "You're, like, a genius." I looked for sarcasm in his expression and couldn't find any.

"Seriously," he continued. "I'm good for A's in English and humanities, but you get A's in math and science and everything else? Pretty impressive, Naomi." I liked the way he said my name.

"It is *very* impressive," Mrs. Fairweather agreed. "Do you play any sports, do any clubs?"

"I'm in the LGBT-Straight Alliance," I said. It was true. Skags made me join because she said if I didn't, it meant I was homophobic. And, anyway, she needed my vote for president. It ended up that no one else ran against her, so she automatically won. But I'm still glad I joined. It's like the only fun club at our school.

"And what is that?" Mrs. Fairweather asked. My mother looked less than delighted.

"It's the lesbian-gay-bisexual-transgender-straight alliance," I said. "We march in the Gay Pride Parade every year in Boystown, and we make 'It Gets Better' videos and stuff."

"How nice," Mrs. Fairweather said dryly.

When we ordered appetizers and our entrées, Delilah made

Teddy order for her, whispering into his ear. It creeped me out only slightly more than his flirting with her mother did.

Misti brought out our food, carefully balancing the plates of lobster and sautéed scallops and fried oysters and popcorn shrimp and, for the mothers and Delilah, three undressed arugula salads.

"You all get started without me," Teddy said abruptly, rising from the table. Delilah didn't look up from the arugula she was halfheartedly pushing around her plate.

"Guess I drank that soda a little too fast," he added offhandedly, and headed in the direction of the bathroom.

Suddenly all I could think about was all the bottles of water I'd drunk on the plane, and on the SUV ride to the Downtown Manhattan heliport, plus a Coke at Baxley's, and how it was all kind of straining my bladder. I tried to sit still and listen to Mrs. Fairweather talk about Senator Fairweather's diplomatic trip to Canada, but I honestly couldn't concentrate. My mother had drilled into me at a young age that it's customary for only one guest to excuse him or herself to the bathroom at a time, "because more than one guest missing interrupts the flow of conversation." I knew that rule as well as I knew her other etiquette lessons, like the one about leaving your napkin folded on your chair when you went to the bathroom, and of course, the classic no-elbows-on-the-table rule. But my need to pee was rapidly approaching emergency status, and there was no sign of Teddy returning.

"I'm sorry," I blurted out finally in the middle of Mrs.

Fairweather's criticism of the Canadian health-care system. "I just—uh, I really need to excuse myself for a minute."

My mother waved me away dismissively, never breaking eye contact with Mrs. Fairweather. Relieved, I got up from the table and fairly dashed to the ladies' room. I inherited my tiny bladder and my tiny boobs from my mom—although she got the latter surgically enhanced the first time her catering business turned a profit.

Here's another thing I got from my mom: a terrible sense of direction. It's the only thing that explains why I took a left out of the bathroom instead of a right. Baxley's is in a big old Victorian house, so it's got some twists and turns to it. Anyway, I took a wrong turn out of the bathroom and ended up in the wrong dining room, so I just kept going and ended up in the wrong corridor, which concluded with the wrong glass door, which looked out at the back of the restaurant, and with my luck it was the exact wrong moment because there was Teddy Barrington shoving Misti hard against the wall. She staggered a little.

And I swear to God, at the exact freaking second I realized what was going on, Misti-with-an-i looked up and locked eyes with me. I immediately spun around and started walking away, but I heard the door crash open behind me and felt a big paw on my shoulder. I jumped and spun around to look at Teddy. He looked panicked, but he seemed to relax when he saw how afraid I was of him.

"I'm not—I didn't—" I tried to get the words out. "I didn't

mean to spy. I just got lost coming back from the bathroom." I saw Misti the waitress behind him, looking terrified. Half her face was a little red.

"It's okay," Teddy said soothingly, putting his other hand on my other shoulder. He turned his head to Misti. "Why don't you get back to work." It wasn't a suggestion. It was an order. Misti obediently scurried past us, shooting me a nervous glance.

I was trapped.

"I'm sorry you had to see that," Teddy said, frowning. "The last thing I want to do is put you in an uncomfortable position."

I didn't know what to say, so I kept my mouth shut. This seemed to please him.

"Look, Naomi," Teddy said, staring so deeply into my eyes I felt really exposed and uncomfortable. "Delilah and I are going through a rough patch. We've talked about being in an open relationship, and I think that's really what she wants. But it isn't official yet, and Misti's upset because, well, she wants to be with me. But Delilah tends to get depressed, and I really think it would be unhealthy for her to hear about this. It could really cause some serious problems for her. With her health. Do you know what I mean?"

I just wanted to get the hell out of there, so I nodded vigorously and said, "I won't say anything. It's none of my business."

"No, it really isn't," Teddy agreed. Then he flashed his big white smile at me and patted me on the head. "You remind me of my sister," he said.

"Oh." I wasn't sure how I was supposed to respond to that.

"She's dead," he said.

"Oh." I *really* wasn't sure how I was supposed to respond to that. "I'm . . . I'm so sorry."

"Yeah, it's really sad, but it was a long time ago," he replied. "Thanks for understanding about this whole thing, Naomi. How 'bout I head back to the table first, and you wait a minute and then follow?" I was about to protest that I didn't know the way back to the table, but he was already gone. I waited the Teddy-prescribed minute and then found a busboy who pointed me in the right direction.

I sank down at the table between Jeff and my mother. Teddy, who had his arm around Delilah, was too busy teasing Mrs. Fairweather to look up. Delilah was actually giggling, as was my mother.

"What happened?" Jeff asked quietly. "You look really pale."

"I am really pale," I said.

"Yeah, but something freaked you out."

"How do you know? We just met two hours ago."

"I can tell." He lowered his voice even further. "Let me guess—it had something to do with Teddy being gone so long."

I sipped my water quickly.

"You saw him with her, right?"

I almost spit my water out, like they do in movies.

"Shh!" I hissed, glancing nervously at the other part of the table. "They'll hear you."

"No, they won't," Jeff said. "Giovanni always puts rum in Delilah's and Teddy's Cokes, so they're a little drunk. Your mom and Delilah's mom are each on their third glass of wine, so they're *definitely* drunk. No one is paying any attention to us. And besides, I know about the whole thing, anyway. Teddy's my best friend. Everybody in town knows, too. If Delilah doesn't know, she's an idiot."

"If he's your best friend, then why are you talking to me about this?"

"Because it's interesting. It's an interesting turn of events, to have you drawn into it. This changes the game a little bit. It'll require a slightly altered strategy on his part."

"Do you always talk about people's lives as if you're talking about a round of golf?"

"Usually," he replied.

"Great," I said.

"Misti's dating the bartender," he said. "He's twenty-one. She's, like, nineteen. They're from up-island. Babylon, I think. Italian, if you couldn't tell. Their families own a bakery together. Immigrants. The American dream." He chuckled to himself. I purposely turned away from him and pretended I was interested in Mrs. Fairweather's conversation.

"You know they love Delilah on the blogs," she was saying to my mother.

"On *all* the blogs?" Teddy asked innocently.

"What's that one that writes about you—the one that called you the next big modeling sensation, the return of the super-model?" Mrs. Fairweather asked Delilah, ignoring Teddy.

"*The Wanted*," Delilah said, and even looked a little proud.

"That's it," Mrs. Fairweather said. "*The Wanted*. All the kids are just in love with it. Of course, it's all about *them*, so why wouldn't they be?" She laughed lightly.

"I've never heard of it," I said. "Is it like *Perez Hilton*, or something?"

"Sort of," Delilah said. "It's mostly a fashion and style blog, but it's about people who go to independent schools in Manhattan." It's so funny how rich people have invented a less hoity-toity term for "private schools." As if we normals don't know it's the same thing.

"But she does bigger stories, too," Delilah continued. "She covers Fashion Week in New York, plus social events the rest of the year—parties and stuff like that. Sometimes she writes about models. I guess she thinks I'm good." You could tell Delilah was underplaying it, because even she couldn't hide that she was kind of excited by the attention.

"All the girls at Trumbo are obsessed with *The Wanted*," Jeff said. "If they get mentioned on it, it's like they won an Academy Award."

"The girl who runs it will grab photos from Trumbo parties off Facebook and analyze what everyone's wearing," Teddy added. "It's probably not even run by a chick. It's probably some thirty-year-old dude in his mom's basement." He and Jeff snickered.

Delilah ignored them and looked at me. "It's a really pretty site. And the girl who runs it goes by Jacinta, even though no one knows if that's her real name. She takes a photo of what she's wearing each day, but you only ever see her from the neck down. She could be anybody."

"It's me!" Teddy announced. "I'm Jacinta!"

"Oh, you are *so* not Jacinta," Delilah said. "Jacinta has perfect taste."

As if on cue, Misti showed up for the mothers and Teddy to sign their account cards. She murmured, "Thank you." I saw her hand shake a little as she took away the cards. Our eyes met for a moment, and she flicked hers away.

"She's going to have to be more subtle than that," Jeff whispered.

In the car on the way home, Teddy drove faster than was absolutely necessary.

"Teddy!" Mrs. Fairweather said, giggling. "Slow *down*."

But he didn't, and we ended up at my mother's house rather quickly. Her house is lovely and expensive, but it's no mansion— "just" five bedrooms, and only three bathrooms (the shame of two bedrooms that aren't en suite!), a finished basement with a game room and home theater, a living room, dining room, big kitchen, and a spacious back deck. It has a nice view of the narrow, northern end of Georgica Pond, which laps the edge of the property. It's not the fancier, Steven Spielberg-y end of Georgica—it's nearer the highway, and the public landing where clammers and fishermen are allowed to enter, but you can make out the back of the Fairweathers' house across the water. The property is still considered desirable, though not as desirable as beachfront real estate—but, as Mom never tires of pointing out, some people even prefer the pond as more private and less touristy than the beach.

"Our humble abode," my mother said wryly when Teddy screeched to a halt at the bluestone driveway.

Mrs. Fairweather said, "I have always thought your cottage is darling. I remember when the Timothy Stanford family owned it, and they always had the loveliest eggnog and caroling at Christmastime."

"Well," Mom said darkly, "I'd like to make some improvements, but I won't have anything more done to it until I can find the perfect restoration experts to maintain the integrity of the original layout." Mrs. Fairweather nodded approvingly.

"Weren't you talking about putting in a pool with a water-slide in the spring?" I piped in. Jeff held in a snort.

"I most certainly was *not* talking about anything of the sort!" my mother snapped. "I did have an idea for a nice Zen garden with a reflecting pool, but it wouldn't be for swimming. And of course it would be *nothing* like the one next door." The house next door was something of an infamous legend among my mother's friends. A three-story cedar-shingled castle, it fairly towered over Mom's house. It even had a couple of turrets in the Queen Anne's style. And while Mom had one very well-maintained acre of land, the house next door sat on over two acres. It even had a moat, sort of.

A winding pool designed to look like a river dominated the backyard. It snaked along the right side of the yard and then doubled back, curving along its original path and then snaking out along the left side of the yard before curling around and returning to meet the place where it started. I imagine from above it looked like a giant bubble letter U drawn with squiggly blue borders, with perfect green lawn filling in the space between. There were a few rustic-on-purpose foot-bridges scattered along the river pool's path, and here and there, little waterfalls built from smooth stones. There were even a couple of story-high waterslides. It was actually really cool, and ever since I was eleven, I'd secretly longed for a chance to swim in it.

"Who lives in the Disney castle, anyway?" Teddy asked. "We've never been introduced." You could tell by "we" he meant the entire great and powerful Barrington Oil clan. Super-rich people never really think of themselves as individuals—they're forever blessed, or doomed, to be an extension of a glamorous genetic web.

"Neither have we," said Mrs. Fairweather.

"God knows we haven't, either," my mother said with a touch of resentment. "Some Europeans who never actually visit. They rent it out to summer families and, I'm telling you, Merilee, they pick the people with the *noisiest* children. Last year it was a Saudi family who let their boys swim until three o'clock in the morning. Nine-year-old twins. *Screaming* little madmen. You can imagine how much we loved that."

"They were just excited to have that pool," I said, not sure why I was defending a pair of rich Saudi boys. "It wasn't their fault their parents let them stay up."

"I'm not saying it was their fault, Naomi, darling," my mother said testily.

We were all silent for a moment.

"Well," Mom said brightly, "it's time we got ourselves to bed. We should be able to sleep through the night this year. No kids next door." She leaned forward to peck Mrs. Fairweather near the cheek, and then began to clamber out of the SUV.

"Who *is* staying there this year?" Delilah asked with mild interest.

"Just some young woman, as far as I can tell," my mother said. "She has a cleaning service come in every week, and the florist is over every few days. When I got here in May, she had an interior decorating service over for a full week. I can't imagine any owners would let her redecorate if they knew about it."

"Maybe she's doing it in secret," Jeff suggested. "That would be a very East Hampton sort of crime."

"Like wearing white after Labor Day," I said.

"Or not going to a top-tier university," Jeff added.

"Oh, you two," Delilah said. She giggled mischievously.

"We should hang out sometime, if you want," Jeff said in a low voice as the adults chattered to each other. "I'm a pretty nice guy. Really."

I looked at him and cocked an eyebrow. "We'll see," I said. He grinned at me, and I had to admit, he looked really good.

I got out of the car, and we waved goodbye as Teddy tore off.

Once the car was out of view, my mother and I stood outside the front door and looked at each other. Neither one of us was particularly pleased with what she saw.

"I'm going to bed," she said abruptly. "Do you need anything?" Now that no one else was around, she had dispensed with the doting mother act.

"I'm just going to hang out here for a bit," I said. "Stretch my legs."

"Be careful. Don't wander or get lost."

"Mom, this is like the safest place in the entire world. *Nothing* bad ever happens in the Hamptons."

"Okay, okay," she said with a sigh. "I forget that you know everything. Just remember to lock the door behind you when you come in. You've got your key, right? I'll take your suitcases in."

"Thanks," I said.

"Don't go on some kind of artistic walk through the yards and scare the neighbors," she said. "The last thing I need is for you to get arrested for trespassing."

"What the hell is an 'artistic walk'?" I asked.

"You know what I mean," Mom said with a sigh.

She gave me a dry kiss on the forehead and took my suitcases into the house. I stood and watched her go. She turned off the front porch light and the front walkway lights, leaving me suddenly awash in near-total darkness. And aside from the dramatic spotlights on the river pool, the enormous house next door had not one light on, either. As my eyes adjusted to the dark, the almost-full moon cast enough glow to allow me to wander without too much trouble.

On impulse, I took off my Docs and socks and dropped them on the front porch. It was summertime, and that meant I could go barefoot, building up the resistance on my feet until I could walk on even a hot sidewalk without wincing. I've always liked going barefoot in the Hamptons. It's so clean that you don't need to fear stepping on a needle or in dog crap like you do in Chicago. And it made me feel vaguely scandalous. When I get away from my mother for a solo journey in town, I'll slip off my flip-flops and put them in my beach bag, wandering down the sidewalk "just like some kind of dirty hippie," as my mother once said in disgust when she caught me. I don't care, though. I'm a Chicagoan through and through, which means I instinctively shed clothes (not in a whorish way) every time the temperature passes sixty degrees. So my feet get a little more sun. So what?

If moonburn were a thing, the tops of my feet would've been fried that night. The moon seemed to glow brighter and brighter with each step I took, acting like a giant lantern in the sky. I walked around the side of the house and watched the moonlight sparkle on the water through the trees.

Something strange caught my eye, an unusual light from an unusual spot. It was tiny, and at first I thought I'd imagined it, but I hadn't—it was a pinprick of green, and it was coming from some inscrutable spot on the back deck of the castle house, in an area shadowed by one of the big turrets. It seemed to hover in midair, and for reasons I can't quite explain, I crept closer to the neighboring yard than I ever had before. I got so close, in fact, that I managed to make out the shape of a person cradling whatever it was that glowed green.

Then, all of a sudden, light flooded the person's face, and I realized it was a she. And what's more, she had just snapped open a laptop. The green light had come from the charging dock on the laptop, where a power adapter was plugged in. I could see now that the adapter cord ran to an outdoor outlet on the castle's deck, and she had set the laptop down on a small table before her.

I felt a little stupid, but my embarrassment was soon over-whelmed by fascination with what I beheld. The girl was beautiful, with a white-blond bob and blunt-cut bangs that glowed in the light of the computer. Her big, thick-lashed eyes were trained intently on the screen, which I couldn't see from my vantage point. She had high, prominent cheekbones and full lips. She was so ethereally thin that she looked as if she might blow away in the light evening breeze and turn into a firefly, or a star. She could've passed for a teen angel, or maybe a fairy. Illuminated as she was by the computer screen, she didn't look entirely of this world.

Maybe it was because she didn't seem real, but I actually thought about talking to her. It would've been completely out of character for me, and chances are I would've just freaked her out, probably, and then had to hide from her scornful gaze every time I sat on my mother's deck. She didn't look like the type who could generate scorn, but if she was anything like every other girl I'd met during my East Hampton summers, scorn was her second-favorite feeling, after boredom. Instead, I stood, frozen and silent, and watched, for what must have been several minutes, as she read and typed on the computer.

Then she did something I'll never forget. The girl stood up, facing the lake. The white light from the laptop screen lent her face an unearthly glow from below as she stretched out her arms toward the twinkling houselights in the distance. She held it for a long moment, like some kind of yoga pose, just reaching and reaching for something I couldn't identify. Then, after what seemed like hours, she scooped up the laptop and went into the house, leaving me alone in the moon-drenched yard. I lingered for a moment, listening to the sound of the spring peepers and other frogs calling to one another from the muddy banks of Georgica Pond. I turned back toward my mother's house. I knew it was time for me to go inside, too.

# CHAPTER FOUR

S kags and I have an issue with the term "brunch," as in, we think it's stupid. I mean, if you're having a meal and it's in the a.m., that's breakfast. If you're having a meal and it's in the p.m., that's lunch (or dinner, if it's after 5:00 p.m.) I don't care *what* you eat. French toast at 1:00 p.m.? Lunch! Hot pastrami sandwich at 6:00 a.m.? Breakfast.

Naturally, my mother loves brunch.

I will say that the woman can cook. By the time I got up at 10:00 a.m., she already had a spread laid out on the table on the back deck—popovers, strawberry-flavored butter, mixed berries, scrambled egg whites with local (of course) goat cheese, and fresh-squeezed orange juice. She'd done it all herself in the space of about thirty minutes, probably less. She may fall short of the mothering ideal in most regards, but when it comes to whipping up a fantastic meal, she's just about perfect.

"Hey, Mom," I said blearily, blinking my eyes in the bright

sunshine as I joined her on the deck. "Thanks for breakfast. This looks awesome."

She turned toward me with a smile that faded quickly as she took in my ensemble (a ratty basketball T-shirt and a pair of paint-splattered drawstring shorts.)

"Still in your pajamas?" she asked, a clear note of disapproval in her voice. I was, but I decided to mess with her a little.

"Naw," I said breezily, sitting down and buttering a golden-brown popover. "I figured I'd go over to Baxley's for lunch by myself, then maybe stop by the Marc Jacobs in the village and drop by the Fairweathers' for tea." Her look of horror was so classic that I snorted, cracking up.

"Don't joke about things like that," she said, shaking her head and delicately spearing a berry with a fork. "I don't understand why you can't just give me an honest answer. I know you think your father just hangs the moon, and you two have always been buddy-buddy, but that doesn't mean I'm going to stand for you giving me nonstop attitude for yet another summer."

"Oh my God, this strawberry butter is so good," I interjected suddenly. "Did you use that wild strain you found at that farm last year?"

"Yes," she said, her expression lightening. Nothing brightens my mother's mood like flattery. It's like lighting a candle flame in front of a moth: instant distraction.

Her cell rang, and she checked the incoming number and snatched it up.

"Hello, Merilee," she sang sweetly. "How are you this

morning? I'm . . . oh, *Delilah*. Hello, darling. You'd like to talk to Naomi?" Her eyes lit up with glee, and she snapped her fingers in front of my face, actually bouncing up and down a little with excitement. "Of course, dear, here she is." She handed me the phone, mouthing unnecessarily, *It's Delilah! For you!*

While it's true that this phone call from Delilah was an unprecedented development, my mother's freak-out hardly seemed necessary. She stared at me expectantly, a dopey grin stretched across her face. I could tell she was going to hang on every word of this conversation.

"Hey, Delilah," I said, turning away from my mother, the hyperactive puppy. "What's up?"

"Sorry," she said. "I didn't have your number, so I just thought I'd call your mom. Teddy and Jeff and I want to go to the club to play tennis, and Jeff needs a partner. Want to come?"

I am not athletic in the least, and while the prospect of seeing Jeff was kind of tantalizing (even though I wasn't quite convinced he was the nicest guy), the surrounding circumstances would undoubtedly prove annoying and embarrassing. These kids came out of their mothers' wombs wielding tennis rackets, and I'd only played once, when Skags decided we needed to get more physical activity (actually, she had noticed a hot girl at the public courts in our neighborhood and wanted an excuse to run into her).

And besides, I'd planned to spend the day studying my SAT book and doing a practice test, which takes a few hours. I know that sounds incredibly lame, but (and this sounds even lamer) I've wanted to go to Harvard since I was a little kid and saw *Legally Blonde*, which is the sort of guilty-pleasure movie you wouldn't think a nerd like me would like, except that it is perfect, and makes me wish the Beasts at our school were anywhere near as kind and awesome as Elle Woods. The unfortunate reality is that beautiful blond popular girls usually *are* superficial bitches, and not good-hearted humanitarians like Elle.

"Thanks for asking, Delilah," I said, "but I promised myself I'd study my SAT book today." I could actually hear my mother go into a conniption behind me. She hurried around the side of the table to face me and glare.

"I know that sounds completely dorky," I added hastily, averting my eyes from my mother's gaze, "but I'm trying to get into Harvard early action, so I have to take the SAT at the end of the summer."

*What are you DOING?* my mother mouthed. I turned away from her, toward the backyard, and she let out an audible groan.

"Is everything okay over there?" Delilah asked, sounding concerned.

"Oh, that's my mother," I said. "Her cake just collapsed in the oven, and she's mourning the loss."

"My cakes never collapse," Mom hissed at me, plopping down in her chair and folding her arms in a huff.

"Well, I totally understand about the SAT thing," Delilah said. "You're not a legacy, are you?"

"No," I said. "My dad went to the University of Wisconsin."

I didn't add, "And my mother went to nowhere," because she was already pissed about the cake crack.

"Well, my father and grandfather and great-grandfather and great-great-grandfather all went to Harvard," Delilah said. "And my father is on the alumni board. So if you need any help when it's time to apply, just let me know. I'm applying, too." She did not add, "And I will automatically get in," although we both knew that was true.

"That's really nice of you," I said. "I might actually take you up on it." The thing with rich people is that they often offer to help you with a fancy connection, but you usually can't tell if they genuinely mean it or if they just want to show off their fancy connections. But I wanted to go to Harvard so bad that in this case, I didn't really care. It was worth a shot.

"Please do," said Delilah. "Well, I understand why you're not coming, but Jeff's going to be pretty disappointed."

I blushed. "Really?" I said in a squeaky voice. Then I blushed again, because a squeaky voice is like the number one sign you're nervous about something, and being nervous about a guy means you're into him, and I guess I kind of was.

Delilah laughed. "We'll all get together really soon," she said. "Every day can't be SAT day."

We said our goodbyes and hung up. I looked at my mother.

"She *invited* you out, and you said no," she said flatly. "I put you in contact with these people and provide all these opportunities for you, and you just turn them down, time and time again."

I rolled my eyes.

"You're the only mother I know who would get pissed that her daughter would choose studying over playing tennis," I said.

"She invited you to *tennis*?" Mom moaned. "And you said no?"

"I just don't feel like engaging in any activity where balls fly at my nose," I said, quoting *Clueless*, another favorite movie.

"Well, you should!" my mother snapped, rising to her feet. "That's how people make friends in this town!" I cracked up, and she stamped her foot in exasperation. She's such a child.

"I'm going to town," she said. "To BookHampton, to sign some stock." My mother loves doing that—popping into any bookshop in the world to see if they have her cookbook, and then magnanimously offering to sign any copies. I would love it if, just once, a bookshop owner said, "Nah, we're cool." But they all flip out like she's this big star, which I guess she actually is.

"See ya," I said, returning to my breakfast. She gave an exaggerated sigh and made her customary dramatic exit.

I felt strangely drained as I tried to eat my popover and eggs. Well, I guess it's not so strange—my mother is kind of an emotional vampire at times. I decided to revive myself with a phone call to Skags. Her real name is Tiffani Skagsgaard, but if you call her Tiffani, she will hunt you down and destroy you. It's always hard for her the first day of school, when the teacher calls out "Tiffani Skagsgaard?" and is confronted with this very boyish-looking young lesbian furiously shouting, "It's SKAGS!"

She picked up the phone on the second ring. "S'up?" she grunted.

"My mother is the most superficial person on the planet," I said.

"And water freezes at zero degrees Celsius. Tell me something everyone in the world doesn't already know."

"That's the thing, Skags—not everybody in the world knows it. In fact, I'd say most people in the world don't know it. They think she's this warm, loving culinary goddess who nurtures people with love and food."

"Hold up—I don't think anyone would ever mistake your mother for *warm*. She's not Rachael Ray. She's an ice-queen-prom-princess type. And I assume she's already ruining your summer."

"Yeah, and get this—she made me take a *helicopter* from Manhattan to East Hampton just because she wanted to kiss up to Senator Fairweather's wife. It was the Fairweathers' helicopter, and I had to ride with Delilah and Teddy Barrington and this kid Jeff."

"*The* Teddy Barrington?" Skags shrieked in a high-pitched, girlish tone. "Dreams do come true!"

I laughed a little. "He's totally bizarre," I said. I told Skags about the shoving incident I'd witnessed at Baxley's.

"Dude, that is *seriously* messed up," she said. "Jesus. That poor waitress. She's, like, the abused mistress. How's Montauk Barbie this year? You think he hits her, too?"

"No, I don't think he does," I said. "Delilah's actually pretty good, I think. You know she's always nice to me. I think she's trying to hook me up with this Jeff kid."

"Is he hot?"

"He's not your type."

"Well, obviously not. Why do you think she wants you to mate with one of the jet set?"

"I don't think it's like this big plan, I just think she thinks we'd go well together. He's cute enough"—I was downplaying the situation, obviously—"and he doesn't seem like he's a complete idiot. Kind of has an attitude, but whatever. Delilah called me this morning and asked me to go play tennis with her and Teddy and him today, but I said no because I'm doing my SAT book."

Skags groaned. "You and that freaking SAT book are like the lamest pair in history, you know that? You've been glued to it for months. Why don't you just go out and play some tennis?"

"You sound like my mother."

"Gross! No, I don't."

"Well, she was all pissed that I'm not going."

"That's just because she's obsessed with Montauk Barbie's Republican robot mom. I'm the one with your best interests at heart here: some good old-fashioned physical activity, bonding with the local teen population, getting out of that stupid fancy house for a reason that doesn't involve your mom dragging you to some dumb party. I don't care if it means you have to hang out with some Waspy teen-dream hooker."

"She's not a hooker. She's just—she's a nice girl who happens to come from a very stupid world. And I feel kind of bad for her about the cheating thing—Jeff said everybody in town knows."

"You've always been a Delilah Fairweather apologist. Every summer you call me up and tell me the dumb stuff she does and says, and every summer I'm like, 'This girl sounds like an empty shell of a human being,' and you're like, 'No, she's nice, it's the other kids who suck.' Someone has a girl crush."

"I'm not *gay*, Skags."

"A girl crush is different from being gay, dude. A girl crush is like when one girl is so into another girl that it's *almost* sexual, but not quite. A girl crush is way creepier than being gay, which is not at all creepy and, in fact, is completely awesome, in case you were wondering."

"I wasn't."

"Have you ever seen *The Roommate*?"

"No."

"Dude, it's got Leighton Meester from *Gossip Girl*. Blair freaking Waldorf! It's so much fun." One thing you should know about Skags—despite the fact that she considers herself cooler than everyone else, including me, she is in love with Netflixing old episodes of *Gossip Girl*. She pretends it's because she thinks Blake Lively and Leighton Meester are hot, but actually she gets really into the soapy story lines and has passionate opinions about whether Dan should be with this girl or that girl. She's seen every single episode at least twice.

"I don't have a girl crush on Delilah. I just appreciate the fact that she treats me like an actual person. None of the other kids around here have ever given me the time of day."

"Except for *Jeffrey*, the new love of your life." Skags went into her impression of my mother. "And what do his parents do, Naomi, dear? Are they in plastics? Coal? Mass-produced sex toys?"

"Yes," I said. "They're vibrator moguls."

"Oh, Naomi, darling, that is just *delicious*!" Skags cracked herself up and broke character. "Oh, dude! Change of topic, but such a good one. Guess who came into the DEBJ yesterday?" Skags works at a little café called That's a Wrap, which we refer to as the De-Ethnicized Burrito Joint.

"Who?"

"*La reina de las bestias.* The queen of the Beasts!"

"Jenny Carpenter?"

"JCarpz herself. She rolled in alone, ordered a chicken wrap with extra guacamole, and then told me she's been eating non-stop since she broke up with Taylor Cryan."

"Did she look fat?" I asked evilly.

"Dude! No. I mean, her boobs looked big, but they always look big."

"Gross."

"Deal with it. Anyway, it was pretty obvious she wanted me to know she was single, because she's completely into me."

"Double gross."

"Is this 1992, Naomi? Who says 'double gross'? More like double *hot*. I'm gonna hit it by the end of the summer, I swear."

"You're such a guy."

"No, Naomi, I'm a young woman who subverts the conventionally accepted gender paradigm because I refuse to conform."

"Oh, right. I forgot."

Skags switched gears abruptly. "Listen, for real, you sound exhausted. I know your mom is sucking the life out of you. Why don't you skip the SAT book and take a nap? You know you get sick when you don't get enough rest." There was a sudden note of concern in her voice that was kind of sweet. Sometimes I think Skags is more like a mom to me than my own mom is. Which is weird, because Skags is actually really similar to my dad, which maybe means I have two dads? I don't know.

Anyway, a nap sounded good to me, so I bid Skags farewell and brought the plates inside. I knew Mom's weekly housekeeper was coming that day, but I still scraped and rinsed the plates and put them in the dishwasher myself. I'm aware this doesn't make me some kind of heroine, but it's behavior that my mother actively discourages, especially if other people are around.

"Darling," she once said at one of her beloved afternoon iced tea parties, emitting a peal of shrill laughter, "you don't need to do that. Give the help something to do!" Then her assembled "friends," all of them social climbers in their own right, laughed as well. It made me kind of hate her in that moment.

I went upstairs to my bedroom, which Mom had done in this obnoxious boat theme: blue and white stripes everywhere, with antique ships in bottles and old framed maps. She dubbed it New Nautical Chic, and when *Town & Country* came to photograph the house, she made me wear the most heinous sailor dress and pose by the bed. I was twelve and sported those blond highlights her stylist, Jonathan, had put in, plus a bunch of makeup he piled on me. I looked like an overgrown version of one of those beauty pageant toddlers. Skags, who still went by Tiffani back then, taped a copy of the article to the front of my locker the first day of seventh grade. I didn't talk to her for a week.

But just like she really knows her stuff when it comes to breakfast preparation, my mother is a genius when it comes to picking out bed linens. Still in the pajamas that had so horrified her, I slid between the 1,200-thread-count Egyptian cotton sheets and drifted off to sleep almost immediately. I have a dim recollection of noting the time on the antique wall-mounted clock in the corner (taken from an old lighthouse, natch)—11:07. I figured I'd get up at one.

When I woke up, the clock read 6:00 p.m. I'd slept for (as Skags would say) seven *freaking* hours. I don't know what had me so tired, or why my body felt it needed to store up so much sleep. At least my mother wasn't home—she really would've flipped if she found out I ditched a day of tennis with Fairweather and Barrington offspring in favor of just sleeping. I mean, my mom doesn't even like it when I sleep more than seven hours a night. She regards sleep as a necessary evil, and essentially a waste of her time. She'd eliminate it from all our lives if she could.

I wandered down to the kitchen to make myself an iced

coffee. I swear I had all the best intentions of actually cracking open that SAT prep book, but when I looked out the window above the sink, I was astonished by what I saw.

Something truly faaaaaabulous was happening at our next-door neighbor's place. In all the years I'd been coming to stay with my mother in East Hampton, I'd never seen anything like it.

Gleaming red-and-white-striped tents lined the left and right borders of the backyard. The tent flaps were down on three sides, but the side facing the river pool was open. Some of the tents contained catering stations—I could see two Baxley's vans parked in the driveway—while others displayed games you might see at a carnival. You know that one where you shoot a stream of water into a clown's open mouth and fill a balloon that rises above his head? That was one of the games. There was also a game of Whack-a-Mole, one of those horrendous weight-guessing booths, a dart challenge where you had to try to pop a balloon to win the prize listed on its tag, a beanbag toss, a ring-the-bell competition with a big old-fashioned mallet, a miniature rifle range, and a bunch of other activities that would've seemed perfectly at home at the Jersey Shore but which seemed hilariously out of place in stuffy East Hampton.

As two white-gloved cater waiters struggled to set up a giant tub of lobsters near a grill, I noticed with delight that Baxley's was not the only food provider on-site. It seemed the hostess next door had seen fit to engage the services of a company that did carnival snacks like funnel cakes, grilled corn on the cob, cotton candy, roasted peanuts, ice cream, and (my absolute favorite) sno-cones! I don't know what it is that I so love about pouring a bunch of artificially flavored and colored high-fructose corn syrup over ice, but I'm a big fan. *Big*.

And to top it all off—and this was what I really couldn't believe—there was a Ferris wheel! I mean, a pretty, romantic, old-fashioned, classic Ferris wheel. It wasn't giant like an amusement park Ferris wheel, but it was pretty large! It even matched the rest of the décor, being red and white. They'd centered it in the backyard along the rear perimeter, practically in Georgica Pond, and it dominated the entire scene, dwarfing the tables and chairs that were set up around the U-shaped river pool. The footbridges that crossed the river pool here and there had been festooned with red and white balloons.

As I watched a small army of workers rush around lighting the tiki torches that lined the river pool, I thought I heard a knock at the front door. I figured I was just hallucinating, so I stayed in the kitchen spying on the circus unfolding next door. It occurred to me that my mother would absolutely lose it when she saw that her peaceful evening of silent cupcake contemplation was going to be ruined by some kind of noisy party next door. I honestly would've assumed it was a party for little kids, except that one of the red-and-white-striped tents was a fully stocked bar—manned, I noticed with some surprise, by Giovanni, the kid from Baxley's. As I looked around at the other cater waiters, I recognized quite a few faces. I even saw Misti-with-an-i, straightening the spotless white tablecloths on the white circular tables and adjusting the perfect white cushions on the white folding chairs. Each table was anchored by an expensive-looking crystal bowl in which floated white candles and red roses. Misti yelled something at Giovanni, and he hurried over with a lighter and began attending to each candle. Even from my vantage point, I could see the look of scorn she shot him as she watched him work, her hands on her hips.

We still had a couple of hours until sunset, but all the lights in the house were blazing, and a harried-looking woman wearing a headset kept rushing in and out of the back door, surveying the progress in the yard and barking orders to various sweaty men who were hoisting boxes, pushing hand trucks, handling armloads of red and white flowers, and doing a seemingly endless series of other tasks involving color-coordinated objects. I caught a good look at the woman's face and realized that I actually knew who she was—this was Greta Moriarity, my mother's favorite party planner (though, of course, Anne Rye never liked to publicize the fact that she used a party planner—she liked people to think she did everything herself). I'd met Greta a few times over the years, and she had always vaguely terrified me. Now, as she screamed at a large man carrying a giant red-and-white vase, I could see that she terrified other people, too.

Conspicuously missing from this whole scene was my neighbor, the gorgeous angelic creature I'd seen the previous evening. It seemed as if this horde of caterers, construction workers, carnival barkers, and—were those guys in dark suits security guards? Why yes, they were—other employees had just spontaneously descended upon the castle-like house and elaborate grounds next door and magically made this spectacle come to life. I was sure they'd been at work outside for the duration of the seven hours I'd been asleep—and I had a feeling Greta had been directing activities inside the house since before I woke up in the morning. Suddenly I heard the door to the garage slam. My mother's shrill voice called out, "Naomi!"

She swept into the kitchen, loaded down with bags from Marc Jacobs and Calypso and Citarella, and stared at me with disdain.

"You haven't changed?" she demanded.

"Wait, I haven't?" I shrieked, staring at myself in mock shock. I couldn't help it.

"That's disgusting," she said, huffing around the kitchen and noisily unpacking fancy cheeses and jars of expensive tapenade. "That's really disgusting. You haven't even showered today, have you?"

"Just been really focused on studying," I lied.

"Well, if you haven't noticed, there's an absolute circus unfolding next door," she said. "I doubt we're going to get much peace and quiet tonight. I didn't think anything could be worse than those Saudis, but this girl next door is clearly about as gauche as it gets."

I edged out of the kitchen and toward the front staircase in order to beat a hasty retreat, but stopped when I noticed something affixed to the front door. It was a little pink envelope. I grabbed it quickly and went back into the kitchen.

"Hey, Mom," I said. "Somebody left this for you." I gave it to her, and she stared at it with a furrowed brow. (Well, her brow would've been furrowed if it hadn't been so loaded with Botox.)

"But it's got your name on it, Naomi," she said, a touch of wonder in her voice as she handed it back to me. "And look at that gorgeous handwriting."

I looked. She was right. There on the front of the pale pink envelope was my name in the most exquisite cursive. It looked as if the writer had used a calligraphy pen, but the handwriting was so lovely that I wondered if it had been done professionally. Every Christmas, my mother throws an eggnog soiree at her big Manhattan apartment, and she always hires this fancy stationer, Dolores Weathers, to address the invitations and fill out the place cards. The writing on this pink envelope was even prettier than anything Dolores had ever cooked up.

My mother's eyes lit up. "Perhaps Delilah is having a party!" she said excitedly. "I'd think Merilee would've mentioned it to me—we met up for lunch today, it was wonderful—but it's possible she wanted it to be a lovely surprise for you." I was intrigued, for sure. I tore open the envelope ("You're ripping it up!" my mother scolded me. "This might be something you want to keep!") and unfolded the white note inside. It was a substantial piece of card stock, the sort of thing one might print a wedding invite on, and it contained the same elaborate handwriting:

*Dear Naomi:*

*Hello, love! We've never met, but I'd love to remedy that situation by welcoming you to my carnival party this evening. You're welcome to bring anyone you like. The party begins at 7 and should conclude around 1. Please give your mother my apologies for any inconvenience it may cause her—I'm afraid I've been a terrible neighbor and haven't found the time to introduce myself yet. I'll admit, I'm a bit shy! Rather appropriate for a blogger, I should think. Anyway, I admire her so much and hope to meet her in person soon. And I really hope to make your acquaintance tonight. Come ride the Ferris wheel—it's going to be so beautiful under the moon.*

*Best regards,*
*Jacinta Trimalchio*

I scanned down to the bottom of the page and read the small print there: ARE YOU WANTED? THEWANTED.COM.

"Oh, wow," I said. "This is *that* girl."

"What girl?" my mother asked eagerly, snatching the invitation from my hand. She scanned it quickly, her mouth curving up into a smile when she read the part about how much Jacinta admired her. Then she seemed to notice what was at the end of the note.

"TheWanted.com!" she gasped. "Isn't that the online internet website Delilah was talking about?"

"Yes," I said. "I am pretty sure that is the online internet website Delilah was talking about."

My mother's eyes lit up. "Ooh," she said. "Let's look at it, darling. This girl is famous!" I could tell any resentment she held toward the new neighbor was gone forever.

I popped open my laptop and went to TheWanted.com. The pink background matched the pink envelope, and the header displayed "The Wanted" in Jacinta's distinctive handwriting. The site was designed with a simple elegance—no bells and whistles, no distracting pop-up ads (God, I hate those). The navigation bar below the header displayed the categories: Parties, Fashion, Beauty, Models, and What's Jacinta Wearing? I clicked on the last category and brought up a seemingly endless page of daily posts of Jacinta from the neck down.

"She's so *thin*," my mother said admiringly. "Is she a model?"

"I don't think so," I said, scrolling through the entries. "But she sure seems to have a lot of clothes." I paused on one post from the previous October entitled "Birthday Suit." In the photo, Jacinta's lithe frame was outfitted in a lavender bouclé pantsuit with bright gold buttons down the front of the jacket and a bold, showy white lace ruffle encircling her long, swan-like neck. The hem of the pants stopped above her ankles. She wore lavender-and-white saddle shoes and lacy white ankle socks. It was one of those outfits that was completely weird and would've gotten her laughed out of school if she'd tried it in Chicago, but it made sense on some fancy style blog. The post read:

As if I even need to tell you this is Vivienne Westwood! The asymmetrical collar should've given it away, loves. The best 18th birthday present I could've asked for was a new box of Viv for—and you know I'll always be honest with you about this—free, free, free! So yes, they wanted me to blog about it, and yes, I'm doing it, but only because it is actually this fabulous. For those of you who've been accusing me of sporting too many high-fashion freebies lately: I thrifted the shoes, socks, and the blouse with the incredible lace collar. And you can't see my makeup (anonymity is the spice of blogging, angel faces), but it's cheapy-cheap stuff from the drugstore. Just so you know I'm still your down-to-earth fashionista! All my love, Jacinta.

And there, at the bottom, was her beautiful signature.

"I like what she's doing," my mother said a little dreamily. "Her branding is fantastic. A mix of high-end and DIY. Aspirational yet accessible. Fresh." I could tell my mother was going into one of her marketing term fits, when she stops speaking like a human and starts spouting terms that she and her business associates throw around.

"And of course," Mom added, "I love the lavender. It's not my style, but it's very young and now. Oh, darling, I'm *so* thrilled she's invited you to her party! You are going, aren't you?" Through the kitchen window behind her, the Ferris wheel suddenly lit up with a dazzling panoply of twinkling white lights. It seemed party time was drawing nigh.

Maybe it was the almost pathetic look of hope in my mother's expression. Maybe it was my natural curiosity about this fabu fashion goddess next door. More likely it was the fact that I've always loved carnivals. Whatever the reason, I found myself saying, "You know what? I am gonna go." My mother followed me upstairs, jabbering all the way.

"Now, don't wear all black like you did yesterday," she said. "My God, you looked like you were going to a punk-rock funeral. Let me see what you've packed." Uneasily, I let her go through my suitcase. As she combed through T-shirt after T-shirt, she heaved several disappointed sighs in a row.

"Do you possess *anything* that doesn't have a cartoon character, a band, or a snotty saying on the front?" she asked, holding up one of my favorites, a green shirt that read, "I'm a big fan of your work."

"Not that I'm aware of," I said.

She opened her eyes wide and met my gaze with a steely determination. "I knew something like this would come up eventually," she said, straining to remain calm. "So you know what I did, dear? I stocked up on some Marc Jacobs basics, just for you."

I groaned. "I hate when you shop for me," I said.

"It's for your own good," she called over her shoulder as she rushed downstairs to get the bags. "You dress like you're mentally unstable. You're seventeen years old, Naomi. It's time to start dressing like a woman, not an angry child." In a flash, she was back upstairs with her bags.

"At least it's not Lilly Pulitzer," I said, and my mother blanched. Lilly Pulitzer dresses look like the most boring person in the world barfed on some fabric and fashioned it into a frock. When I was a kid, my mother was a Lilly Pulitzer devotee until some socialite whose event she was catering told her she ought to change into her real dress before the guests arrived. (I'm not kidding—this actually happened.) Ever since then, Mom has hated Lilly Pulitzer with an all-consuming passion.

"Watch your mouth," she said, and for a moment her Chicago accent came out. Then she pulled out a dress and showed it to me.

I had to admit, it was actually nice. Marc Jacobs does good stuff that isn't too flashy and embarrassing but still manages to be pretty. My mother had selected a color-blocked twill sheath dress that was dark blue on top and green from the waist down. It had an empire waist, which looks fine on me because I've got no curves to speak of. The straight up-and-down thing suits me just perfectly.

"How much was it?" I asked suspiciously.

"You are your father's daughter," she said with a sigh, rolling her eyes. "Four hundred."

"For *that*?" I was incredulous. "I mean, it's pretty, but it's so simple. It probably cost seventy-five cents to make. And the three-year-old in Indonesia who sewed it probably made, like, a nickel."

"It's perfect," my mother said. "And you're going to wear it."

Of course, then I wanted to wear literally anything *but* the dress. My mother's tone made me feel for a moment I'd actually prefer wrapping myself in toilet paper and sashaying across the lawn. But the truth was that I looked good in it. For the first time in years, I let her brush my hair. She pulled it into a simple low ponytail and wrapped a piece of hair around the elastic band to hide it, then curled the tail with one of her eighteen thousand beauty appliances. She would've put makeup on me herself, but I howled in protest when she pulled out the medieval-looking eyelash-curling contraption. I just used some of her Guerlain mascara and put on a little lip gloss. She insisted I borrow a pair of simple pearl earrings and a strand of pearls. I drew the line at heels, so she gave me a pair of dark blue Ferragamo jelly flats with a peep toe. I watched her try unsuccessfully to hide her horror at my lack of a pedicure, but I guess she figured she'd won the sartorial battle and didn't need to push her luck by demanding I paint my toenails.

We both looked at my reflection in the full-length mirror inside her enormous walk-in closet. For the first time since I got those highlights back when I was twelve, I saw my mother's eyes light up with pride.

"See," she said triumphantly. "You really *can* be a pretty girl when you try."

"Um," I said. "Thanks." It was as close to a genuine compliment as I was going to get from her.

I waited in the kitchen and watched through the window as the first hour of the party unfolded. Thankfully, my mother was holed up in her home office on a conference call with her lawyer about something or other and didn't nag me about arriving on time. Everybody knows you don't get to a party right when the invitation says it starts. You run the risk of being the first person there, with no one to talk to, which is even worse than getting there when all the other people have gathered. Then at least you might have the chance to strike up a conversation with someone you know.

Of course, it occurred to me that I might not know anyone at this party. I tried my best to make out the people parking in Jacinta's long driveway and along our street, and I thought I saw some of the regulars from the clambakes at Baxley's. I grabbed my mother's binoculars (she claims to be a birdwatcher, but I think she just spies on people across the pond) and peered through them.

There were the Fitzwilliams sisters, Audrey and Katharine, who were notable for being Kennedy cousins and for getting drunk at every clambake or garden party I'd ever seen them at. Their parents never seemed to notice or care, which is probably why they kept drinking. They had each paired off with a Stetler brother, neither of whose first names I could recall, and they all made a beeline for the bar tent as soon as they rounded the corner of the house and entered the backyard. None of them seemed particularly surprised or delighted by the carnival surroundings. I saw Audrey Fitzwilliams give the Ferris wheel a dispirited glance before downing the first of what would undoubtedly be many shots that evening. One of the Stetler brothers put his hand on her butt as if that were perfectly normal public behavior.

I didn't recognize any of the other people streaming into the backyard. The girls all wore pretty dresses and sported perfect tans, while the boys wore polo shirts or short-sleeved button-downs with khaki pants or shorts.

"Naomi!" My mother's voice behind me startled me. I turned around, and she folded her arms in disapproval. "Are you going to just stand there and watch, or are you going to join in the fun?"

I looked at the clock, which read 7:55 p.m.

"I guess it's time for me to join in the fun," I said. "But I might be back in five minutes, if it sucks."

"Give it an hour at the very least," Mom said. "Anything less would be terribly rude."

She stood on the back deck and watched me as I walked across the lawn and, my heart beating extra-fast, rang the bell at Jacinta Trimalchio's castle door. In the gathering darkness, the lights shone bright through the windows. Though I could hear a crowd chattering inside the house, no one answered the door. Nervously, I looked across the lawn at my mother, who gestured that I should ring the bell again. I obeyed, but still no response. Somewhat relieved, I was about to turn around and head home when the door swung wide open, and Jeff Byron greeted me.

"Jeff!" I said in surprise.

"Naomi!" he said, mocking me—but with a big flirtatious grin. "Come join the circus." He put his arm around me and put his hand on my back, leading me inside.

"Oh my God," I said, staring at the luxurious, crowded foyer in which we found ourselves. "This is—"

"Tacky? Fun? Ridiculous?"

"All of it," I said in wonder.

It was a soaring three-story foyer with a white marble floor and an enormous crystal chandelier that had been fitted with pink lightbulbs. A huge white marble butterfly staircase dominated the space, its white marble balustrade resplendent with bright red bunting. Everywhere I looked, I saw red roses: garlands of them hanging from the chandelier, draped around gilt-framed mirrors, peeking out from behind the ears of New York's wealthiest young women. White-jacketed cater waiters with red flowers in their lapels circled among the dozens of guests hanging out in the foyer, offering raw oysters and fried oysters, glasses of red wine and glasses of white wine, flutes of pink champagne, and bits of fruits and meats and cheeses intermingled in complicated, fancy haute cuisine ways that my mother would've identified and judged immediately. And up on the landing of the butterfly staircase, where the stairs met the second floor of the house, sat a white-and-red-clad full band banging out old-fashioned music that sounded like something from Skags's other favorite Netflix show, *Boardwalk Empire*.

"How many people our age do you know who'd throw a party set to Jazz Age standards?" Jeff said, grabbing two glasses of champagne off a passing waiter's tray and handing me a flute.

"Is that what that music is?" I asked, taking a big gulp of my champagne. I'm not much of a drinker, but the dazzling lights and sounds and colors had me feeling like some kind of relaxing substance was in order. I made a split-second vow to myself that I wasn't just going to be Naomi the confession receptacle at this party. I was going to—participate, whatever that meant. Champagne seemed like a start.

"Yup. I know it sounds pretentious, but I love jazz." He pressed his hand into my lower back and led me up the staircase, so we could stand closer to the band. "This is 'Always' by Irving Berlin," he said into my ear. I shivered a bit and drew a little closer to him.

"How do you know so much about music?" I asked.

"My dad owns a record label," he replied casually. "He's into all kinds of music, but he loves 1920s and 1930s jazz the best of all."

"My dad coaches a public high school basketball team," I said, taking another swig of champagne. Already, I felt less awkward than I usually did at these East Hampton parties.

"Your dad sounds like more fun than my dad."

"Your dad sounds richer than my dad." I was kind of tipsy already.

"Maybe, but he's kind of an asshole," Jeff said with a hint of bitterness. "You'll never meet anyone more obsessed with the size of his house or the price of his car. Everything is like a trophy to him. You wouldn't believe how superficial the guy is."

"Oh, you'd be surprised," I said, swallowing more champagne and thinking for a moment about how cute Jeff's floppy brown hair was.

"So what kind of record label does your dad own?" I finished my champagne and reached out for another as a waiter passed.

"Hip-hop," Jeff said.

"Naturally," I replied. "It's clear that you lead a thug life."

"Absolutely. See these pants? Ralph Lauren. My mom bought them for me. Hard. Core."

"I assume you're in a gang—I hear Trumbo is full of them."

"Oh, it's a dangerous place. Our school motto is 'Ride or die.'"

"Let's go outside," I said suddenly, grabbing his hand without thinking. I downed more champagne.

Jeff looked at our hands in amusement. "Whatever you say, madame." I led him back down the staircase and through a palatial living room and an epic dining room—no, a dining *hall*—both of which were a blur of red and white flowers and table runners and tablecloths and cushions and vases and also, of course, shiny gorgeous people. The rear wall of the dining room was made of floor-to-ceiling panels of glass, one of which was an open sliding door. We walked out onto the crowded two-level deck, where another band was playing more of that jazzy, bubbly music ("'Doin' the Raccoon,'" Jeff said. "Late twenties."), and gazed at the extravaganza unfolding in the backyard.

"So this Jacinta girl—do you know her or what?" I asked, taking another generous sip of bubbly.

"Not at all," Jeff replied. "I didn't even think she was real, and then when we were done with tennis today, I got this hand-written note back at my house."

"With the most incredible handwriting, right?"

"Yeah, it was like John Hancock or somebody had written me the Declaration of Invitation." It wasn't that funny, but I found myself giggling inanely. Champagne and a cute boy will do that to anyone, I guess, even a smartass girl from Chicago who knows better.

"For a while, people thought she was one of the girls at Trumbo, but I guess she's not. All of the girls and some of the gays—like the stereotypical gays—are obsessed with being her Facebook friend. But even her Facebook doesn't show her face, or where she really lives." I could hear an irritated Skags inside my head going, "And what *exactly* is a 'stereotypical gay,' you heteronormative fascist?" but I knew what Jeff meant.

"Then right at the end of the school year, she tweeted that she was going to spend the summer in East Hampton. Everybody went nuts. But I don't even know if she's here. It's kind of impossible to tell, you know?"

"I don't get why she singled me out," I said, grabbing another glass of champagne from a passing waiter.

"You aren't kidding around, are you?" Jeff said, chuckling. He patted me on the head, a gesture that for some reason infuriated me.

I was about to say something bitchy, but I saw a plate of fried oysters floating past me and realized I was incredibly hungry.

"Wait!" I fairly shouted at the passing waitress, who obediently paused and walked toward me. I realized too late that it was Misti. She recognized me, too, and looked momentarily terrified.

"Um," I said. "Hi." Her eyes wide with nervousness, she simply nodded at me. Gingerly, I took a fried oyster, and Misti darted off in another direction.

Behind me, I heard one girl say to another, "You know, *that's* the girl who . . ." She lowered her voice at that point, but I caught a few words—"Teddy" and "Fairweather" and "disgusting." Then both girls giggled merrily and walked past us into the house.

"Teddy's behavior is gonna bite somebody in the ass one of these days," Jeff remarked dryly. "Not him, of course. Never him. But somebody."

"Excuse me," I said haughtily, remembering his condescending attitude about my drinking. "I am going to find the bathroom." Without waiting for his reaction, I turned around, wobbled for a moment, and then set off on my quest. I did really have to pee.

I wandered around the first floor through the dining room, living room, foyer, slightly smaller second living room (people were already making out on couches), incredible kitchen (my mother would *die)*, cigar room (it smelled nice), billiards room (it was stuffed with drunk guys smoking cigars and playing pool), and two-story *Beauty and the Beast*–style library (perfection) before I found the bathroom. I opened it without knocking and swiftly walked right in, shutting the door behind me. Against the white marble countertop, right beside the canyon-size white marble sink, leaned two lithe brunettes snorting white powder off an oversize white marble-backed hand mirror.

"Oh," I said, suddenly really uncomfortable. "Oh. I'm—I'm sorry."

"You want some?" one of the girls asked cheerfully. Her companion giggled.

"N-no thank you," I replied, backing up. "I just have to pee."

"Go ahead," said the first girl. "I don't mind."

"Just make sure it's *just* pee," her companion tittered, and they both burst into high-pitched laughter.

"Right," I said. "I'm gonna go." And I did, getting the hell out of there.

The bathroom was located next to the kitchen, beside an unobtrusive back staircase. I hurried up the steps, passing a couple in the midst of a heated argument ("I *told* you Daddy doesn't want us to take the boat out on our own!"), and bypassed the second floor in favor of the third, where I practically ran directly into a tall, stunning rail-thin girl with long red curls and dramatic cat's-eye makeup.

"Oh, I'm sorry," I said. "I'm just looking for the bathroom. Do you know where it is?"

"No worries, love," she said lightly. "There's one in each of the bedrooms."

"How many of them are there?" I asked curiously.

"Six. Red, orange, yellow, green, blue, and indigo, just like the rainbow," she said. "Only thing the owners missed is violet."

I drunkenly thought for a moment and then declared, "I would like to pee in the blue bedroom."

She laughed as if I were the cleverest and funniest person

in the world. It was a pretty, gentle sound. "The blue *bath*room, love," she reminded me with a grin. "I don't think the blue bedroom is the right place for that."

I considered this. "True," I said. "I'm not *that* drunk." Laughing again, she linked her arm through mine and led me through a magnificent blue bedroom to a pretty blue bathroom. It was far larger and more impressive than even the white marble masterpiece of a downstairs powder room I'd previously visited. There was a claw-foot blue bathtub that rivaled the size of the shark tank at the Shedd Aquarium back home in Chicago. There was a blue-tiled shower that could have easily fit six people. There was even a wall-mounted flat-screen TV set facing the throne-like blue toilet. I resisted the urge to switch it on.

I emerged to find the redhead sitting on the four-poster bed. Drunkenly, I plopped down next to her.

"This is some crazy party, huh?" I said.

"Crazy in a good way or crazy in a bad way?" she asked anxiously.

"Oh, in a good way. Everything is so beautiful and red and shiny," I slurred. "I got invited today. I live next door. I mean, I don't *live* next door, I just stay there for the summer with my mother, who is a crazy person." The girl laughed her lovely laugh again. "I'm serious. She is nuuuuuuts. But anyway, this girl, Jacinta—I never heard of her, but I guess she's famous? Like she writes this famous blog?"

The girl looked at me and smiled kindly. "That's me, love.

*I'm* Jacinta." I squinted at her and realized this was indeed the beautiful alien girl from the other night, clad in a wig and a boatload of makeup. Those big green eyes—how had I missed them, just because they were encircled by loads of smoky liner and shadow? They seemed unmistakable now, as did her ultra-thin form.

I blushed. "Oh my God," I said. "I'm sorry."

"Sorry?" Jacinta looked worried for a moment. "Why would you be sorry?" She put her arm around me and smiled, her big eyes sparkling with friendliness. "I'm actually wearing a wig," she said, tugging at a red curl. "I love dressing up and playing pretend. Don't you?"

"I haven't done it in years. I used to go through my mother's closet and pretend to be a princess, but then one time I was wearing this super-dark lipstick and I stained one of her favorite dresses, so I got banned from dress-up for life. I'm Naomi, by the way. Naomi Rye. Thank you for inviting me; it was really nice of you. Like, really nice. I don't usually get invited places. I mean, here. I just—why did you invite me, by the way? Is that rude to ask? I don't mean to be rude." I had a full-on case of the Nervous Naomi Babbles.

Jacinta smiled warmly. "I invited you because we're neighbors, and because I'm interested in you and what you do," she said.

"Oh, I don't do anything, really," I said, wondering for a horrible moment if she just wanted to get to my mother. Once in a while somebody will suck up to me because of who my mom is, but usually it's some fawning housewife type, not a skinny teenage alien fashion priestess.

"Sure you do," Jacinta said brightly. "You were in a bunch of photos on Facebook last summer from different charity events. There was the Metropolitan Museum of Art Costume Institute Subcommittee Tea, and the after-party honoring Robert Caro for the East Hampton Library Authors Night, and the Friends of the Central Park Turtle Pond tapas fiesta." The casual way she rattled off the different names startled me.

"Man," I said. "I barely remember the reasons for those parties. You must have a great memory."

"Well, they were all at Senator and Mrs. Fairweather's house," she replied, as if that explained everything.

"Oh. Right."

"It seems as if your family and the Fairweathers are quite close," she said with a studied casualness.

"I guess my mom is friends with Mrs. Fairweather," I said.

"And you must be friends with Delilah Fairweather, then?" she said with a hint of eagerness that slightly confused me.

"Um," I said. "I guess. I mean, she's a really nice girl. I usually see her a handful of times each summer. She asked me to play tennis today, but I couldn't. Maybe I'll play another time soon." At this, Jacinta smiled and looked pleased.

"Usually my mother just makes me go to things with her, and it's so awkward because I know I don't fit in," I continued. "But this party, *your* party, is such a fun party."

"Well, that's the whole point, love," Jacinta said. "Fun. I

want everyone to have the most fun they've ever had in their entire lives. I want it to just be the most perfect party, the most perfect summer. For everyone."

"I've never had that much fun here," I confessed. "My mother can be—difficult."

"Well, we're going to change that," Jacinta assured me. "Not your mother—we can't do anything about her. But you're going to have a wonderful summer. I'm going to throw the best parties, and you're coming to each and every one. You have guest-of-honor status. I was thinking of doing a pirate-themed one, with lots of rum drinks and live parrots and a ship-shaped sandcastle in the backyard—my party planner says she knows an artist who will do one for me."

I didn't know how on earth I'd achieved guest-of-honor status simply by peeing in this girl's blue bathroom, but she was so genuinely friendly that I figured I'd just go with it. It was possible that, behind her gorgeous otherworldly façade, she was actually a completely normal human. Like back home in Chicago, it's not considered wild or out of the ordinary for a person to be nice. People say hello and when they ask how you're doing, it seems like a lot of them actually care about your answer. It's hard to find someone like that in East Hampton— someone who is nice to you just for the sake of being nice, not because they want something from you.

"The jazz bands are so different from anything I've seen at a party before," I said.

Jacinta looked worried again. "You don't think they're too

much, do you?" she asked. "I could've hired a DJ, or I could've just put my iPod on shuffle, but I wanted to do something that people would really remember. Something really different from all the other parties. But maybe I went overboard with the music."

"You've got a Ferris wheel in the backyard, and you're worried the *jazz* is overboard?"

Jacinta's brow furrowed for a moment, and then she smiled. "I guess you're right," she said ruefully. "I just wanted to make a big splash."

"It's awesome, Jacinta," I said honestly. "The whole thing. The roses, the music, the carnival in the backyard, everything. People are having a great time."

Suddenly she happily wrapped me in a big hug, the way a little kid might. She released me quickly, looking nervously at me, and I could tell it had been an impulsive move. I smiled at her to show her that it was okay. She visibly relaxed.

"Let's go outside," she said. "I want to see if— I want to see which guests have arrived. I actually haven't even been down-stairs yet."

As we walked downstairs, I really took a look at her outfit for the first time. Unlike most of the guests, who looked as if they'd stepped out of a Ralph Lauren ad, Jacinta's ensemble was quirky and funky. She wore a long, translucent vintage-looking pink camisole over what looked like a vintage Victorian black corset (like me, she had nonexistent boobs, so the effect was pretty and elegant rather than va-va-va-voom sexy) and a black lace slip. Her black kitten-heel sandals matched her black-painted toes and nails, which also sported a constellation of tiny rhinestones. I could just imagine my mother's face if I showed up with black fingernails with *rhinestones*. One arm was loaded with black plastic jelly bracelets, while the other was bare. And except for her white-blond eyebrows, you'd never know she wasn't a natural redhead. Really, she was one of the most interesting-looking people I'd ever seen.

The white marble butterfly staircase was loaded with revelers, but the crowd parted as Jacinta regally descended. I followed, a little shyly, because suddenly all eyes were trained on us. Chatter fell to a hush, and the jaunty music would've had the spotlight if it hadn't so obviously been occupied by Jacinta.

I felt someone grab my arm. Startled, I turned to face Audrey Fitzwilliams. She and Katharine, clearly wasted, stared at my new friend, openmouthed.

"Is that Jacinta Trimalchio?" Audrey asked loudly. Her voice echoed in the quiet. Jacinta, halfway down the staircase, turned and smiled sweetly.

"It is, love," she answered. "And you two are wearing the most gorgeous shoes I've seen since I got out to East Hampton. I *adore* espadrilles for summer." I watched as the girls nearly fainted into the arms of their respective Stetler brothers.

"You look amazing," Katharine told Jacinta reverently, and I watched as several of the assembled girls nodded in agreement. Jacinta walked back up the steps toward them.

"Katharine and Audrey, yes?" she asked. They bounced up and down like eager puppies and nodded.

"You looked *divine* at Alexandra Fox's birthday party earlier this year," she said. "I reposted a few snapshots of you two on the blog."

"Oh, we saw," they said in unison.

"It was the coolest thing," Katharine said. "The coolest thing ever."

"We took a screenshot and printed it out and hung it up!" Audrey nearly shouted. She was one of those people who gets louder and louder as she gets drunker and drunker.

"I'm so glad you two are here," Jacinta said sincerely, wrapping them both in a spontaneous hug. Their eyes nearly popped out of their heads as they hugged her back. You would've thought God himself had descended from heaven to embrace them.

We continued on our way down the staircase, with people falling all over themselves to say hello to Jacinta. Those who tried to shake her hand invariably got a hug. She paused and asked about a dozen people how they were doing, and if the food was all right, and did they need something else to drink, and had they tried the Ferris wheel yet? Word rapidly spread through all the rooms in the house that Jacinta Trimalchio had made an appearance, and an ever-growing crowd followed us through the house as if Jacinta were the Pied Piper of Hamelin. As we slowly made our way to the back deck, I caught snatches of chatter.

"I heard she's a distant cousin of Prince William," one girl said to her friend.

"She's definitely not American—you can tell she's trying to hide an accent," a boy in a peach bow tie said to his date (a boy with whom he was holding hands).

"She's soooooo thin," a tiny girl in pink ballet flats said to her friend. "I mean, like thinner than L.A. thin."

"Her parents are dead," a drunk guy announced to no one in particular. "She's this orphan heiress."

If Jacinta heard any of the comments, she didn't let on. She was too busy sweetly greeting strangers and telling them how honored and delighted she was that they'd made time in their schedule to come to her little party. I'd never seen someone so obviously rich display so much genuine gratitude. Even in her wig and layers of makeup, Jacinta was the most authentic person at the party.

On the deck, Jeff Byron immediately came over to me.

"I didn't know where you went," he said, and something in his voice pleased me. He wasn't whining, exactly, but he hadn't been happy about my exit. I liked that.

"Miss Naomi," Jacinta said, "do you want to ride the Ferris wheel with me?" Jeff looked at her, startled, taking in the unusual getup and those Cleopatra eyes.

"I'm Jacinta," she offered, opening her arms for a hug. "And you're Jeffrey Byron. I'm such a fan of Byron Records. I'm *so* glad you could make it!"

Jeff looked bewildered as Jacinta enfolded him in her arms. When she stepped back, he said, "You're Jacinta Trimalchio?"

"I am," she said. "Are you enjoying yourself? Did you like

the appetizers? If you're still hungry, there's lots of food in the backyard. The grilled lobster is really, really great. And how do you know Naomi?"

"We just met yesterday," I said. "We have a—friend, I guess, in common."

"Really?" Jacinta said, her eyes lighting up. "What friend?"

"Delilah Fairweather," Jeff said. "Do you know her?"

Jacinta's eyes widened, and she smiled so energetically I thought she might break her own face.

"We were just talking about her upstairs," she said. "She is my favorite up-and-coming model. I think she's just absolutely amazing. Jeff, you're friends with her boyfriend, Teddy Barrington, aren't you?"

"Yeah," Jeff said, looking a little surprised.

"I see you together in photos on Facebook all the time," Jacinta said by way of explanation. Then she let out another sweet laugh. "Oh God, that sounds a bit stalker-ish, doesn't it? It's just that I've got to go through all the party photos to pick the best ones for my blog."

"Trust me, I know," Jeff said reassuringly. "All the girls at Trumbo are obsessed with *The Wanted*."

"I was hoping Delilah and Teddy would come tonight," Jacinta said. "I was too shy to send *them* invitations, but I figured if their friends were here . . ." Her voice trailed off.

"I'm sure they were just busy," I said. "Next time you should send them invitations."

"I've really been wanting to meet Delilah," Jacinta said,

looking out at the Ferris wheel. "I think she's the next big supermodel. In a couple years, everyone will know her name."

"And her father may be president," Jeff interjected.

"Oh, but she'll be famous on her own," Jacinta said wistfully. "She's too good to stay unknown."

She turned her big green eyes on me, and I watched her hesitate. Finally, she said, "Would you ever have her over to the house, and invite me over, too?"

I was surprised by the timidity with which Jacinta issued the request. You'd think a girl who could summon two hundred strangers to a party wouldn't be too worried about meeting a new person, especially not a person she'd already praised several times in public on the internet. I was beginning to think Jacinta was something of a Delilah Fairweather fangirl.

"Of course I will," I said. "Any time you want."

"Oh, Naomi!" Jacinta exclaimed, wrapping me up in another tight hug. "I would be soooo grateful! I'm so glad we're friends!"

"Me too," I said, my voice muffled against her armpit. She was much taller than me.

A horde of excited girls descended on Jacinta then, asking if they could take photos with her, and she graciously obliged them. As they jabbered at her like hyperactive geese, Jeff leaned over.

"It's *the* Jacinta Trimalchio?" he whispered without a trace of sarcasm. "I mean, it's really, really her?"

"It's really, really her," I whispered back.

"Wow," he said in wonder. "I can't believe she's real. Any

Trumbo girl who missed this party is going to be seriously pissed off."

My stomach was starting to growl, which always happens when I've had too much alcohol. I had determined that several glasses of water and some food were in order, lest I wake up hungover the next day. I'm a real lightweight when it comes to alcohol, and Skags has taught me some tricks over the years to prevent the dreaded morning-after headache and stomach trouble. The funny thing is that Skags doesn't drink at all, but she says she likes to watch out for her stupid friends. She's sweet that way.

"Let's go down to the carnival," I suggested. "I want to check out the food tents."

"Oh, you just want me to win you a stuffed animal," Jeff said.

"I'm a feminist, Jeffrey. I will win my *own* stuffed animal."

"Do feminists ever ride Ferris wheels with men they've just met?"

"Feminists do whatever they want. That means I'll see how I feel *after* I get some grilled lobster in me."

He took my hand and led me down the stairs, past the lower level of the deck, and into the backyard wonderland of lights and music and delicious food smells.

We ate grilled lobster, grilled corn on the cob, funnel cake (we split one), homemade gelato (I got salted caramel; he got mint chocolate chip), and cotton candy. At the bar tent, we ordered a ginger ale for me and a beer for Jeff, who high-fived Giovanni as if they were old friends.

"How you doing, man?" Jeff asked.

"All right, man, all right," Giovanni said, pouring our drinks with an easy grin.

"Working hard as usual, right, my man?" Jeff said.

"You know it," Giovanni responded, handing us our beverages.

"You're doing a great job," Jeff said.

Maybe I was just still drunk, but I thought he had the peculiar feigned ease of a rich person talking to a less-than. It's the way my mother talks to her housekeeper. It's not condescension, exactly. It's like there's this knowledge hanging in the air that one person has more power than the other, and we're supposed to pretend everything is nice and normal and equal, but in reality, luck or chance has showered benefits on one person that the other person couldn't dream of. I didn't like it, but I brushed the feeling aside, reminding myself that Jeff was actually fun and smart and, as far as I could tell, not all caught up in the social-climbing game.

He was also the best shot I had at getting a beach boyfriend, something I'd always secretly wanted—not that I'd ever, ever, *ever* admit it to anyone, *especially* not Skags. All the boys in East Hampton had always seemed so douchey, but Jeff was actually intelligent. Another thing that separated him from the pack was that he displayed an interest in me, something no East Hampton boy had done before. To be fair to them, I wasn't exactly warm and inviting—but neither were they! Oh, it's a chicken and egg thing, I guess.

Jeff and I walked over to the Ferris wheel and got on board. While I buckled myself in, he murmured something to the attendant. I didn't catch it.

The wheel moved slowly and kept creaking and groaning. What looked from afar like a sparkling new carnival ride was actually pretty worn-out.

"You're not afraid of heights, are you?" Jeff asked when we were almost at the top.

"You ask me that *now*!" I laughed at him. "Wouldn't the ground have been the place to make that inquiry?"

"Probably. But you're not, right? Afraid of heights?"

"Nope," I said. We were almost, *almost* at the top. Georgica Pond spread out before us, a wide patch of darkness punctuated by occasional twinkling lights on the shore. The party noise had faded somewhat, and I could see Jacinta's red wig sparkling like a ruby under the lights on the deck. She was still mobbed by people.

"So this isn't going to bother you," Jeff said.

"What isn't going to bother me?"

We reached the top, and the Ferris wheel shuddered to a halt.

"How did you know it was going to—"

"I told the guy to stop us up here."

"*What?*" I was utterly confused. For a second I thought about this rich kid in Chicago, this guy who grew up in a penthouse on Lakeshore Drive, who got super-wasted at a party and was all pissed off at his girlfriend, so he *pushed her off a balcony.*

I know it seems weird that my first thought would be that Jeff might *murder* me, but I was still a little drunk, and it's not like I had much experience with guys. "I just wanted to do this," Jeff said, and he leaned over to kiss me.

I had never been kissed before—I know, I know, I was seventeen and that's old, but whatever, it just hadn't *happened*, unless you count the time Alan Scott pecked me on the lips during Spin the Bottle in seventh grade—so you'd think I would freeze up, but actually, I seemed to know exactly what to do. I just leaned over and kissed him back. It was kind of odd, because if you think about it, having your lips on someone else's lips is just inherently weird—there's no, like, evolutionary need for it, as far as I know. It doesn't aid in reproduction, although apparently foreplay is important to the sexual act, according to this sex book my mother sent me when I was fifteen in lieu of having an actual discussion with me about sex. Getting that book in the mail and opening it in front of my dad was one of the single most embarrassing experiences of my life. He grunted, "Oh. Um," and promptly left the room. But I did read it.

Anyway, we kissed and it was nice, and I had this strange feeling of triumph, like I'd checked off a box on the grand list of Things You Must Do While You Are a Teenager. Then I immediately wanted to text somebody and tell them, but who was I going to tell? Certainly not my mother, and definitely not my dad. Skags would just say that straight make-outs were gross. I wished I had a girly girlfriend I could tell. It's fun being BFFs with the butch future first lesbian president of the

United States, but sometimes I do want to have the kind of stereotypical girl friendship where you paint each other's nails and talk about boys.

"Thanks, bro!" Jeff yelled down to the ride operator. "You can let us down now!" The guy heard him, and soon we were slowly lowering toward the ground.

"You want to go up again?" Jeff asked, raising an eyebrow impishly.

"Just don't touch me," I said. "That was guh-*ross*."

"Yeah, it was pretty disgusting," he agreed. "Never again!"

"Never again!" I repeated.

We made out for, like, the next three revolutions of the wheel.

Eventually, other people started boarding the ride, which was annoying because the Ferris wheel would squeak to a stop and then jerk to a halt every minute. We decided to get off and head back to the bar tent. Jeff held my hand on the way, and I looked down and blushed when he greeted a couple of guys he knew from Trumbo.

I was about to order another ginger ale when Jacinta appeared, trailed by a gaggle of admiring girls. She was holding her camera—not a crappy little thing, but a real-deal, professional-style digital camera with a big round lens and a light that she held in one hand.

"Naomi!" she exclaimed, hugging me like I was her best friend in the world. This girl gave out hugs like it was her job. "Let me photograph you for tomorrow's blog post!"

"Is it for a Spotlight?" one of the girls asked tremulously. I recognized her as Ainsley Devereaux, a tobacco heiress who I'd never seen express any feeling other than cool boredom.

"It is," Jacinta said, and the assembled fangirls collectively gasped.

"What's a 'Spotlight'?" Jeff asked, amused.

"It's a special feature I do once in a while when I think someone looks particularly fabulous," Jacinta explained. "Usually it's once a month. During Fashion Week I'll do six or seven."

"It is a *huge* deal," Ainsley said urgently, grabbing Jeff's arm for emphasis and shaking it. I looked at her hand on his bicep and instantly hated her.

Jeff laughed and freed his arm from the rich girl's tight grasp. "Yeah, you don't need to resort to violence to convince me, Ainsley."

"That was not *violence*, Jeffrey," Ainsley said, rolling her eyes. "It's a big, big deal. All the other fashion blogs and some of the gossip blogs pick it up. Sometimes it's even on Page Six." I knew about Page Six because my mother was on it sometimes— it was the *New York Post*'s legendary gossip page, and it was stupid and bitchy but apparently very influential.

"Delilah holds the record for Spotlights," Jacinta said as she quickly redid my ponytail. "Five times. I'll have to talk to her about that when we have our little get-together at your house." She bent down by my feet.

"Little get-together? Oh, right." I felt slightly awkward that Jacinta was straightening my hemline and brushing bits of grass off my sandals.

Jacinta stood up, switching from stylist mode to photographer mode, and pursed her lips, looking at me with an artist's critical eye.

"I want you to put your hands on your hips," she said. "No, not like you're angry. Like, naturally."

"I don't naturally put my hands on my hips," I said. At this, Ainsley got involved, repositioning my fingers and pushing my hands higher on my waist.

"Now put one foot in front of the other, like this, love," Jacinta said, demonstrating. "And lean forward just a little bit."

"Hinge at the waist!" Ainsley said.

"Hinge at the waist!" Jeff shouted.

"I'm hinging!" I shrieked. "I'm hinging!" He and I dissolved into laughter. Jacinta smiled good-naturedly.

"This is serious," Ainsley said. "What's your name again? Natalie?"

"Naomi," I said. "We've met every summer since we were eleven." It couldn't have been the champagne any longer, but *something* sure had me feeling saucy.

"Okay, I'm bad with names. Naomi. This is a big deal. A. Big. Deal. You want this photo to look amazing. So hinge at the waist." Obligingly, I hinged at the waist. Jacinta began snapping away from different angles, encouraging me to grin, then to smile slightly, then to look serious, and to open my eyes wider. Eventually, she was satisfied and lowered her camera.

"Perfection, love," she said.

Ainsley nodded authoritatively. "I agree," she announced

with an imperious air, as if anyone cared. Jacinta ignored her and wrapped me in yet another hug. "Don't forget about Delilah, okay?" she murmured into my ear.

"I won't," I whispered back.

"Jacinta," Ainsley said eagerly, "I'm going to get something to drink. Would you like something?" Jeez. Ainsley Devereaux wasn't the type of person to care about anyone's needs other than her own. She must really be starstruck by Jacinta Trimalchio.

"I would, Ainsley," Jacinta said. "And so would Jeff and Naomi, I'm sure, wouldn't they?" Ainsley looked briefly horrified by the prospect of being a cocktail waitress, but she quickly hid her distaste for the task by smiling insincerely.

"I'd like a ginger ale, Ainsley," I said sweetly. "Thank you *so* much. You know what? Have him put some vodka in there for me. Why not?" Jeff patted me on the back approvingly.

"Fetch me a Stella, won't you, Ainsley?" he said with his usual charming smile. Ainsley rolled her eyes at him.

"And I'll have a lemonade, love," Jacinta said, lightly resting her hand on Ainsley's shoulder. Ainsley immediately brightened up at her touch.

Ainsley caught sight of Misti passing by, and reached out and thumped her on the shoulder. It struck me as quite rude, but that seemed to be Ainsley's style.

"Hey, can you get us a Stella, a lemonade, a gimlet, and a vodka ginger ale?" she said. It was more of an order than a question.

"Sure," Misti said automatically, with a forced smile.

"Thanks," Ainsley said, her voice dripping with fake honey. "You know, I *heard* you were very . . . accommodating. Really giving. And now I see it's true!" She smiled brightly, and a few of the other girls fought back snickers. Misti ignored them and went off to get the drinks.

"Ainsley," one of the girls whispered with delight. "You are *so bad*!"

Ainsley laughed. "What? I was just being friendly."

"You're friendly like a snake is friendly," Jeff said. Ainsley stuck her tongue out at him.

Jacinta led Jeff, Ainsley, and me back to a table near the house. She flagged down one of the fangirls, who brought us caramel popcorn at Jacinta's request.

"Popcorn for the big show," Jacinta said.

"What big show?" Jeff and I asked in unison.

As if in response, the sky above us exploded in sparkling red and white peonies and chrysanthemums and starbursts. On top of everything else, Jacinta had arranged for a fireworks display. An obsequious Misti brought us our drinks and hurried away quickly.

"How'd you get a permit for this?" Jeff asked as everyone in the house poured out onto the back lawn to watch the fireworks.

"Oh, I didn't worry about a permit," Jacinta said, laughing lightly. Ainsley copied her, laughing too.

"You've got chutzpah, Jacinta Trimalchio," Jeff said admiringly, clinking his beer bottle against her glass of lemonade.

"What is a 'chutzpah'?" Ainsley asked.

"It means guts in Yiddish," Jeff said as another round of white stars blasted the sky above us and a cheer went up from the crowd. "Kind of like courage. At least, in the modern sense, that's how it's used."

"I always forget that you're Jewish," Ainsley said. "That's so cute."

"Yes," said Jeff. "We're just adorable." He grabbed my knee under the table and squeezed, and I did the same to him. Suddenly the two girls I had seen getting high in the bathroom rushed past us, squealing and giggling.

"Pool party!" one of them shrieked, stripping down to her underthings and jumping in the river pool, which was illuminated from below by lights. Then the Fitzwilliams sisters, seemingly even drunker than before, took off *everything* and splashed down, followed by the delighted Stetler brothers. The crowd roared its approval, clapping and hooting and whistling, while the fireworks concluded overhead and the band on the deck struck up another jaunty tune. More girls and guys followed suit, some jumping in fully clothed, some in their underclothes, and a few more girls completely naked. I hate girls who do stuff like that just for attention. They reminded me of a couple of the Beasts back home, Melissa Donnelly and Madison Delaney, who were famous at school for getting drunk and making out for the football team's benefit at every single Homecoming dance. Skags calls them fauxbians.

"Ugh," Ainsley sniffed. "That's disgusting."

"I don't know," Jeff said with a smile. "I think it's lovely—from an artistic perspective, of course." I punched him on the arm, and he cracked up.

It was getting pretty late, and the party seemed on the verge of devolving into some giant drunken orgy. I wasn't really up for that. I'd already shown up at an East Hampton party by myself, made out with a boy I'd just met the day before, and posed for some big-deal blog. Enough personal firsts for one night.

"I think it's time for me to head home," I said. Jacinta was visibly disappointed.

"Oh," she said a little sadly. She clasped my hand in hers. "Well, you *must* come over again soon. And at the next party, you must come early and get ready with me. You can always stay over afterward in the blue room if you want!" With some satisfaction, I noticed Ainsley's look of jealousy.

"I'll get going, too," Jeff said, rising. "It's been a wonderful party, Jacinta. Thank you so much for inviting us."

"You were *invited*?" Ainsley asked, aghast.

"Yes, of course," Jeff said. "You think we'd just show up at some stranger's house without an invitation?" Ainsley's bitter silence made it clear she had done just that.

"Oh, Ainsley, love, I simply didn't get to send out invitations to everyone I wanted here," Jacinta said graciously. "In fact, I *only* managed to get notes out to Jeff and to Naomi today. I just put the word out and figured all my favorites would make it here—and most of them did." Her smile faded for a moment, but just when I noticed its absence, it popped back into place.

"Now tell me about your bag, love. It's absolutely precious." Mollified, Ainsley smiled and launched into a monologue about Louis Vuitton. Jeff and I backed away slowly. Jacinta blew us kisses.

"Do feminists mind gentlemen walking them home?" he teased.

"This feminist does not," I said. "After all, who knows what dangers lie between here and the house next door?"

"Georgica Pond is typically a hotbed of gang activity," Jeff said.

By the time we reached my back deck, the sounds of splashing, shrieking, and music had gotten a little softer, although it was still pretty noisy. Jeff asked me if he could see me again soon, and I said he could. Then he gave me a long, lingering kiss that left me tingling from head to toe. When he walked away, I wondered for a second if we could fall in love. Then, of course, I felt like a complete dork, because I'd only gotten my first kiss like an hour previously and I was *already* thinking of L-O-V-E. It must be because I was a little drunk. That vodka and ginger ale hadn't exactly sobered me up.

I opened the sliding glass back door as quietly as I could, and crept up to my bedroom. I flopped down on the bed, still fully clothed, and stared up at the ceiling. It had been a weird but awesome night. I waggled my feet in the air and looked at my sandals. They were actually really pretty. So was my whole outfit. Maybe my mom wasn't so stupid. Maybe East Hampton wasn't so stupid. Maybe this summer wasn't going to be as stupid as previous summers.

Then I noticed the ceiling was spinning gently, and I flopped my legs back down, dropping one foot to the floor for stability (another trick Skags taught me). I focused on my breath and soon drifted into a pleasant, boozy sleep. The last coherent thought I had was that I hoped my mom would make popovers and eggs again the next morning.

# CHAPTER FIVE

y phone buzzed with an incoming text, and it sounded like a cluster of killer bees had descended on my room. When you're hungover, everything is louder.

I groaned and rolled over, noticing that my sandals were still on. I kicked them off, and they thudded to the floor.

I groped for my phone, which rested atop a side table assembled from discarded wood that had been used on some dead rich person's yacht. (In my mother's house, every object has a fancy origin story.)

The text was from Delilah. It read, *Sounds like SOME-BODY had a pretty sexy night! ;)*

I blushed and texted back, *Not SEXY. I don't move that fast!* ☺

She wrote, *LOL. I'm soooooo glad you had fun! Next time don't say no to tennis!* ☺

I wrote, *I won't. Promise!*

The weirdness of girly-texting with Delilah Fairweather was actually less intense than I'd thought it would be. Could I be getting used to talking to her like a real friend? And if I were used to talking to her like a real friend, did that mean she *was* a real friend?

This summer was getting odder by the day. Since when did I happily and comfortably swill champagne with the sons and daughters of America's finest families? I started to analyze the previous evening the way I always do the morning after a party, but I stopped after a few seconds. Maybe it was my hangover. Or maybe it was something else—a conviction that I was going to do things differently this summer. Maybe I didn't need to overthink *everything*.

I checked the time on my phone: 12:00 p.m. I was really surprised my mother had let me sleep that long. Had some spirit of kindness possessed her? Or had she been so enormously pleased by my decision to go to the party that she'd decided to indulge my love of sleep?

It turned out to be the latter reason. When I shuffled off to the bathroom to take a shower, she ambushed me in the hall-way, full of questions.

"Was it fun? Did you have a good time? You must've had a good time—you're still in your party clothes! Whom did you meet? Any boys? What was the Jacinta girl like? Did Delilah go to the party?"

"I'll tell you after I shower," I said.

The hot water felt incredibly good on my skin, and I realized to my relief that I didn't have a monster headache or stomachache—I was just tired and a bit out of it. Because I knew it would give my mother a little bit of a thrill (I couldn't say why I cared to give her one, but I guess I was in the mood to be nice), I put on one of the new Marc Jacobs dresses she'd hung in my closet—a simple, sleeveless cream-colored cotton sundress with an A-line skirt. I checked myself out in the mirror, and I had to admit I looked good in it. I was starting to realize that my mother had smart instincts with clothes sometimes.

Downstairs on the back deck, my mother actually clapped a little when I came outside and sat down.

"Oh my God, Mom," I said. "Seriously?"

"No cartoon T-shirts or ratty jeans!" she said. "You look fabulous. Now sit down and tell me everything."

She'd laid out oatmeal in simple white bowls with small white containers of honey, brown sugar, chopped walnuts and almonds, and mixed fresh berries. This was accompanied by a mini-omelet. My mother loves making miniature versions of regular food. "We all know Americans need to eat less," she said once on a very special Thanksgiving episode of her Food Network show. "And I'm delighted to be part of the solution." She went on to teach everyone how to make mini–organic turkey meatloaf with wee servings of organic mashed potatoes and organic gravy. I doubt anyone obeyed her command to "eat less this Thanksgiving, for your waistline and your world," but I can say with authority that at that Thanksgiving, she ate exactly one spoonful of mashed potatoes and a small arugula salad.

I attacked my omelet first, surprised by how much I was craving grease and protein. Of course, with my mother's cooking, you got very little grease—the concept of fatty foods grossed her out—but the protein was there in abundance. After I inhaled the omelet, I set to work on the oatmeal, which was delicious. She'd flavored it with cinnamon and a touch of nutmeg, so it tasted like Christmas.

"So tell, tell," Mom said, pouring me a glass of fresh-squeezed orange juice. "Who was there?"

I recounted as best I could the list of attendees. I hadn't been able to identify too many people, but I told her about Ainsley Devereaux, the Fitzwilliams sisters, a few friends of Delilah I'd seen jumping naked into the pool (I didn't tell her that part), the Stetler brothers, and Jeff Byron.

"Jeffrey Byron!" my mother exclaimed delightedly. "You know, his father has expressed interest in buying shares of Bake Like Anne Rye!, Inc. when we go public later this summer."

"No, I didn't know that," I said, shoveling berries into my mouth. "His dad's a music producer, right?"

"Darling, don't speak while you're chewing. And take your elbows off the table. Yes, Herman Byron owns Byron Records. I couldn't tell you any of the names of his artists, but I know he's *very* successful. He's on the Vineyard for the summer."

"With his new girlfriend. I know."

My mother raised her eyebrow and looked at me inquisitively. "And how would you know that? It wasn't in any of the papers."

"Jeff told me."

My mother's eyes widened with sudden excitement. "Jeff told you! Oh, he must like you if he confided in you." She withdrew a tube from her purse and delicately patted a bit of moisturizer with sunscreen on her face. My mother is obsessed with avoiding the ravages of time and sunshine.

"I don't think it's a secret in his world."

"But you talked to him!"

"Sure. The other day when we came from Manhattan, and last night at the party. He's nice. We . . ." I tried to stop myself from saying it, but part of me just really wanted to tell someone. "We rode the Ferris wheel."

My mother let out a little squeal and clapped her hands again. I turned red and felt a flush of anger.

"Oh, I can't believe it! You chose the perfect summer to start acting like a real girl." She sighed happily. "Anne Rye's daughter and Herman Byron's son. Thank you, darling. This is going to be so good for me."

"It has exactly nothing to do with you, Mom," I snapped. "Would you just let me have something of my own for once? And there isn't even a something to talk about. We rode the Ferris wheel. That's it." I immediately regretted putting on her stupid dress.

"Don't get an attitude with me, Naomi," she snapped back.

"You may not care about your social life or your future—or mine—but *I* do. I've spent your whole life caring enough for the both of us, and now it's starting to pay off."

"Are you seriously taking credit for this? God, you're a narcissist."

"And you're a brat." We glared at each other. Just then, a smiling face appeared at the side of the deck. Jacinta's white-blond bob and enormous Fendi sunglasses were a welcome distraction from my annoying mother.

"Hello!" Jacinta said. "I hope I'm not interrupting your brunch. I just wanted to pop over and introduce myself." She smiled winningly at my mother, who immediately shifted into her public mode, all perfect posture and poise.

"Come on up," I said. "Your timing is perfect." My mother shot me a side glare as Jacinta walked up the steps and popped her sunglasses up on her head.

"I'm Jacinta Trimalchio, the girl next door," she told my mother, shaking her hand. My mother beamed.

"Oh, Jacinta," she said. "It is so wonderful to finally meet you! I was just looking at your world wide website yesterday and marveling at how lovely it is. Naomi is a *huge* fan."

"Well, I'm a huge fan of Naomi's," Jacinta said. "She's featured on the site today, in her Marc Jacobs dress from the party."

My mother smiled at me triumphantly. "I picked that out, you know," she said proudly.

"How wonderful," Jacinta said. "You have exquisite taste.

In fact, you inspired me! This is Marc Jacobs as well. A bit less subtle, but I do enjoy it." She was wearing a long, silky red sleeveless dress splashed with colorful flowers.

"Darling, sit down." My mother patted the chair beside her. "Shall I fix you an omelet or some oatmeal, dear?"

"Oh, thank you, Ms. Rye. I don't want to pass up on a chance to try your cooking in person, but I've already eaten breakfast." Jacinta settled her long, impossibly thin frame into a chair. "But I would love a glass of orange juice."

"Call me Anne. And you *are* tasting my cooking, because I squeezed it myself not twenty minutes ago." Mom giggled as if it were the funniest thing in the world. Jacinta took a big sip.

"Perfection," she said, and my mother shot me a satisfied smile, as if she'd won whatever secret competition she thought we were in.

"I hope the noise last night wasn't too awful, Anne," Jacinta said apologetically.

"Not at all," Mom said. "I barely heard you. But then, I'm a heavy sleeper." I wanted to add that her over-fondness for Ambien might have something to do with it, but I kept my mouth shut.

"The police did pay us a visit right after you left, Naomi," Jacinta said. "It was the fireworks. They were nice, though, and didn't give me a citation for that or the underage—um, or anything else."

"Personally, I think liquor laws in this country are an atrocity," my mother sniffed. "In France, where I trained, children are educated about wine drinking as an art form." I tried not to roll my eyes.

"I came over to steal Naomi away for lunch, but I see you're brunching," Jacinta said.

"Oh, Naomi can go," my mother said. "She only had her little omelet and half her oatmeal. I'm sure she's got room for more, don't you, Naomi? You always did have a big appetite."

"Yeah, you know what?" I said. "I'd really like to eat something different. Let's get out of here." I stood up quickly, nearly knocking over my glass of orange juice.

"We'll take my car," Jacinta said.

"Good," I said. "Because I don't have one, so otherwise we're walking."

Jacinta's car turned out to be a spotless, shiny little white Mercedes-Benz convertible she'd leased for the summer. The car would've immediately caused a stir on my block in Chicago, but here in East Hampton it was just one of the many luxury vehicles lining the town's streets. We drove into the Village of East Hampton and parked near BookHampton. Jacinta told me she wanted to take me to "the most *divine* new restaurant, love. It's called Crave."

It wasn't exactly divine, but it sure was out of this world— out of the world of East Hampton, anyway. It felt more like a hip spot in Soho or Tribeca, with its sleek interior, exposed pipes, minimalist modern furniture, and thumping music. Even the model-gorgeous waiters and waitresses seemed to have been imported from an episode of *Sex and the City*. It was the kind of fancy place where the waitress looks bored by your very presence and where the daily specials include things like gently tormented brussels sprouts and severely slapped salmon with a blackberry attitude reduction. It was too trendy for my mother, but she would've approved of the tiny portions.

Jacinta seemed eager to tell me her life story. I still couldn't figure out why she singled me out, but I didn't want to question it. "I'm a year older than you—I'm eighteen. I just graduated from a teensy little boarding school in Switzerland, nothing anyone here has ever heard of. It's really itty-bitty, barely forty students. But I was only there for my senior year, because before then I was traveling all over the world, popping in and out of schools for a semester here and there, but mostly being privately tutored."

"Homeschooled?" I asked.

"No, tutors. My mother and father are diplomats, and they're too busy to spend time teaching me calculus and French. My father is from an old Spanish family—they're aristocrats— and my mother is from a family of Montana ranchers. The wealthiest cowboys in the Wild West, she used to say." Jacinta laughed and took a sip of her passion fruit–watermelon iced tea.

"So where did you grow up?"

"Oh, everywhere. All over. Too many places to name," she replied, and I immediately felt the ember of suspicion in my mind. Given my question, most people would proudly rattle off a list of cities to prove how well traveled they were. Either Jacinta was just humble or she was lying.

"So can you speak Span—"

I hadn't even gotten the question out before Jacinta swiftly answered, "No, my father never taught me."

"Oh."

"Just English, and French, from school."

"Ah," I said.

"I grew up in so many places that I never had the chance to really put down roots or make friends," Jacinta continued in what sounded a little like a rehearsed speech. "That's why I'm so glad to meet you, Naomi. It'll be so fun to have a real friend this summer."

"Where are your parents, anyway?"

"Oh, they're on assignment, love. In Europe," Jacinta said. It all sounded very exotic to me.

"I decided I wanted to have some fun on my own this summer," she said. "You know, without Mother and Father."

I was about to ask another question, when a pretty thirty-something woman with long brown hair and expensive-looking highlights approached our table. She wore those oversize late '80s–early '90s glasses that always look so ridiculous in movies from that time period (and in real life, if you ask me, but I'm not exactly up on trends).

"Excuse me. You're Jacinta Trimalchio, aren't you?"

Jacinta smiled at her. "That's me, love."

"Oh my gosh," the woman said, sounding starstruck. "I'm Erica Rawls. I'm the associate style editor at *Vogue*."

"Erica!" Jacinta cried, standing and throwing her arms

around the startled editor. "We've corresponded! Oh, what an honor to meet you."

"No, the honor's mine, really," Erica gushed. "You're just so incredible, and I'm so inspired by you. Some days when I'm feeling stuck, I'll just look at your site and get all kinds of ideas. We all think you're just amazing."

If Jacinta's story was even a little bit exaggerated, her reaction to Erica was 100 percent genuine. She got very quiet, and her eyes grew enormous.

"At—at *Vogue*?" she whispered. It was almost as if she were speaking to herself. "*Vogue* thinks I'm amazing?"

"Completely," Erica said.

Jacinta put her hands over her heart. She opened her mouth and closed it soundlessly. Her big green eyes shone. For a moment I thought she might weep. But she quickly regained her composure. If she blinked away any tears, I didn't catch sight of them.

Erica gave me a cursory glance, then decided I wasn't worth acknowledging. I've had this experience plenty of times with my mother, when press people or fans assume I'm just her assistant, and don't bother shaking my hand or even making eye contact with me. I end up being invisible. Not that it really bothers me, but it does tell you something about a person. Erica Rawls had quickly achieved "not a nice person" status in my book.

Jacinta was too kind to let me dangle there in silence for too long, so she quickly said, "And this is my dear friend Naomi Rye."

"Hi," Erica said with as little effort as possible. "Jacinta, it's so fabulous to see you out here. Do you think you'll come to the city soon?"

"Well," Jacinta said, "I've finally got a September coming up with a clear schedule. For once, I won't be traveling everywhere. I can actually go to Fashion Week. I suppose you'll be there, too?"

"I always am," Erica said. "We really should talk—I could use a good guest correspondent with a really fresh, young approach." She handed Jacinta her card. Jacinta accepted it almost reverently, handling it like a precious jewel.

After Erica bid us farewell—in other words, air-kissed Jacinta and ignored me—Jacinta looked at me gleefully.

"*Vogue* magazine!" she whispered. "Can you believe it?"

"You're really getting influential," I said.

"Oh, I've only just begun," she replied. I believed her. I didn't know how much of Jacinta Trimalchio was real and how much was fake, but she was clearly a force to be reckoned with. I'll admit it—I was impressed at how snooty-snoots like Erica Rawls and Ainsley Devereaux fell to pieces when they met her. A little over-the-top, but that's part of what made her so fun to be around. As if she were reading my mind, Jacinta said, "About last night . . ."

"Yes?"

"Remember when I asked if you could have Delilah Fairweather over so that I could meet her?"

"Of course."

"Did you mean it when you said that was all right, love?"

"Sure. I wouldn't have said it if I didn't mean it."

"Oh, goodie!" Jacinta clapped her hands together like a little girl and let out an excited mini-shriek. I laughed at her childlike enthusiasm. It was kind of adorable.

"Jeez," I said. "You must really be a Delilah Fairweather fan."

"Oh," Jacinta said. "You have *no* idea."

As we drove home, I asked Jacinta if she had a boyfriend.

"No time for a boyfriend," she said. "No time for anything, really, but my work. I guess you could say I've been waiting for the right one for a long time."

I thought of Jeff, wondering if he could be the right one. Then I told myself I should calm down. We'd only kissed a few times.

Jacinta pulled into her driveway, worriedly pointing out the divots in the grass where drunk girls' high heels had sunk into the sod.

"I'll have to get a lawn man over to fix that before I meet Delilah," she said.

"I thought we were having her over to my house," I said.

"Oh, to start. But of course I'll want to bring her over to see my house, too."

"Of course."

"I hope she likes it," Jacinta said wistfully. "Do you think she'll like it?"

"I don't know her well enough to say," I said. "But I can't imagine anyone not being impressed by this house. And by you."

She gave me one of her signature big, tight hugs. "Thank you, love. I am *so* glad we're friends."

"Me too," I said, and I meant it. My summers in East Hampton were usually awfully lonely. But this year, within the space of a couple of days, I had acquired two friends and a maybe-possibly-not-to-be-a-dork-but-it-could-happen boyfriend.

Jacinta and I put each other's numbers in our phones. Then I walked home in the afternoon sunshine, leaving Jacinta behind to poke around in her rented lawn, a look of concern on her pretty face. I wondered why she cared so much.

# CHAPTER SIX

After I left Jacinta examining her lawn, I went into the house and sequestered myself in my room, curling up with a Noam Chomsky book my Honors US History II teacher had recommended the previous year. I finished it in two hours and moved on to an old favorite, *Anne of Green Gables*. After that, I went through another old favorite, the L. M. Montgomery book *Emily of New Moon*. I fell asleep with an almost-finished *Emily of New Moon* clutched in my hand, my clothes still on.

I woke up the next morning to the buzz of a text from my mother. It read, *Emergency meeting at HQ—tell no one.*

I rolled my eyes and texted back, *Oh, so I shouldn't post it on Facebook?*

*That's not funny*, came the response.

My mother and I have slightly different senses of humor.

I put the phone down and rolled over to go back to sleep.

I was drifting off quickly when my phone buzzed again. I was prepared to fire off a bitchy retort to my mother, when I saw that the text was from Jacinta. It was an 813 number. I wondered where 813 was, anyway.

*Have you called Delilah yet?* the text read.

*Not yet,* I texted back. *But I will soon.*

☹

*I'll call her now,* I texted. For some reason, I didn't want to do anything to make Jacinta unhappy—even if what would make her unhappy was waiting a completely reasonable amount of time to meet Delilah Fairweather.

*T H A N K Y O U T H A N K Y O U T H A N K Y O U XOXOXOXOXO* ☺ *<3,* came the response.

I'm not the biggest fan of talking on the phone, unless it's to Skags, because my phone voice gets kind of high-pitched and weird. I'm sure there's some complex, deep-seated psychological reason for this phenomenon, but as yet, I can only attribute it to performance anxiety. I hate saying the wrong thing, because then I revisit it in my head over and over again for days after. I don't know where I get it from, because my dad seems to have no trouble barking orders on or off the basketball court, and my mother has probably never wasted a single moment of time feeling embarrassed over anything she's said, no matter how dumb.

I called Delilah's cell. It rang a few times and she picked up, sounding kind of out of it.

"Hellllloooo?" she said lazily.

"Hey, Delilah, it's Naomi," I said in my high-pitched phone squeak. "Naomi Rye."

"Well, of coooourse it is," she said in her breathy Marilyn Monroe voice. "You're the only Naomi I know. The number one Naomi!" She giggled through a yawn. "Sorry. I get a little loopy when I sleep late."

"I was wondering if you'd like to come by today," I said. "My mother's gone to the city, and I thought you could meet my neighbor, Jacinta Trimalchio. She threw this amazing party the other night."

"Ooh," Delilah said. "Ooooooooooh. Jacinta Tri*mal*chio. I would *love* to meet her. Was her party as fabulous as everyone said?"

"It was really fun," I said, thinking of Jeff and the Ferris wheel.

"Well, of course for *you* it was, you naughty thing," Delilah said. "By the way, have you talked to Jeff?"

"Not since the night before last," I said.

"That's no way for a gentleman to act!" she said, sounding playfully indignant. "You don't make out with a girl and then not at least text her the next day. I must speak to him about this *immediately*."

"No, no—it's no big deal," I said quickly. And at that exact moment, my phone buzzed with an incoming text from Jeff.

*Want to come to the beach?* it read. *No Ferris wheels, but I'll buy you a lobster roll.* They sold lobster rolls at the beach snack shack in East Hampton for, like, sixteen dollars a pop, but it was at the public beach. I guessed Jeff's rented house didn't come with access to a private stretch of beach. "You'll never guess who just texted me," I told Delilah.

"Shut *up*," she said. "Is he psychic?"

"Maybe he's . . . *magical*," I said dramatically. We giggled together, just like Skags and I did when something cracked us up. Well, almost like that.

"So it's what, ten?" I said. "You want to come over for lunch at, like, one o'clock?"

"That should give me enough time to pick out something fabulous to wear," Delilah said. "And to get myself together."

After we hung up, I texted Jeff that I couldn't do the beach but might be able to hang out later in the day.

*I demand to know why you shall not be accompanying me on a sunbathing excursion,* he wrote.

*I shall be otherwise occupied with a ladies' lunch,* I texted back.

*Which ladies, madame?*

*Madame Jacinta and Madame Delilah, sir.*

*Well, should your schedule permit, please do contact me later, dear lady.*

*Perhaps I shall. Perhaps I shall.*

Despite the good looks and the money, he was really kind of a dork. I liked that about him. I don't feel comfortable with guys who aren't at least a little bit weird.

Not even two minutes after I stopped texting Jeff, which was not even three minutes after I stopped talking with Delilah, which was not even ten minutes after I got off the phone with

Jacinta, the doorbell rang. Even though I was still wearing my dress from the previous day and obviously hadn't showered or brushed my teeth, I decided to answer the door. I figured there was probably only a 1 percent chance it was Jeff, anyway.

Outside my mother's front door, I found a very jittery Jacinta standing and shifting her weight from one leg to the other, like a little kid waiting in line to see Santa. She was wearing some kind of old-fashioned white peignoir with a long white silk nightgown underneath, and her white-blond bob was all messy and unkempt. She looked like she'd just rolled out of bed in 1962 or something. I opened the door and grinned at her.

"She's coming over at one," I said.

Jacinta let out a whoop and actually danced a little jig. I laughed out loud—she was so unself-conscious in her delight. I mean, the girl was wearing white fluffy bunny slippers on someone's front lawn in the Hamptons in the blazing mid-morning sun, and she clearly couldn't have cared less if anyone saw her.

Then Jacinta rushed past me into the house and started going over everything with a critical eye, as if she were investigating a murder scene.

"Mm-hmm," she'd say while examining a set of family photographs hanging on the wall. Or "aah" when glancing over the décor in the dining room.

"Uh, Jacinta," I said tentatively. "What are you doing?"

"Just getting a feel for the place, love," she said distractedly. "You won't mind if I have flowers brought over, will you?"

"No, I mean, flowers are always nice," I said, confused. "Are they for my mom or something?"

"Oh no," Jacinta said, as if the very idea were unimaginable. "Oh no, they're for Delilah. She loves red and white roses."

"Oh," I said. "Of course." I didn't ask how Jacinta knew what kind of flowers a total stranger loved. I assumed she'd seen it on Facebook or something.

She whipped her cell phone out from the pocket of her peignoir and called up a florist to order six dozen roses—three dozen white, three dozen red. There was a feverish look in her eye.

"Are you feeling all right?" I asked.

"Oh, I'm perfectly fine!" she said unconvincingly. "Just want to make sure everything's right. You wouldn't mind if I had my housekeeper bring over cookies, would you? She's over today, and she usually cooks a few days' worth of meals for me. . . . It wouldn't be any trouble to have her bake cookies—I ask for them all the time anyway."

"Just as long as she doesn't bake them in my mother's kitchen," I said. "Anne Rye is a territorial animal when it comes to anyone else touching her stove, unless she's hired them herself."

"She'll do them at my house," Jacinta said. "I'll have her run them over just as soon as they're done. You said Delilah's coming at one, yes? I suppose I ought to have the housekeeper bake them so that they're out of the oven at twelve thirty, and they'll be just the right temperature at one. But what if Delilah is early? If it's twelve forty-five, the cookies might still be too hot. And if she's late, they might start to cool off too much."

She was pacing, talking to herself almost as if I wasn't even there. I had never seen a girl so nervous about meeting another girl.

"I have to go home and get ready," she said suddenly. "Oh, Naomi, thank you so much!" She threw her arms around me and hugged me close. I hoped I didn't smell too bad, pre-shower.

"Hey, Jacinta?" I asked before she could leave.

"Yes?"

"Where's 813?"

She cocked her head and looked at me curiously. "Why do you ask?"

I was a little taken aback. "Um, I don't know, I was just wondering when I saw your phone number."

"Oh, my phone number," she said, chuckling. "When I was fourteen, my parents thought I should get a dose of real American living. So they sent me to boarding school in Florida. It was awful. I was back with them in Europe after three months! But I kept the cell phone, and I use it whenever I'm in the States."

"Oh," I said, thinking that I'd never heard of anyone being sent to boarding school in Florida.

And then, as quickly as she'd come over, she was gone. I watched her dash across the lawn, practically accosting a woman who was carrying cleaning supplies from a humble-looking car into the house.

I showered and put on another one of the dresses Mom had gotten me at Marc Jacobs. This one was a simple black shift, and my mother probably would have told me it was too dark and sophisticated for daytime entertaining, but thankfully she was still stuck in New York having her company emergency. I went into the kitchen and put on one of the prototype aprons my mother's company was considering releasing after "evaluating the success of our inaugural product line launch" or something similar my mother had babbled at me when showing me the aprons. It was made of some kind of super-fabulous organic white cotton and had a line drawing of my mother's smiling face emblazoned on the front.

I may not be Anne Rye, but I'm still her daughter and I've picked up a few things in the kitchen over the years. I sort of had to—she used to tote me around to her catering gigs like a combination personal assistant/trophy, dressing me in clothes that matched her own and teaching me about all the cooking and prep work. People thought it was so cute when the caterer's eight-year-old daughter stood behind a warming tray, spooning out apple compote or mashed potatoes or whatever was on the menu. When Mom opened the cupcake bakery in New York, sometimes I'd help out in the kitchen. That was in the early days, back when my mother did all her own handiwork, before she became a Brand Name™ and could hire loads of people to do things for her.

Still, I'm no slouch in the kitchen. And I make a mean mac and cheese—not that boxed Kraft stuff, but the real deal. As in, I use three kinds of cheese: Pecorino Romano, Gruyère, and sharp white cheddar cheese. And my mother taught me long ago that fresh pasta is almost always better than dried, boxed, or bagged pasta, so she either makes her own for dinner parties or keeps some fresh pasta from a specialty store on hand. She happened to have fresh elbow macaroni from Citarella in the fridge, so I was in luck. Throw in some nutmeg, pepper, milk, flour, bits of bread (yes, bread—makes it soooo good), salt and butter, and boom! I had whipped up a truly kickass version of a classic American treat. At the last minute, I decided to take some bacon my mother had bought from the butcher, fry it up, slice it into little pieces, and add it to the mixture. I did this for two reasons: one, bacon makes everything better; and two, my mother is disdainful of the trend in which people add bacon to things that don't require bacon (like ice cream, milk shakes, salads, you name it—people are nuts for bacon these days). Then I cut up some watermelon into cubes and tossed it with some balsamic vinaigrette, arugula, and feta.

The doorbell rang at eleven thirty, and the florist and her assistants marched in with three big vases of red roses and three big vases of white roses. I didn't know what to do with them, so I just kind of spread them around the first floor. I even put one vase in the bathroom, because why not? The bell rang again at noon, while the macaroni was gently bubbling in the oven. I took off my apron and went to the door to find Jacinta wringing her hands on the front steps.

"Jesus," I said when I opened the door. "You look amazing."

She was wearing purple eye makeup that set off her enormous green eyes, and a beautiful mint-green sleeveless dress that consisted of finely wrought lace over a satiny sheath. Little, slouchy green leather elf boots and lavender fishnets completed the look. It was delicate and sweet and sexy and hip.

"She's not here yet," Jacinta said, looking at me with mournful eyes. "She's not coming, is she?"

"It's only noon," I reminded her, ushering her into the house. "She's coming at one. Did you decide about the cookies?"

She looked at me blankly. Then something seemed to register.

"Oh, the snickerdoodles," she said. "Delilah's favorites. They're coming at twelve forty-five."

I put a hand on each of her arms and looked up at her. I'm not the type of girl who touches people a lot, but this girl was a serial hugger, and I figured I wasn't crossing any boundaries. "Jacinta," I said. "Are you okay?"

"I'm freaking out," she whispered.

I steered her over to the couch. "Lay down," I ordered. "Or lie down. I never know which one it is."

"I don't know, either," she said faintly, obeying me.

I made a mental note to check my SAT book. That was exactly the kind of trick they'd probably use to make you lose points.

Then I heard the oven timer ding.

"That's the mac and cheese," I told her. "I've got to take it out to cool."

"Mac and cheese?" Jacinta repeated, looking confused. "Like Kraft mac and cheese?"

"No way," I said. "I don't mess with that Kraft garbage. This is the real deal. Homemade with fancy cheeses."

Jacinta looked a little relieved that I had made a properly pretentious version of comfort food. I left her on the couch and went to the kitchen to get the dish out of the oven. Then the doorbell rang, and it was Jacinta's housekeeper with the snickerdoodles. *Then* I realized I still hadn't set the table on the deck, or made fresh lemonade.

I bustled about, feeling like Suzy Homemaker, and set out what my mother would have called "an exquisite spread" on the table on the back deck. I was so consumed in my activity that I jumped a little when the doorbell rang.

Delilah Fairweather stood on the front porch wearing a red shirtdress that had probably been a gift from Ralph Lauren himself. She looked like the epitome of an all-American girl. Skags would've scolded me for the thought, pointing out that America is a vast mosaic of individuals of different ethnic backgrounds, colors, shapes, etc.—but Delilah certainly had that classic Barbie look down pat.

"Hello there," Delilah said.

"C'mon in," I said, ushering her into the foyer.

"Your house is beautiful," she cooed. "Your mother has perfect taste."

"She's an expert shopper," I said. "Can I get you something to drink?"

"You couldn't do a mimosa, could you?" she asked mischievously, her big blue eyes sparkling.

"Sadly, no," I said. "I know I sound like a nerd, but my mom would flip if she found out I'd opened any of her champagne."

"Oh, that's no problem," Delilah said. "I forget that most people's parents actually notice if they steal their alcohol. Merilee isn't the most—attentive mommy." She giggled.

"I just made some lemonade. Want any?"

"You made it yourself?" Delilah sounded truly impressed. "Of course I'd like some!" Then her eyes widened in surprise. I looked over my shoulder in the direction she was looking, and there in the doorway to the living room was Jacinta Trimalchio, pale as could be in her little dress and elf boots. Delilah instantly generated a friendly smile and looked at me expectantly.

"Oh," I said, a little confused. "Delilah, this is my neighbor, Jacinta Trimalchio."

Delilah gave a squeal of delight.

"Oh my gosh," she said, grinning wide. "I *adore* your site. It's *such* a pleasure to finally meet you." Jacinta appeared frozen by some invisible force, so I gamely put my arm around her waist and pushed her forward. I may get a case of the Nervous Naomi Babbles now and then, but I don't think I've ever appeared this terrified when being introduced to a new person. Jacinta, on the other hand, was looking at Delilah as if she were a ghost.

"Jacinta," I said after an uncomfortable silence. "This is Delilah Fairweather." It was such an unnecessary statement that I immediately felt embarrassed.

"Why don't you sit down and tell me all about the site," Delilah suggested, and I felt a rush of gratitude toward her.

Here she was, confronted with a freakishly silent girl, and she was really making an effort to make her comfortable. Without a word, Jacinta obeyed. The two girls sat on opposite ends of the living room couch staring at each other, while I stood with hands awkwardly clasped in front of me.

"For how long have you been blogging?" Delilah asked politely.

"S-since I was fourteen," Jacinta said in a voice barely above a whisper. "Four years."

"Well, I've been a *huge* fan for the past three," Delilah said, soldiering onward. "I remember the first time you featured me in a Spotlight, when Mom and I did the red carpet for the Whitney Museum benefit. I couldn't believe it. I was so excited."

"That's lovely," Jacinta said faintly.

I could tell this was going to be a complete disaster. Jacinta was acting completely out of character. Okay, so it occurred to me that I didn't exactly know her character very well, but she sure wasn't the confident, bubbly girl with whom I'd gone to lunch.

"I'm going to get some lemonade and cookies," I announced in an unusually high-pitched voice. "Be right back." I turned on my heel and left, and heard someone rush after me.

"I'm freaking out," Jacinta whispered urgently as we walked into the kitchen.

"What's going on?" I whispered. "You were so excited about meeting her."

"I'm just—I guess—oh, I don't know," she fretted as I poured three glasses of lemonade and set them on a tray. "I've wanted to meet her for so long, and now I just don't know what to say. She's so—*her*, you know?"

I tried hard to conceal my growing annoyance. I hate awkward social situations, and it feels like they're *always* happening around me. I put some snickerdoodles on the tray and pushed it toward her.

"Here," I said in a voice that sounded oddly like my mother's. "She's your guest. You bring her the cookies and lemonade."

"Don't leave me alone in there with her!" Jacinta pleaded.

"I have to make a phone call," I said, sounding colder than I'd intended.

Practically shivering, Jacinta sighed and picked up the tray, walking into the other room. I got out my cell phone, walking out onto the deck and shutting the door carefully behind me.

"What's up?" Skags asked when she picked up her phone. "How's everything in the land of moneybags and Botox?"

"Completely weird," I said. "I had Delilah over to meet this girl who lives next door, Jacinta. She's this style blogger who thinks Delilah is the next big supermodel, and she threw this crazy party the other night with a Ferris wheel and carnival games and fireworks in the backyard."

"Look at you, socializing," Skags said. "Your mother must be delirious with excitement. Her little girl's making plastic friends!"

"Ugh," I said. "I don't think Delilah's going to be my friend after this. This girl Jacinta is acting crazy. It's like she can't even talk because she's so starstruck."

"Starstruck?" Skags snorted. "Over *Delilah Fairweather*?"

"They're in the living room right now, and it's just so awkward," I said.

"You left them alone?" Skags laughed. "Yeah, you're a really great hostess, Naomi."

"Well, what else am I supposed to do?" I hissed. "Jacinta's the one who made me have Delilah over, and I made lunch for us and everything, but I seriously don't think I can suffer through another hour of this weirdness."

"Dude, I don't know what to tell you," Skags said. "But I gotta go. I've got a tennis date at two."

"With that hot girl we met at the courts that one time?"

"Nope." Skags sounded very self-satisfied. "You'll never guess who I'm playing tennis with."

"Carter?" Carter was our extremely preppy gay guy friend. He was always trying to get us to play tennis or croquet or some other fancy activity.

"Jenny Carpenter."

"*What?*" I gasped. "Just the other day she was buying a burrito from you, and now you're tennis buddies?"

"Dude, I told you," Skags said. "The girl freaking loves me."

"No way. Absolutely no way. That girl is straight as an arrow."

"She asked if I wanted to play tennis. It's totally a date."

"But—but—we're talking about Jenny *Carpenter*. The

Queen Beast!" I was thoroughly baffled. "I mean, she doesn't even talk to girls who don't have Louis Vuitton purses."

"Well, she talks to me," Skags said a little huffily. "I gotta go. Good luck with Barbie and her Web stalker." She hung up abruptly, and I felt a little guilty for dismissing her Jenny Carpenter fantasy.

I groaned aloud. I knew I had to go back into that living room, but I really, really, really didn't want to. I stalled in the kitchen for a few minutes, wiping down surfaces that didn't need to be wiped down, before I resigned myself to reentering the living room.

When I returned to the living room, I was confronted by a sight that confused me even more than Jacinta's earlier behavior had.

Jacinta and Delilah had both kicked off their shoes. Jacinta sat on the couch with her feet tucked under her, her head propped up in her hand, her elbow resting on the back of the couch. She was leaning toward Delilah, her eyes rapt with attention. For her part, Delilah had stretched out on the couch and draped her legs over Jacinta's lap. When I walked in, Delilah was laughing gently at something Jacinta had said. The energy in the room couldn't have changed more drastically. The two seemed like the absolute best of friends.

I stood in the doorway for what seemed like an eternity before Delilah looked up and noticed me.

"Oh, Naomi!" she exclaimed in her sweet girly voice. "We're having the *best* time. I can't believe I *finally* got to meet the girl behind *The Wanted.*" She shot Jacinta a look I couldn't read, and Jacinta appeared to stifle a giggle.

"Oh, um, that's great," I said, waiting for Jacinta to look at me and say something. But she remained facing Delilah, her expression blissful.

"Did you guys want lunch?" I asked lamely.

At this, Jacinta turned and smiled at me. "I was just asking Delilah over to see my house, love," she said. Then, almost as if an afterthought, she added, "And you're welcome to come, too. But then, you've already seen it."

"Not the whole place," I said. "Like the non-blue bedrooms. Maybe after that we could come back and have lunch?"

"Of course," Jacinta said, and she and Delilah rose to their feet.

We walked over to Jacinta's mansion, the girls murmuring and giggling conspiratorially in front of me while I trailed after. It wasn't hard to feel left out, though my feeling of exclusion was trumped by my absolute astonishment at the 180-degree turn-around in the girls' attitudes. "I *must* see the pool first," Delilah announced, and Jacinta obliged her by leading us out back to the river pool. Delilah squealed with delight at the waterslides, the footbridges, the whole setup.

"It looks like it's got a *current*," she said with wonder, looking at Jacinta.

"It does," Jacinta said. "You should come over to swim. Or just to float."

"I'll come *every day*," Delilah said, and she almost sounded as if she really meant it.

Then it was time for the tour of the indoors, which took quite a while because the place was so huge. Turns out I'd only seen part of the house. On the first floor, I was familiar with the bathroom, main kitchen, dining room, living room, foyer, slightly smaller second living room, cigar room, billiards room, and library. But I hadn't seen the home theater or the greenhouse attached to the far side of the house, the side not facing my mother's place.

That greenhouse was really something. When we walked in, I heard Delilah gasp. The whole place was blooming with red and white rosebushes. She looked at Jacinta in wonder.

"It was empty when I got here," Jacinta said by way of explanation. "I put in a big order at the nursery."

"It's *beautiful*," Delilah whispered reverently.

"Better than the snickerdoodles?" Jacinta asked. I cast a curious glance at her. One thing didn't seem to have much to do with the other.

"I don't know . . . the snickerdoodles were *pretty* great," Delilah said.

"Would you call them 'scrumptious'?" Jacinta inquired. This cracked Delilah up for some reason. I had the uncomfortable feeling that I was a truly unnecessary addition to this little social gathering—a real third wheel.

"Oh, but you haven't seen the upstairs yet, love!" Jacinta suddenly cried, and Delilah clapped excitedly. Delilah held her hand out to Jacinta, and Jacinta's eyes widened. When she took the proffered hand, you could fairly see the electricity crackle up her rail-thin arm. Together, she and Delilah floated in some invisible cloud out of the green room, down the long hall and into the foyer, where they ascended the stairs as if by magic. I couldn't have been less a part of their world if I'd actually left the house and gone home—something I was strongly considering.

Upstairs, we went through the rainbow of rooms and bathrooms in reverse order—indigo, blue, green, yellow, orange, and finally red.

"This is my favorite part of the entire house," Jacinta said proudly, pointing to what looked like a closet door.

"Is it a walk-in?" I asked, trying to reinsert myself into the conversation. Both girls looked at me with surprise, as if they'd completely forgotten I was there.

In response, Jacinta flung open the door to reveal a set of display shelves, dramatically lit from above. On the shelves was a series of similar-looking handbags in a rainbow of colors. They didn't look too impressive to me, but Delilah seemed bowled over. She stared at the bags, her blue eyes filling with tears.

"They're—they're so beautiful," she said softly, her voice catching a little. "They're all Birkins, aren't they?"

Jacinta nodded.

This was unprecedented. I'd never seen Delilah cry, ever. I'd never even seen her get teary-eyed. And suddenly it occurred to me that I was an intruder in a private moment I hadn't been meant to see, and though I couldn't imagine why or how it had all come to this—Delilah Fairweather crying over handbags in the bedroom of some blogger—it was time for me to go.

"I'm going to go put the macaroni and cheese back in the oven," I said. "If you get hungry for lunch, come over." I turned around and left them there, not waiting for a reaction, since I was pretty certain one wasn't forthcoming anyway.

I walked back across the lawn in the shining afternoon sun and cleared the table on the deck. I stored the mac and cheese and salad in the fridge and grabbed my cell phone, intending to call Skags. Instead, I found myself dialing Jeff Byron.

"How's it going?" he asked cheerfully.

"Too weird to explain," I said honestly. "Want to come over and watch a movie?"

"Screw the sunshine," he said.

He was over in fifteen minutes.

Jeff stayed through dinner, and I served him the meal I'd intended to give my original guests. While he scarfed down two bowls of mac and cheese, I told him all about Jacinta and Delilah.

"That's so bizarre," he said. "And by the way, adding bacon to this was a genius move."

"Thanks," I said. "So what do you think? I mean, does Delilah usually cry at handbags?"

He laughed. "Delilah doesn't usually cry at anything. That girl's life is perfect."

"It was so weird," I said with a sigh, spearing a piece of watermelon with my fork.

"I'll tell you one thing," he said through a mouthful of mac and cheese.

"Yeah?"

"Those chicks are totally making out right now," he said, cracking himself up.

"Gross!" I said, throwing a balled-up napkin at him. He laughed harder and tossed it back at me. I threw some watermelon at him, and he returned with a volley of arugula. We were about to launch into a full-scale food fight when my mother swept into the room.

"Hello, darlings," Mom said brightly in the super-fake voice she only uses in front of important strangers. "Jeffrey, lovely to see you again."

"Hi, Mrs. Rye," he said.

"Hi, Mom," I giggled.

She looked at the small mess we'd made and opened her mouth to say something, then shut it and smiled tightly.

"I've had a *very* long day," she said. "Naomi, take care that all the lights get turned off, yes? I'm going to bed."

She disappeared upstairs, and pretty soon Jeff and I were back in the home theater in the basement. We stayed down there long after the movie ended.

# CHAPTER SEVEN

I t's weird how plans change.

Before I got to New York for the summer, I figured it'd be the usual routine each day—wake up when my mother yelled at me, eat some of her amazing food, dive into some books, break for lunch, hit the books again, and have dinner at home alone while she went out to some social function or another. Of course, there would inevitably be times when she'd drag me against my will to the Horticulture Society benefit or some boring polo event, and on certain days I'd actually feel like trekking to the beach for a bit, but generally my life in the Hamptons would follow a very familiar pattern.

Then Jacinta Trimalchio entered my life, and everything changed.

Because of what happened on the Ferris wheel at her party, I had a boyfriend for the first time in my life. We didn't use that word or anything, but it's basically what Jeff Byron instantly became to me.

We hung out all the time, watching movies—or pretending to, anyway—going to the beach, hiking, and trying the lobster rolls at every beach shack and fancy restaurant for miles around. Jeff said he wanted to learn how to cook, so I taught him how to make his favorite things: mac and cheese, pizza, spaghetti with meatballs, and even pad thai. He took me waterskiing, which was mildly terrifying but also incredibly fun. We talked about politics and history and lay around listening to NPR podcasts, our fingers intertwined. Once my mother walked in on us quizzing each other on SAT words in the living room in the middle of the night.

"It's two o'clock in the morning," she said wearily. "As long as you're awake, shouldn't you be at a bonfire on the beach or—or something fun, dears?"

"This is pretty fun," Jeff said.

"You two are perfect for each other," Mom said, sighing. She turned around and went back to bed.

I liked almost everything about Jeff except for the fact that my mother approved so wholeheartedly.

During the hours when I wasn't with Jeff, I was with Jacinta—and, usually, Delilah. They were always throwing little tea parties and slightly-more-adult-beverage parties over at Jacinta's house in the afternoons. Ainsley Devereaux would come over and divide her time between kissing up to Jacinta and fawning over Delilah. The Fitzwilliams sisters would show up, and a pair of girl cousins whose family owned the *New York Times*, and other girls whose names I had trouble remembering. They seemed interchangeable to me—they all had horses, and long shiny hair, and bright white teeth, and plans to go to Harvard or Yale or Princeton or wherever their fathers and grandfathers had gone. A few of them carried that type of bag Jacinta had stockpiled upstairs—the Birkin, Delilah had called it.

Once, we all sat on the deck drinking mojitos and trading sex stories. Obviously, I didn't have much to contribute, even though I was gaining more experience with Jeff on that particular front. And Jacinta kept herself busy freshening everyone's drinks, so she didn't speak up much, either. When Ainsley mischievously asked Delilah how it was with Teddy, Delilah rolled her eyes.

"Ugh," she said. "We hardly ever do it anymore." The Fitzwilliams sisters exchanged a look, and Ainsley Devereaux wore a pert smile. I remembered how she'd treated Misti at Jacinta's party. Then I remembered how Jeff said everybody knew about Teddy and Misti. I wondered if Delilah knew.

Jacinta smiled gently and poured Delilah another mojito.

The girls were all perfectly nice to me, warmer with each subsequent visit. There were group beach excursions where Ainsley exclaimed over the flatness of my stomach ("You mean you don't even have a *trainer*? God, I am so jealous!") and the Fitzwilliams sisters asked me which clubs in Chicago checked IDs. (I had no idea.)

And something funny started to happen, something that

had never happened before during all the summers I'd spent in the Hamptons. I started to feel like I almost *belonged*. I didn't come from the kind of pedigree these girls had, and I didn't get all their references to private schools and Swiss ski resorts and high-end designer this-or-thats, but for the first time, I was one of them. I began to realize that they weren't so bad, at least not all the time. You just had to ask them questions about things *they* were interested in: shopping, parties, horses, guys. Sometimes I would bake surprises for our afternoon get-togethers, and the girls would squeal with delight over my creations (when they weren't moaning that I was going to make everybody fat by the end of the summer).

The most fun, though, happened after the other girls left, drifting home to parentally mandated dinners. That was when Jacinta and Delilah and I floated lazily on mini-rafts in the river pool, letting the current take us, talking about everything and nothing. But at times I'd catch them staring at each other with what I could only describe as longing. Something was developing between them that went beyond friendship. It was like they got high off each other, and every mutual encounter was another chance to feel some sort of pleasure that was very specific to their union. There was me, and then there was the Delilah-Jacinta combo, a two-headed blond creature. It was almost like watching two people fall in love. I didn't feel left out, but there always came a certain moment when I knew it was time for me to leave them alone. I'd excuse myself to go to the bathroom or just to walk outside for a moment, and when I returned, I always felt as if I were interrupting something. But they took pains to make me feel welcome, so I stayed. I could tell they both genuinely liked me. It felt good to be genuinely liked, especially in a place where I usually felt genuinely ignored. Even with Skags, I was always the beta friend. I knew a lot of people at school saw me as her sidekick. But when Delilah Fairweather trained those big blue eyes on you and told you she was glad to hang out with you and you alone, you believed it. I believed it, anyway.

Since they knew I was invariably going to see Jeff in the evening, they assured me I needed to look super-hot each time. It was like I was their pet project. I protested that I was giving him an unrealistic impression of my own grooming habits—left to my own devices, I'd go bare-faced, with my hair in a pony-tail. But Jacinta and Delilah seemed horrified by the prospect of my leaving the house in anything but a full face of makeup.

"It's not that you aren't naturally beautiful, love," Jacinta said one day as she carefully applied lipstick to my mouth with a lip brush. "It's just that—well—what would you say, Delilah?"

"A guy likes to see that a girl has made an effort for him," Delilah said helpfully.

"I think you're both nuts," I said, laughing. "You're like the fussy older sisters I never had." Skags would've probably said that they were forcing me to embody conventional, narrow-minded notions of femininity—and that I was woefully complicit with my own subjugation—but Skags wasn't there. And we weren't talking all that much these days, so it's not like I gave her the details. She wouldn't have understood. She would have said I was turning into a Beast (one of the evil ones, not her newly beloved Jenny Carpenter), and I couldn't take her judgment when I was this happy.

After I was all done up, Delilah would leave for dinner with Teddy, either at the Barringtons' place or at her parents' place. She and Jacinta seemed to have an unspoken understanding that while her days belonged to Jacinta, her nights belonged to Teddy. And because Jacinta always seemed a little sad to see Delilah go, I'd stay awhile, sipping tea with her on the back deck. Eventually it would be time for me to meet Jeff, and I'd give Jacinta a hug goodbye. When I left, I always paused for a moment on the lawn and looked back at her house. It gave me a tiny pang to leave her there all alone, though I couldn't have told you why.

One day, after everyone else had gone home, Jacinta shut the door behind Delilah and walked into the kitchen looking particularly forlorn.

"I hope you don't get this sad when *I* leave," I joked, trying to coax a smile from her.

She looked at me quite seriously and said, "Well, it's a completely different thing with you and me than it is with me and Delilah."

"Ah," I said, trying not to feel insulted.

"We just . . ." She hesitated a moment and peered at me closely, as if she were searching for something. I guess she found it, because she continued, "We've actually known each other a bit longer than we let on. We knew each other when we were kids. Briefly. So this has all been a bit of a reunion for us."

"Oh," I said. "That makes sense, actually. It sometimes seems like you are speaking your own language. Why didn't you tell me?"

Jacinta smiled a little. "I guess we wanted to keep it to ourselves a little while longer. We used to play together every day as kids. Her housekeeper used to call *everything* 'scrumptious,'" she recalled fondly. "Like, literally everything. And she always baked us snickerdoodles. And we had matching mini-Birkins when we were kids. Hers was red; mine was white. Don't tell anybody though, okay?"

I thought about this new revelation on my way across the lawn to my house, where Jeff was going to pick me up for dinner. I didn't begrudge the girls their friendship, or their semi-secret past. It just seemed a little . . . intense for just a regular friendship, actually. And I still didn't understand why they hadn't been open with me about the fact that they used to hang out when they were little, but I didn't know them *that* well, after all.

I tried to call Skags a couple of times, but either she couldn't talk more than a few minutes or she didn't pick up the phone. I guess I could've tried harder to call Skags, or at least to text back and forth, but it seemed like something else was always coming up—a clambake, or a day at the village spa with Jacinta and Delilah, or a long bike ride with Jeff. Usually I spent all summer wishing I were back in Chicago, but at some point that summer I stopped thinking about home.

# CHAPTER EIGHT

I was so involved in my newly busy summer, in fact, that I didn't even remember to call my dad to check in. He had to call me.

We were at the beach when my cell lit up with an incoming call from Dad.

"Hey, Dad!" I chirped with an amount of excitement that astonished even me. I'm not exactly what you'd call perky, but suddenly I sounded like a cheerleader hopped up on cotton candy and Pixy Stix.

"Hey there, kiddo," he said. With his Chicago accent, it sounded more like "Ey dere, kiddo."

"Whatcha up to?" he asked.

I looked around. Jeff lay on his back on our huge beach towel, napping. I traced the lines of his body with my eyes, admiring the muscles I was growing to know so well. He had that thing some super-buff guys get (I don't know what it's called, I haven't taken anatomy yet) when a couple of their lower abdominal muscles make this sort of V shape that points directly to—

Well.

Anyway.

That's not the sort of thing you tell your dad.

"I'm not up to much," I said, turning my attention to my toes, which had been painted pale pink a few days before during a spontaneous mother-daughter pedicure downtown. I'd been wandering around killing time, waiting to meet Jeff after his golf game, and I ran into my own mom outside a salon. She suggested we get our toes done, so we did. It was kind of nice and she only annoyed me, like, twice in thirty minutes. That's got to be a record for her.

"No time to call your dad, though," Dad said a little gruffly. "I'm used to hearing from you at least once a week when you're over there."

"I'm sorry, Dad. I guess I have been kinda busy. Hanging out with friends and stuff."

"Friends?" He sounded surprised. "Since when do you have friends at the beach?"

"Since, I don't know. This year. It's not as lonely."

"You still reading that SAT book?"

"When I have time," I lied. The truth was that other than our late-night study session that so surprised my mother, I'd largely been ignoring my SAT book. It was just that there were always other things to do, like hang out with the girls or go night-swimming at the beach with Jeff or go biking around the neighborhood with Jeff or go hiking on some of the old horse trails with Jeff. There was also frequently dinner at Jeff's house with his post-divorce-depressed mom, who always seemed to perk up when I was around. And at night—especially at night—there were other things to do with Jeff.

I talked to my dad for a few more minutes about the summer basketball camp he was running, the classes I had signed up for the first semester of senior year, what was happening in the neighborhood back home—stuff like that. Then he asked the question he always asks on these phone calls, maybe to be polite, or maybe because he actually still cares about her in some way.

"How's your mother?" he asked, clearing his throat.

Usually, I respond with "She sucks" or something similarly hostile, and then he gives me a mini-talk about how I've got to be nice, or at least patient, and that the summer will be over soon and I won't have to see her again until Thanksgiving. But this summer was kind of different, and so was my answer.

"She's okay," I said. "She's all into her company going public, so she's in the city a lot. Mostly she stays out of my way, but I see her sometimes, and it's not too bad."

"Wow," my dad said, sounding surprised. "I think that's the best report I've ever gotten from you, kiddo."

"Well, it's not like I *like* hanging out with her," I said defensively. He laughed.

"It's okay to not hate your mother," he said.

"Whatever," I said, a little irritated. I'm not used to feeling irritated with my dad, so I figured I'd get off the phone before I said something crappy.

We exchanged a few more words, and I told him I loved him, and then the call was over.

"No mention of your hot summer lover?" Jeff said without opening his eyes.

"Ewwww," I said. "'Lover' is such a gross word."

"Lover," he said, sitting up and grinning at me. "Lovaaaah, lovaaah, lovaaah."

"Oh, nasty," I said, punching him lightly in the arm. He grabbed me and started tickling me, shouting "lover, lover, lover" over and over again while I cracked up. I had just started fighting back and was tickling him in slightly inappropriate places when I heard someone walk up. I looked up, and there was Jacinta Trimalchio, carrying a vintage-looking robin's-egg blue parasol with pretty white ruffles.

Because Jacinta Trimalchio could never wear anything run-of-the-mill, she was sporting what looked like a 1920s bathing costume—a long black tank with little shorts attached, seemingly made of a jersey cotton instead of Lycra or Spandex or whatever is usually in bathing suits these days.

"Do you ever say to yourself, 'Hey, I think I'm just gonna go for a subtle look today'?" Jeff asked, teasing her. I looked at his dimples and almost melted.

"No," Jacinta said seriously. "Why would I do that?"

"I don't know," Jeff said. "To fit in?"

"Fitting in is overrated," Jacinta said simply. She turned her attention to me.

"Delilah's at a model agent's in Manhattan today," she announced, apropos of nothing. "Ford Models. They've launched the careers of so many of my favorites, I can't even count."

"Oh," I said. "That sounds nice. Yeah, I haven't really seen you girls for a couple of days."

"A break in your busy tea party schedule," Jeff said.

"We've been . . . ," Jacinta began, and then her porcelain face flushed. She was opening her mouth to say something else when another girl wandered up. This girl was short and curvy, with breasts so large that they almost appeared aggressive in their need for attention. She wore a white bikini and white sandals and carried a white straw beach bag that probably cost more money than one semester of tuition at Trumbo. There was something about the tilt of her chin and the way she pursed her lips that made me immediately dislike her.

"What's up, Olivia?" Jeff said lazily.

Great. Another pretty robot from Trumbo. I restrained myself from rolling my eyes and tried to act friendly.

"Not much," Olivia said. She looked at me with slight interest.

"You're Anne Rye's daughter, right?" Her expression was hard to read behind her giant sunglasses, but I could tell she was trying to be friendly.

"Yeah, I'm Naomi," I said. "Nice to meet you."

"You too," she said with a syrupy-sweet smile. "All I hear

about at home these days is good things about your mom's company."

"Really?" I asked, surprised.

"My parents are investors," she said, as if that were a normal job to have. "And," Olivia added, "they've been looking at your mom's company."

"Oh, that's—that's really nice," I said. "Yeah, she, um—she works really hard."

"Trust me, I know *all* about it," she said with a friendly little laugh. "You should come over for dinner sometime. My parents would ask you about a zillion questions."

"Is it weird for you that your mom has fans?" Jeff asked.

"Oh, they're not *fans*, exactly," Olivia said quickly, frowning at Jeff. "I mean they're looking for a good investment."

"That's genuinely fascinating, Olivia," Jeff said, and I tried not to laugh. He could be such a nonchalant asshole sometimes, and it was hilarious.

Olivia ignored him and turned back to me. "But really, you ought to come by sometime," she said.

"Sure," I said without enthusiasm. I'm not an idiot. I can tell when people are being nice to me just because they know who my mom is. Then Olivia turned to Jacinta, acknowledging her for the first time, and her demeanor completely changed.

"You're Jacinta Trimalchio," she said frostily, as if it were an accusation. Jacinta smiled warmly.

"Yes, I am," she said. "And I know who you are, love. Olivia Bentley. *Young Hamptons.* I *adore* your blog."

"I'm sure you do," Olivia said nastily. "I see you using my party photos all the time."

"Oh, I hope that's all right," Jacinta said apologetically. "I always give credit and link back to *Young Hamptons*."

"I noticed," Olivia said. "I get more traffic from your blog than from anywhere else." You could tell she wasn't so much grateful as bitterly resentful.

I looked at Jeff. He looked at me.

*Catfight!* he mouthed, grinning. I widened my eyes and nodded in agreement.

It was more like a cat-puppy fight than anything. Olivia had her claws out, but Jacinta clearly just wanted to make friends and play.

"We should collaborate sometime!" Jacinta suggested brightly. "Cross-posting features, or writing a post together, something like that. You have the best Hamptons coverage of anyone, year-round."

"I can tell you think so," Olivia said. "I mean, based on how often you post about things that I've just posted about."

Jacinta looked at her in surprise. I think it was just beginning to occur to her that Olivia might not have the best intentions. Jacinta was kind of mysterious and possibly a liar or at least a major exaggerator, but she was *not* a bitch. I don't think she had a mean bone in her entire long, skinny body.

"So you're European, right?" Olivia asked, popping her sunglasses up on her head.

"Yes," Jacinta said a little cautiously. "Well, partly. My

mother's family is from Montana. My father's family is Spanish."

"That's funny," said Olivia. "Because 'Trimalchio' is an Italian name. Isn't it." She raised an eyebrow. She was acting like a cop who was just beginning to interrogate a perp on *SVU* or something.

"Spanish by way of Italy," Jacinta said without missing a beat.

"I'm sure," Olivia said. "And where did you go to school?"

"Oh, all over," Jacinta said. "Tutors, mostly. A bit of time in a Swiss boarding school."

"Which one?" Olivia asked, widening her eyes with the fakest curiosity you ever saw. "My sister teaches in Bern."

"In—oh, she's in *Bern*," Jacinta said. "Yes, well, we were out in the countryside—far, far away from Bern. Little boarding school. Only about fifty students. No one has ever heard of it."

"My cousins all go to a little boarding school in the Swiss countryside," Olivia said. "I wonder if it's the same school."

"Probably not," Jacinta said.

"I think it's so interesting," Olivia said, "that you comment on all these parties and what everyone's wearing, but you're never actually *at* any of them."

"Well, I've been traveling a great deal," Jacinta said. "Living all over the world. This has just sort of been a hobby of mine."

"Looking at strangers' party photos and writing about their outfits," Olivia said.

Jacinta looked her straight in the eye, with a level expression.

"Exactly," she said firmly. "That's how I have my fun." Then she smiled brightly.

I could've hugged her. She wasn't backing down in the face of this jerk's attitude, and she'd dispensed with trying to win her over.

Olivia looked frustrated, and then she shoved her sunglasses back over her eyes.

"Well," she said. "Nice talking to all of you." Her tone indicated that it had been anything but nice.

"Lovely to meet you," Jacinta said sweetly.

Without responding, Olivia turned on her heel and stalked off down the beach.

"She's a real charmer," Jeff said when Olivia was a safe distance down the beach.

"Jacinta, come sit with me," I said, scooting over so that I was sitting in the middle of our giant beach towel. Jacinta gratefully plopped down next to me and gave me a little side-hug.

Jacinta asked Jeff about his most recent golf game, and he lit up and started talking about how he'd almost hit a deer on the back nine. Surprisingly, Jacinta seemed to know a lot about the big golf stars (I couldn't have given a crap), and she and Jeff were trading facts about some guy named Graeme McDowell when something suddenly blocked the sun and cast an enormous shadow over the three of us. It was quickly joined by two slightly smaller shadows. I looked up and right into the eyes of Teddy Barrington.

"Hi, Naomi," he said with a broad smile. "It's so great to see you. Where have you been?" His two companions, who looked like less handsome carbon copies of himself, looked at me with curiosity.

I cringed inwardly. I hadn't seen him since the night I caught him shoving Misti at Baxley's. I could tell he was doing the "everything's totally fine and completely normal" thing, and that I was expected to play my part.

"Hi, Teddy," I said uncomfortably.

"Theodore," Jeff said, reaching up.

"Jeffrey," Teddy said, and bumped fists with him.

"Brock, Reilly," Jeff said, bumping fists with each of the other guys in turn. It was like watching some weird male-bonding ritual. I felt like an anthropologist in the field.

"Guys, this is Naomi," Teddy said, gesturing to me. "She's friends with Delilah and *special* friends with Jeff."

"We're more like buddies," Jeff said, slinging an arm around me. As awkward as I felt around Teddy, I couldn't help but appreciate the warmth of Jeff's skin against mine.

"S'up," said Brock.

"Hey," said Reilly.

"Nice to meet you," I said. "And this is Jacinta."

Teddy raised his eyebrows, and a slow smile spread across his lips. "*The* Jacinta Trimalchio," he said, peering down at her. She looked nervous and twisted her hands a little.

"Teddy Barrington," he said, sticking out his big hand and shaking her delicate one vigorously. When he released his grip,

I could tell by the way she flexed her fingers that they were a bit sore.

"Nice to meet you," Jacinta said faintly.

"She's Delilah's new best friend," he told Brock and Reilly. They nodded in tandem.

"In fact," Teddy added, "they hang out so much, I feel like I barely see my own girlfriend anymore. At least not until the nighttime. But I guess that's when it counts, right?" He let out a dry chuckle. Jacinta's big eyes widened, and for a moment I genuinely felt worried. She looked like a tiny animal confronted by a huge beast. "I'm surprised I didn't recognize you right away," Teddy said, staring at Jacinta intently. "There are so many pictures of you and Delilah on Facebook now."

She gave a light laugh. "Oh, not so many," she said. "Ten. We were just playing dress-up the other day at my house. Doing our hair and makeup. Silly girly stuff."

"Yeah, that's what Teddy and I do when we hang out," Jeff said.

"That reminds me of an episode of *Oh, Those Masons!*" Teddy said, a faraway look stealing over his eyes. "The brothers dressed in drag to get into a hot girl's birthday party. I was in makeup for two hours. The director said I looked pretty in pink."

"That's kind of creepy, bro," Jeff said, cracking up.

"It wasn't creepy," Teddy said seriously. "It was art. You know what I mean, right, Naomi?"

"Uh, sure," I said. "Acting. It's art."

"Exactly," he said, smiling down at me as if I had just said something truly profound. "See, your girl gets me, Jeff. Me and her, we're on another level. She gets it." He winked at me, and I pretended not to notice.

"You been hanging out with Delilah at all, Naomi?" Teddy asked.

"Sometimes," I said cautiously. "I actually haven't seen her for a few days."

"That's too bad," he said. "You should come over for dinner sometime. You can bring Jeff, too, if you have to." He laughed as if he'd said something really funny.

"Thanks, bro," Jeff said.

"Maybe one day you could let Delilah see her old friends," Teddy said, looking pointedly at Jacinta.

"Oh," Jacinta said, looking flustered. "You know Delilah— she does whatever she wants."

"I do know Delilah," he said. "I've known Delilah since we were in kindergarten."

"That's sweet," Jacinta said. "When did you start dating?"

"You mean she hasn't told you the whole story?"

"No, I'm afraid she hasn't."

"I thought boys were all girls talked about. Besides, you know, hair and makeup."

"You're such a feminist, bro," Jeff said, squeezing my shoulder with his hand.

"Oh, we talk about all sorts of things at my house," Jacinta said, twisting her fingers together. "But I guess mostly fashion and style."

"I heard there was a wild party at your house the other week," Teddy said. He turned to his companions. "You guys remember the fireworks, right?"

"Oh, shit," Reilly said, suddenly becoming animated. "The party with the Ferris wheel. I heard about that. That was your place?"

Jacinta smiled and nodded with pride.

"Sounded badass," Brock grunted.

"You better invite us to your next party, Jacinta Trimalchio," Teddy said.

"How about tonight?" Jacinta asked.

I looked at Jeff. Jeff looked at me. We hadn't heard anything about a party at Jacinta's, and you'd think that since we were the only ones who were actually invited last time, she would've given us a heads-up.

"You're having a party tonight?" Teddy asked, raising an eyebrow.

"I am now," Jacinta said simply. "You can come over, have some drinks, see where Delilah's been spending her days." The tilt of her chin and the way she pursed her lips almost made it seem like a challenge.

Teddy looked at Brock and Reilly. Brock shrugged. Reilly scratched the back of his head.

"Sure," Teddy said. "What time?"

"Eight o'clock," Jacinta said. "Delilah can show you how to get there."

"I'm sure she knows the way by heart," Teddy said.

"She does," Jacinta said.

"Cool," Teddy said. "Great. We'll see you then." He and his boys said their goodbyes and walked off down the beach.

"It's one o'clock," I said. "Can you really put together a party by eight?"

"I can if Baxley's can cater it," Jacinta said, whipping out her cell phone. She walked away from us for a few minutes, talking on the phone and gesticulating enthusiastically.

"I like her," Jeff said to me in a low voice. "She's great. But she's super-weird, right? Like, it's not just me."

"She's—different," I said carefully. I knew what he meant, but I was suddenly feeling very protective of her.

Jacinta came back, triumphantly waving her cell phone in the air. "They said yes!" she said. "Which means I have to go to the bakery to get desserts, and to the florist to get flowers, and I've got to rent the chairs and tables—oh, I have so much to do, loves!" She wrung her hands but seemed more excited than nervous.

"Do you need any help?" Jeff asked.

"Just spread the word," Jacinta said, gathering up her parasol. "Text your friends. I'll email everyone, get the message out. This won't be a huge party like last time—I'll aim for maybe a hundred. And it's a white party! Everyone has to wear white."

"Ah," Jeff said. "Only a hundred. All white. Got it."

And then she was gone, swept away in a whirl of excitement.

"I guess we're going to a party tonight," I said.

Jeff put his arms around me and bent his head down to my ear.

"Then we've got some things to do in the meantime," he whispered. "Your mom isn't home, is she?"

"Nope," I said. "Sailing with investors."

"Perfect," Jeff said. "I'll race you to your house."

And so we were busy for the next few hours.

# CHAPTER NINE

Later, when it was time to go to Jacinta's party, I kicked Jeff out of my room so that I could put on my party outfit and makeup. When I came downstairs fifteen minutes later, he whistled.

"Lookin' good," he said approvingly. I was wearing a strapless white playsuit, kind of a '60s look, and my hair was in braids. I wore white espadrilles and had tucked a white gardenia from my mother's bedroom behind my ear.

"We're lucky you already had a white polo shirt with you," I said. "Otherwise, whomever would I take as my date?"

"I'm sure Brock or Reilly is available," he said, pulling me close to him.

"Ew," I said. "I don't date Cro-Mags."

It took us another few minutes to get out of the house, but once we were in view of Jacinta's backyard, I stopped short and gasped in wonder.

"*How* did she do this in just a few hours?" Jeff said in disbelief.

"I think she's magic," I said, and I wasn't really exaggerating.

Somehow, Jacinta had transformed her backyard into a white wonderland. White rose petals were scattered all over the ground like fragrant snow. White rose-shaped candles floated in the river pool. The trees were covered in white Christmas lights and white streamers. White chairs with white cushions, white tables draped with white lace tablecloths, white-clad cater waiters with white gloves serving food on white plates under a white tent—Jacinta had managed to assemble it all. At least one of the 1920s bands was back, dressed all in white and playing pre-Depression hits on the deck, which was draped with white bunting. And near the deck were two objects that would've seemed ridiculous and childish if they weren't so much fun—a giant white bouncy house and a huge white trampoline. One guy was already jumping on the trampoline, a champagne bottle in his hand, while his friends cracked up nearby. A few girls were eyeing the bouncy house, and I knew that as soon as they had a few glasses of wine in them, they'd be shrieking and squealing as they hopped around in their bare feet.

As we wandered the backyard, marveling at Jacinta's lightning-fast party planning, I overheard a few snatches of conversation.

"I got the text at one thirty and was already trying on white dresses by two," one girl said to another. "I had to get Hunter out of his sweaty golf clothes and into a nice white shirt and shorts."

"Oh, you'll use any excuse to get Hunter out of his clothes, you slut," her friend chortled.

"She could've given us more notice," a third girl complained. "She obviously had this planned way in advance—couldn't she have sent invitations last week or something? I had to cancel dinner with my parents, and they *hate* when I cancel."

"Oh my God, look who's working the party again," another girl hissed excitedly. "Think she'll 'serve' Teddy Barrington in the bouncy house?" The girls all dissolved into giggles.

Under the tent, Misti listlessly served grilled lobster and corn on the cob while Giovanni tended bar nearby. I went to get plates for Jeff and me, and I felt like I ought to say something nice.

"I like your dress," I said. It was a pretty white shirtdress with a little white belt—much cuter than the usual cater-waiter gear.

"Thanks," she said cautiously. "It's from Mandee. I'm lucky I had it with me or I would've been outta luck when they told us we had to wear all white. I couldna worked the gig." Then she looked over my shoulder, and her entire bored face lit up like the sunrise. It was so marked a change that I swiveled around to see what she saw.

Flanked by Reilly and Brock, Teddy strode around the side of the house, greeting passersby with fist bumps and hugs, almost like a politician. A few girls stopped and cooed over him, and he leaned down to say things that made them giggle and blush.

Then, about twenty paces behind Teddy, an obviously reluctant Delilah came into view. I glanced back at Misti and saw her face fall.

"Gio!" she yelled over her shoulder at Giovanni. "Make me a rum and Coke!"

He looked over the bar, surprised. "While we're workin'?"

She stared daggers at him. "What did I friggin' say? Yeah, while we're workin'!"

He looked a little scared. "Okay, baby," he said soothingly.

"Baby," Misti muttered, slapping a buttery piece of corn on the cob on my plate so that some of the butter splattered on my wrist. "Yeah, friggin' right." I murmured my thanks for the food and hustled my way back to the table where Jeff and I had set up camp. He was already a couple beers in by the time I sat down.

"You should've seen Misti's face when Teddy walked in," I said, handing him his plate. "She thinks he's like a god or something."

"I can't wait to see how he reacts when he sees *her*," Jeff said through a mouthful of corn. He chuckled a little. "Or even better, how Delilah will act when she sees her."

"Jeez, catty much?" I said. He shook his head and swallowed his food.

"Not catty," he said. "Observant. Interested. I'm fascinated by the strategy of it all. It's like golf. You hit the ball, hoping it goes one place, and sometimes it does. Other times, it doesn't.

Regardless, you've got to play it where it lies. Teddy came to this party, and Misti is here. He wasn't expecting that. So now what's he going to do? How's he going to play it?"

"I've heard enough sports analogies for one lifetime. My dad's a basketball coach, remember?" I dug into my grilled corn and wondered, not for the first time, if Jeff actually looked at people as if they were players in some kind of giant game. It seemed a little cold, but I remembered how Skags and I used to analyze the Beasts' antics back at school for our own amusement—their stupid fights, their little intragroup rivalries, their dumb drama over idiotic boys. Maybe it was kind of like that. And that was harmless, right?

But there was a big difference—Skags and I weren't friends with the Beasts. Well, not until her recent bonding with Jenny Carpenter, anyway. Jeff was supposed to be one of Teddy's best friends. So how could he look at Teddy's life with such amused detachment?

Maybe boys were just different about this stuff.

And anyway, Jeff didn't know anything about Teddy pushing Misti. I was sure he would've been less cavalier about the situation if he knew about that. Maybe I would tell him— eventually. Now clearly wasn't the moment.

"Oh, man," he said in a low voice. "Look at that."

I looked, and saw one of the most uncomfortable scenes I've ever witnessed: Jacinta Trimalchio, wearing a sleeveless ivory dress, plus white heels and a tiny white top hat set askew on her head, gingerly talking to a miserable-looking Delilah, who was wearing a tight white dress that seemed illegally short, and a very animated Teddy, who had his arm slung protectively around Delilah's shoulders. Brock and Reilly stood slightly behind him like sentries, watching the conversation unfold with expressionless faces. As I watched, Teddy threw an arm around Jacinta and drew both girls close to him, lowering his head and murmuring something. Whatever he said, it didn't go over well—Jacinta pulled back and looked startled, while Delilah furiously threw off his arm and snapped at him. This only served to make him laugh, and he cast a glance at Brock and Reilly, both of whom began laughing, too. Delilah stalked off toward the house, grabbing Jacinta's hand and pulling her along.

"I should go talk to Jacinta," I said, standing up so fast I almost upset my glass of wine. "Something crazy is going on."

"You're a good friend," Jeff said. I studied him to see if he was being sarcastic, but he wasn't.

"I mean it," he said, taking another gulp of beer. "I know they're glued at the hip, but I think you're a better friend to Jacinta than Delilah is. Delilah's playing some kind of weird game. You—you just care about people. It's nice." He sounded almost sentimental. I guess it was the beer.

"I'll see you later," I said, grabbing my white beaded clutch and hurrying away. I passed Teddy & Co. on the way to the house.

"Hey, Naomi," Teddy said, and I could tell he must've come to the party already drunk. "You gonna save my girlfriend from that psycho?"

"She's not a psycho," I said, and kept walking.

"You're a good girl, Naomi!" Teddy bellowed after me. "All girls should be as good as you!" I ignored him.

I hurried inside as a steady stream of revelers in white came through the front door and around the side of the house. I recognized a lot of faces from Jacinta's first party—those brothers whose names I couldn't remember; the Fitzwilliams girls; Ainsley Devereaux; and dozens of others. It looked as if Jacinta's party might pass the hundred-guest mark she'd predicted earlier. Whether she'd intended it or not, this was going to be another mega-bash.

I couldn't find the girls downstairs, so I went upstairs and peeked in each of the rooms in backward-rainbow order: indigo, blue, green, yellow, and orange. All had their doors wide open, and all were empty of people. Then I got to the red room, and saw that the door, while not closed, was just slightly ajar. I peered inside cautiously, and there were Jacinta and Delilah, sitting on the bed, Delilah's head on Jacinta's shoulder.

"He was just being a jerk," Jacinta said. "The more you take him seriously, the worse it gets."

"I hate him," Delilah said fiercely, balling her hands up into fists. "I seriously hate him. He's disgusting."

"You need to tell him, then," Jacinta said. "Tell him it's over."

"I will," Delilah vowed. "I can't wait to be free of him. He's the worst. I don't care what my mother says—he's a piece of crap."

"He doesn't understand you," Jacinta said. "He thinks you're just a doll for him to show off. He doesn't know how creative you are, or how smart, or how talented."

"You're so right," Delilah said. She pulled back and looked at Jacinta for a moment. A glance passed between them that I couldn't interpret. But then Delilah did something that needed no interpretation—she leaned forward and kissed Jacinta full on the mouth, just as if she'd done it a hundred times before. And Jacinta wrapped her long, skinny arms around Delilah and kissed her back.

It's not like I'd never seen girls kiss before. My best friend was a huge lesbian who showed it off like a badge of honor; when she had girlfriends, she'd purposely kiss them when they were walking past a church or sitting in a restaurant full of old people, just to see the reaction. I couldn't imagine Jacinta or Delilah doing something like that. In fact, I had the uncomfortable feeling that I'd witnessed something that really wasn't any of my business. As I backed away from the door, the floor creaked loudly. Jacinta anxiously called, "Who's there?"

I had to think fast. I pretended that I'd just walked up to the door and hadn't been standing there for a few minutes. I poked my head in the room.

"Hey, ladies," I said, smiling as if nothing were amiss. "I was just looking for you two."

They visibly relaxed.

"Oh, Naomi," Delilah said. "It's you." She slowly exhaled and then giggled.

"God," she said. "I need to pack a bowl, like, right now."

Wordlessly, Jacinta went over to a drawer and withdrew a glass pipe and a little plastic bag. She handed them to Delilah like she was a mother giving her child a Tylenol and a cup of water.

While Delilah smoked and the air filled with that kind of skunky smell, Jacinta and I stood at the windows and looked out at the party. The bouncy house was in full swing, and a few girls had pulled off their white dresses to reveal white bikinis. They were splashing around in the river pool, giggling and trying to avoid dousing any of the dozens of glowing white floating candles. A few guys, not surprisingly inspired by the girls, had stripped down to their tighty-whities and were "swimming," i.e., trying to take the girls' tops off. More and more people streamed into the backyard, which was getting quite crowded.

"What on eaaaaarth is Teddy doing?" Delilah asked from the bed, her stoned voice back in full effect.

Jacinta looked over in the direction of the food tent. Teddy was talking to Misti, who was leaning toward him over the warming dishes as if she wanted to dive down his throat and build a home there.

"You won't like it," Jacinta said.

Delilah got up, tripping and giggling a little as she did, and sauntered over to the window. She put her arm around Jacinta and gave her a big kiss on the cheek. Then she looked outside.

"Maybe if he likes her so much, he should buy her a new

nose," Delilah said, and this time her giggle had a nasty hard edge to it. Jacinta joined in the laughter, something that surprised me. Jacinta was quirky but never mean. I guess love, or whatever they were in, changes a person. Or maybe it just brings out their true nature.

I looked down and suddenly they were holding hands again, but definitely not like friends do. Delilah was smoothing her thumb back and forth across Jacinta's wrist. Jacinta was visibly trying to hold back a response. I got exactly the awkward feeling I experienced when I went to the movies with Skags and her then-girlfriend, some other high school's lacrosse team captain, a couple of years ago. In that moment, I knew I was a real third wheel. I also knew the other two wheels were about to make out regardless of whether or not I was there. I decided it would be better if I weren't there.

"I'll, um—see you two later," I said, waving lamely as I walked away.

"Lovely to see you, Naoooooooomi," Delilah said. "I've missed seeing you these past few days."

"Me too," Jacinta said eagerly. She broke her grasp with Delilah and enfolded me in a hug so tight I found it difficult to breathe.

I went downstairs and out onto the back deck and was immediately waylaid by Olivia Bentley, who wanted to take a photograph of me for *Young Hamptons*. She made a snarky comment about how she was sure this meant I'd be on *The Wanted*, too, probably within five minutes. I posed for her, but I was kind of frowning in the shot, so when she showed it to me, I said, "Man, I look like a real snob."

"We're all snobs, honey," she said. "I just say it's how I was raised."

"It's not how *I* was raised," I said.

"Sure," Olivia said. "You're here, at this fabulous party, with these fabulous people, all of us looking fabulous in white, drinking the same wine and eating the same food, listening to the same hired band in the same backyard of the same mansion— and you're different?" She laughed a nasty little laugh. "Sure you are."

"Excuse me," I said coldly, and went off to find Jeff.

He was drunker than when I'd last seen him, and knocking back another drink in the kitchen.

"There she is!" Jeff said loudly, leaning over and giving me a boozy kiss.

He looked out the window, and I followed his gaze to see Delilah and Jacinta now curled up together on the chaise lounge on Jacinta's back deck. Then I hesitated for a moment, looked back at the girls, and decided to plunge forward.

"Now, *that* is an interesting situation," I said. Jeff rolled his eyes.

"I don't know if 'interesting' is the word for it," he said. "More like pathetic." There was something in his tone I didn't like.

"Pathetic?" I repeated. He held up his glass.

"To the freak who throws the best parties in town," he said with a laugh.

I put down my drink.

"She's not a freak," I said defensively. "I know you think she's weird, but she's a good person. She's never been anything but sweet to you."

"Oh, I don't doubt that she's a good person," Jeff said. "And yes, she's been very nice to me. But the girl is obviously out of her mind."

"Why?"

"Well, to start, look at what she wears. She always looks like she's dressed up for some costume ball happening inside her own head." I could tell he was drunk and figured I'd give him a pass on that one.

"She's just—I don't know, she's fashionable," I said lamely, hoping he'd get off this track.

"Fashionable. Right. Or she dresses like she just escaped from the mental ward. Also, she's so into Delilah that it's creepy." Okay, that pissed me off.

"It's not creepy," I protested. "They really care about each other. I've spent way more time with them than you have."

"Teddy told me Delilah spends all day, every day, at Jacinta's house and won't talk about it when she sees him at night."

"Well, that's Delilah's choice, not Jacinta's."

"Jacinta is obsessed with her. It's messed up. You see how they are together. I bet they're even weirder when they're by themselves. I mean, look at that." He pointed out the window. "That's not normal."

"What about Delilah? She seems just as into it as Jacinta," I said.

Jeff gave a dismissive wave of his hand. "Delilah's playing the same game she always plays when she's pissed at Teddy," he said. "Usually she starts hanging out with some poor guy who totally worships her. Finally, after Teddy flips out and beats the hell out of the kid, she comes back around and starts acting like a girlfriend again. I guess this summer she decided to get creative, get a female barnacle. Interesting move on her part, I have to say, but this whole thing has gotten old." As if to illustrate his point, he stifled a boozy yawn.

"Maybe they actually love each other," I blurted out, my face heating up. "Ever thought of that? Sometimes real human beings have actual genuine feelings for one another." I hadn't meant to say it, but he was pissing me off with his condescending attitude.

He looked at me and gave a surprised laugh. "*Love* each other?"

I nodded. He laughed again.

"You think Delilah Fairweather would love somebody like *her*? She's Delilah's pet for the summer, someone for her to play with. She'll be gone as soon as the summer ends."

"I just don't understand how you can talk about Jacinta like this when you've been so nice to her face," I said. At this, Jeff cracked up again.

"Oh my God," he said, cackling. "That is adorable. Sometimes I forget you're from Chicago." He tried to wrap me in his arms, but I resisted. I was no longer in the mood to excuse his behavior by remembering that he'd had one too many.

"What is *that* supposed to mean?" I demanded.

He was clearly irritated that I had pushed him off. "Look, maybe you live in some cutesy, perfect little world where everyone is one hundred percent honest all the time, but in the real world, sometimes people act one way when they feel another way. What am I gonna do, tell the girl to her face I think she's crazy?"

"Maybe don't talk crap about her," I said testily.

"Maybe don't act like Jacinta Trimalchio is your best friend forever," Jeff said. "You just met her, too. What do you even really know about her?"

"What do I even really know about *you*?" I shot back. "I just met you, too."

"You're acting nuts," Jeff said. "Is this like some kind of PMS situation?"

"You have *got* to be kidding me."

"Of course I'm kidding!" He smiled at me and poked me in the arm. "I'm trying to make you laugh."

"Well, talking about my period is not the way to do it. And no, it's not a PMS situation. I just think you're being a jerk."

"Fair enough," Jeff said pleasantly, pounding the rest of his drink. He set his glass down and put his arm around me. "I think what we need is some alone time."

"Maybe another time," I said, shrugging his arm off.

He stared at me like I'd grown an extra head. "You're not even kidding, are you," he said after an amazed silence.

"No, I'm not," I said. He looked at me for another moment.

"Fine, fine," he said with his hands up in mock surrender.

I wasn't sure what had just happened, but this night was going seriously downhill. We wandered outside to a table where Brock and Reilly and Teddy were standing and playing flip cup, a dumb game that involves plastic cups and beer, and as far as I could tell, the whole point is just to get drunk. The rules are really inconsequential.

"Naooomi," Teddy said, smiling at me. He swayed back and forth a tiny bit on his heels. "This girl—this girl right here—this girl gets it. She and me, we get it." He took a swig off a champagne bottle and burped loudly. Then he swiveled around and yelled, "Hey, Misti! Misti!"

Misti, still serving lobster, looked up, startled. So did Giovanni at the bar beside her.

"Come play flip cup!" he called. "Come help us play flip cup!"

She blushed happily and waved him off. "I'm workin'!" she yelled back.

"Forget your work!" Teddy roared. "It's flip cup time!"

"I'll get in trouble," Misti called back. She pointed at Giovanni. "My supervisor," she said, making zero effort to disguise the disgust in her voice.

"Oh, him?" Teddy slurred, getting out his wallet. "He's no problem. Me and Giovanni, we go way back. He's my boy." He stumbled over to Giovanni and waved a hundred-dollar bill right in front of the bartender's Roman nose.

"Naomi needs a partner for flip cup," he said, pointing at me. "That girl there? You know her mom? Her mom's the cupcake lady. Anne . . . Anne *Rye*. The famous cupcake lady."

"Hey, man, I'm sorry," Giovanni said stiffly, though he didn't sound very sorry. "I can't let the staff mingle with the guests. It's against our company policy. I didn't make the rule."

"Oh," Teddy said, temporarily nonplussed. Then his expression cleared and he smiled winningly. "But you can *break* the rule! Right? Right?"

Giovanni shook his head. "I really can't. And neither can she." Misti scowled at him bitterly.

"Hey, Teddy, why don't you come back and finish the game?" Jeff called in that talking-to-a-three-year-old voice people use with their super-drunk friends. "Naomi just wants to watch, right?" He gave me a pointed look.

"Right," I joined in. "Yeah, I don't even like beer that much. I like wine."

"So we'll play with wine!" Teddy exclaimed, throwing his arms wide open and staring at the ceiling of the tent like he wanted to hug it. "We'll play with wine!" He reached over and tucked the hundred-dollar bill in Giovanni's collar.

"A hundred dollars," Teddy said. "A hundred dollars for a bottle of wine and your girl for flip cup."

"Wine bottles aren't for sale," Giovanni said evenly. He stared at Teddy.

"And neither is she," he added, looking at Teddy's girlfriend.

"For Christ sake, Gio," Misti snapped. "Just let me play freakin' flip cup. No one gets in trouble unless you tell a manager."

"You don't need any more to drink tonight, baby," Giovanni said, moving his eyes back to Teddy. "You've had enough."

"Baby!" Misti repeated in disgust.

Giovanni removed the hundred-dollar bill from under his collar as if he were holding a shoe covered in dog crap. He held it out to Teddy.

"Here," Giovanni said. "I don't want your money."

"Sure you do," Teddy said, laughing. "Everybody wants money."

"I don't want yours," Giovanni said. His eyes were steely.

Teddy's mood soured then, and he glared back at the bartender.

"That's not what you said last summer," he said. "Only reason I even know your name is you were running that little side business."

"I don't do that anymore," Giovanni said.

"Why not?" Teddy asked.

"My cousin got busted. Scared the hell out of me. I'm not trying to end up in jail, man."

"Jail?" Teddy said, chortling. "Bro, all you'd have to do if something came up was call me. I'd take care of it. You know who my girlfriend's father is?"

"Teddy!" A sharp voice cut through the air like an ax. We

all jumped a little—me, Jeff, Teddy, Giovanni, Misti, even Brock and Reilly.

It was Delilah, followed closely by a nervous-looking Jacinta. But this wasn't the stoned, catty Delilah I'd seen in the red bedroom. This was a very angry Delilah, with fire in her eyes.

"My father," she said, pulling herself up to her full height, "is not a prop you can use to impress your friends from Long Island." The way she spit out *Long Island* meant she definitely wasn't talking about the Hamptons.

I'd never seen Teddy Barrington cowed by anyone before, but it seemed Delilah had found the trick.

"Aw, baby," he said. "I was just having fun."

"Don't call me baby," Delilah snapped.

I realized then that while Delilah had referenced Giovanni and Misti—"your friends from Long Island"—she hadn't looked at them once. She certainly hadn't acknowledged them directly. It was like they didn't even exist. In contrast, Misti was staring at her, gape-mouthed, as if she were looking at a movie star.

"I'm going home," Delilah said.

"But we took my car," Teddy said.

"Exactly. You're going to give me your keys, and I'm going to drive myself home. You can come with me, or you and Brock and Reilly can find another way to get out of here."

Teddy laughed. "Drive home? You? You suck at driving. You'll put my car in a ditch."

Delilah rolled her eyes, deftly removed his keys from his

back pocket, and began walking away. Before she left, she gave Jacinta's hand one last furtive squeeze.

Teddy stared at his retreating girlfriend, then at Brock and Reilly, then back at Delilah.

"But we just got here," he whined.

"Looks like the train's leaving, bro," Jeff said. "I'd get on it if I were you. I'm sorry, you know I'd drive you if I were sober."

Heaving a huge sigh, Teddy trotted off behind Delilah. Brock and Reilly followed suit.

"Well, I guess that's the end of flip cup," Jeff said.

"Hey, man, you need a ride home?" asked Steven Xavier, an oily catalog heir who'd joined us with his girlfriend, some chain-smoking Russian model who fawned all over Jacinta in broken English ("You is famous of blog!" she exclaimed at one point). Steven had explained earlier that he was currently "doing the sober thing," having just finished his third stint at a *lovely* rehab center in the Berkshires.

"Yeah, I guess I do," Jeff said reluctantly. "I've got a tee time at seven tomorrow morning." He looked at me. "Is it cool if I leave my car parked overnight at your house? I'll pick it up tomorrow."

"Sure," I said. He kissed me goodbye, and the three of them left.

"You okay, Jacinta?" I asked. She looked paler than pale, so white she matched everything else at the party.

"I think I'll just sit down, love," she said shakily, before lowering herself into a chair at our table. Around us, girls had begun kicking up their heels and dancing their own versions of the Charleston and other old-timey dances they'd probably only seen in movies or something. More and more people jumped into the pool, some in their underwear, some wearing nothing at all.

We chatted about how she'd gotten the decorations done so quickly ("I had to *beg* the florist, love—*beg*!"), who was wearing the best white dress, who had the best white shoes, and whether it would've been feasible for Jacinta to serve only white foods at her white party. ("Nah," I said. "It would've just been, like, mashed potatoes and white bread. None of these girls eats carbs anyway.") I switched from alcohol to club soda, and we passed a pleasant few hours watching the wealthiest kids on the East Coast do what any kids do at a party: drink, brag, fight, cry, and make out. By the time I looked at my phone to check the time, it was midnight.

The party started to peter out, and Jacinta busied herself flitting around and saying goodbye to folks who were making moves to go. I watched all the air-kissing and the hugging and heard all the declarations of affection (she called people "love" about fifty times) and the invitations to go out on so-and-so's boat, and wondered if any of it was actually real. If Jacinta weren't writing about these people and inviting them to her lavish parties, would they give a crap about her? I didn't think so. And yet, she seemed to genuinely care about each and every one of them, and to legitimately hope that they'd had a fantastic time.

Then the catering staff began breaking down their stations, and the rental folks arrived to collect the tables and chairs, and the post-party cleaning crew fanned out over the property to pick up everything else—soggy candles, cigarette butts, even the rose petals. The evening was cool, and Jacinta went inside for a few minutes, emerging with hot tea and a couple of blankets. We sat on the back deck, watching a small army of people erase every trace of Jacinta Trimalchio's latest grand bash.

"I'm afraid it wasn't fun for her," Jacinta said a little mournfully.

"Of course it was," I said lamely.

"How do you know?"

"Well . . . she looked happy when I came into the red room."

"But you saw her outside before she left. She was so angry."

"She was happy when she was just with you."

This pleased Jacinta greatly, and she smiled. "She was, wasn't she? When it was just the two of us—oh, and, of course, when you were there, too—I think she had a very nice time."

"That's the impression I got," I said. "And the Teddy and Misti thing just threw her off." I lowered my voice when I said Misti's name, since the girl was in the backyard yelling at poor Giovanni about something.

"Which one is Misti?" Jacinta asked curiously.

"The one Teddy was talking to when Delilah yelled at him. She was our waitress at Baxley's the night Delilah and Teddy and Jeff and I took a helicopter from the city." I hesitated and then plunged on. "Can you keep a secret? Like, even from Delilah?"

"Absolutely, love," Jacinta assured me. "I'm a top-notch secret keeper."

In a whisper, I told her about the incident at Baxley's. Her eyes widened with something that looked like a mixture of shock and delight.

"I *knew* he was wrong for her!" Jacinta exclaimed. "I *knew* he was cheating! She has to know it, too. She has to sense it. Part of why she hates him so much. He's really awful."

"Well, don't tell Delilah," I said. "Teddy would probably have Brock and Reilly slash my car tires or something."

"I won't say a word," she whispered. "Not a single word. You know he asked us if we wanted to have a threesome? Just out in the open, tonight, right in front of people."

"Oh, ew," I said.

"Delilah really can't stand him," Jacinta continued, sounding like an authority on the subject. "You can't imagine the stupid things he's done to embarrass her over the years. She's always been such a wonderful person, even when she was little. He's never really understood what he has."

"I believe it," I said.

We sat outside until the very last person had left the property.

"I'll see you again soon, won't I?" Jacinta asked when I stood up to go. She sounded a little worried.

"Of course you will," I said, squeezing her shoulder. "We're friends."

"We are," Jacinta said. "We really are."

I went home then, across the soft cool grass, and curled up in my warm bed. I don't know when Jacinta went to sleep, or if she did. Jeff texted when he got home, *Hey—sorry I made you mad earlier. Didn't mean to be an idiot. Too many drinks.* I texted back, *It's okay,* but the truth was it wasn't okay, and both he and I knew it.

I woke with a start at six the next morning and couldn't get back to sleep. When I went into the kitchen to make tea, I looked through the window and saw Jacinta sitting in the same spot, wrapped in the same blanket, typing on her laptop. The green light glowed, a tiny spot of brightness in the early-morning dim.

# CHAPTER TEN

There were no more daytime or nighttime parties at Jacinta Trimalchio's house that summer. For a brief flicker of a moment, her evening soirees were the talk of the town, and she was the queen of the teen social world. Then, just as swiftly as she'd grabbed the crown, she gave it up. I saw her, but only through the kitchen window. She was often on the back deck with Delilah, always under her blue parasol, while Delilah baked to a perfect golden crisp. Other times they played badminton or croquet or floated around the river pool on a raft built for two. Sometimes I could tell that they were holding hands. They didn't invite me to join them.

I also saw less of Jeff over the next couple of weeks. Partly, it was because summer golf league had kicked into high gear and he was super-busy. The summer golf league was something that kept the boys from the city prep schools occupied during their time in the Hamptons, something that kept their game sharp and their bodies active—or, at least, that was Jeff's explanation. But a pastime had changed with us. I figured I could spend the extra alone time getting back into my SAT book.

The one time my mother was around during those two weeks, she expressed concern that I was hanging out with neither Jeff Byron nor Delilah Fairweather nor "the famous girl next door," but I told her we were all just busy doing our own things. And I guess that was true.

Then one day, while I was sitting on the back deck reading this old novel, *Save Me the Waltz*, I saw a white-blond head pop up.

"Naomi!" Jacinta cried happily. She fairly bounced up the stairs to the deck, immediately wrapping me in one of her tight hugs. I hugged her back and then went and got us both some of the lemonade I'd made that morning.

"I came to invite you to dinner at Delilah's house tomorrow night," Jacinta said breathlessly. "She's having you, me, Jeff, and Teddy."

"Isn't that going to be a little awkward?" I said.

Jacinta shook her head vigorously. "Not at all," she said. "She's only inviting him because she can't not invite him if she's inviting Jeff, and she wants to invite Jeff because she wants to invite you, and she can't not invite Jeff if she's inviting you."

I tried to follow her social calculus, but all I could come up with was, "Okay."

"Can *you* keep a secret?" Jacinta asked with a tantalizing

grin. "You know *I* can. I haven't breathed a word of what you told me about that waitress, love. Not a word."

"Yes," I said. "Tell me what's up."

"She's going to break up with him tomorrow night." Jacinta burst forth as if it were the greatest news ever told. "Not at the dinner, of course—afterward, after we've all left. She's going to end it with him for real."

"Woooow," I said, absorbing the information. "She's finally dumping him? After, what, like a zillion years?"

"She's realized she deserves to be treated better," Jacinta said. "She's realized she deserves everything she's ever dreamed of. Besides, she's going to break so huge at Fashion Week this year that she won't need him, or her family's money, or anything. She'll be booked for months, and the months will turn into years, and she'll make so much money as a super-model."

"As a supermodel," I repeated dubiously.

"She's going to finish out her senior year at Trumbo, and then we're going to rent an apartment together in Brooklyn."

"Together? In Brooklyn?" I tried to picture Delilah Fair-weather living in, or even going to, Brooklyn. It was an image I couldn't summon no matter how hard I tried.

Jacinta was still talking. ". . . and we'll have a garden in the backyard to grow some of our food, and of course, if she *wants* to go to college, she can go to NYU or Columbia, and I'll keep up with my blog and I'll be much closer to the designers, being in New York instead of Florida."

"Florida?" I was confused. "Why would you be in Florida?"

Jacinta looked flustered. "Oh—um—well, you know, Miami is one of the fashion capitals of the world. I was thinking of spending some time down there to, you know, enjoy the weather."

"Okay," I said. "So, Brooklyn, then. With Delilah. In an apartment. Together."

"Yes," she said confidently. "We've figured it all out."

"And until then, you'll . . . what, live in the city?"

Her bright smile dimmed a bit. "That part I'm not quite sure about. Delilah's going to see if I can stay in one of their spare rooms for a while."

"And do her parents . . . know about you two?"

"They know we're friends. That's all they need to know. And they'll come around eventually, once they do know."

"Right," I said, even though she was so obviously, utterly, completely wrong. "I noticed you haven't had any parties lately. Is that because of Delilah?"

"Sort of. I just don't want too many people asking questions. It's very important to her that it stays as private as possible. It's different for her than it is for me. I don't have any—my parents couldn't care less. They're fine with whatever I do. Very European attitude. But her parents are more—opinionated. Conservative."

"Of course," I said. I had a very strong feeling that Senator and Mrs. Fairweather would prefer to be swallowed whole by a monster than to have their picture-perfect, all-American image besmirched by a lesbian daughter. But I wasn't about to say so to Jacinta.

"I've even let my housekeeper go. I just want to have as much time with Delilah as I can before the summer is over."

"So who cleans the house?"

She laughed. "Um . . . no one, really. But there are only two of us ever there, so it hasn't gotten *too* messy just yet."

Her phone buzzed. She looked at it, and her face lit up. "Delilah will be over soon," she announced, as if I wouldn't know who was texting her. "I'd better get back. But you'll come tomorrow night? To Delilah's house, at seven?"

"Of course," I said. "It'll be good to see Jeff, too. I haven't seen him as much since the summer golf league started. He's busy practically every day."

"Then we'll all have a wonderful time," Jacinta said. She kissed me on the top of my head before bounding across the lawn, back to her castle.

Once Jacinta was safely out of earshot, I actually dialed Skags. She picked up.

"Hello, trust-fund baby," she said, yawning. "Thanks for remembering I exist."

I felt bad, but I didn't know what to say. So I pretended I hadn't heard the last part. "You sound like you just got out of bed."

"I'm still *in* bed. I was out all night with Jenny Carpenter."

"Doing *what*?"

"Driving along the lake."

"*What?!*"

"You heard me. Driving along the lake. What's weird about driving along the lake?"

"With Jenny Carpenter? Only, like, eighteen thousand things."

"Well, she's actually very smart and interesting," Skags said primly. "There's a lot going on underneath the surface there."

"Skags," I said. "She's a *cheerleader.*"

"That's just because she's really interested in dance. Experimental dance, actually. Have you ever heard of this group Pilobolus? They're a modern dance troupe out of the Northeast somewhere, maybe Yale or something, and they do the most amazing stuff. We watched all these YouTube videos about them at Jenny's house the other day."

"At Jenny's house?" My world was spinning. "Jesus Christ, is *everyone* a lesbian now?"

"Yes, Naomi," Skags said. "Everyone is a lesbian now. Except for you, the lone straight person carrying the banner of heterosexuality forward for the sake of the future of the human race. You're like a saint. A really boring, heteronormative saint. Who goes to fancy parties and never calls me." Again, I decided to ignore the jab. She was completely right, after all. And apparently, while I'd been ignoring her, Jenny Carpenter had been doing the exact opposite.

"You are not gonna believe what happened here the other night," I said.

"Does it involve that one girl queering off with the other girl?"

"Well—yeah. How did you know that?"

"Duh. Anyone could see that was going to happen."

"Really?"

"Oh, totally. Now give me all the details."

I explained as much as I could while Skags listened. By the time I was done, she'd reached a conclusion.

"Oh, they're not really gay," she said.

"Since when are you the authority on gay?" I asked, even though Skags pretty much *was* the authority on gayness, at least at our school.

"No offense, Naomi, but you don't know anything about women."

"I *am* a woman," I said defensively.

"The point is that I understand chicks better than you do. And what Delilah and Jacinta have is not a real relationship. They are mutually obsessed. Well, Jacinta is obsessed with Delilah, and Delilah is also obsessed with Delilah, so it all works out for them."

"I'm pretty sure they have sex," I said.

"Okay, can I get real with you for a second? If they do have sex—and I really doubt they do, given Republican Barbie's natural inclination toward straight white douches like her dad—it is all Jacinta doing stuff to Delilah."

"Eww," I said. "TMI."

"How is it TMI?"

"I don't know. I just don't want to picture it."

"Well, I'm sorry I offended your delicate Wasp sensibilities, but that's my take on it. Jacinta wants to be Delilah, and

Delilah wants to be worshipped. I gotta go—Jenny and I have a tennis date."

"Have you guys even, like, kissed yet?" I asked, even though I didn't usually like to know the details of Skags's encounters (I still kind of thought of her as a little kid, even though we were obviously all grown up).

"I'm not going to go into that with you, Naomi," Skags said airily. "It's not like you've been particularly interested in what's going on with me this summer. I haven't even told you about my plans for the all-school LGBTQ BBQ in September, or the fact that I've basically locked down an internship with the mayor's office this fall."

"That's awesome," I said sincerely.

"It is," Skags said. "And I'm not going to share any more information with you." I could tell she really was a little hurt, but I knew she'd forgive me.

"That's fine," I said. "Feel free to continue not sharing the fact that you've turned Jenny Carpenter into a total lesbian."

"Jenny Carpenter was already a total lesbian," Skags said fondly. "I just helped her to see it."

We got off the phone, and I marveled at my friend's powers of persuasion. I didn't see Skags as sexy at all—she was a girl who looked and dressed like a boy, and besides, she was my funny best friend. But apparently, she held some kind of fascination for a certain kind of young lady. And now I knew Jenny Carpenter, of all people, was that kind of young lady.

ဢ ဢ ဢ

The next day was a real scorcher. You know those hot summer afternoons when you look into the distance and it's all hazy and wavy because of the heat rising from the pavement? Or those days when you can sense the heat inside somehow, even with all the air-conditioning? It was that kind of day. My mother popped in, presumably to check that her daughter was still alive, and grabbed a few things before zooming back to the city.

"Nice to see you, stranger," I said before she left.

"Why, Naomi," she said, half turning toward me. "You'd almost think you missed me."

I didn't say anything, which pleased her. I *didn't* miss her, not exactly, but it might've been nice to have another time like the one we had at the nail salon. Not that I'd want to plan it out or anything, but if we happened to run into each other for more than five minutes, it might be okay to hang out a little. Maybe.

Then again, I reflected, she'd probably end up saying something to piss me off. So maybe it was better that we weren't up each other's butts that summer.

Jeff came over to pick me up for dinner, and I was already nervous for what was about to transpire. When we got into his car to go over to Delilah's house, we looked at each other.

"This is gonna be so weird," I said.

He grinned. "I know. I kind of can't wait." He rubbed his palms together, and I laughed a little, uncomfortably. Was it too late to fake a stomachache and curl up with my book for the night?

When we got to Delilah's house, a butler let us in with apologies. "I'm afraid the air-conditioning is broken," he said, wiping his brow. "We've got fans going everywhere, but it's not the most comfortable situation. Senator and Mrs. Fairweather, thankfully, are at the townhouse in the city, but the rest of us have got to suffer out here." He sighed and shook his head, then led us to the enormous living room, where Jacinta and Delilah were perched on either end of the couch, wearing nearly identical white cotton sundresses. Of course, Jacinta accessorized hers with a funky white headband covered in big red felt flowers, but other than that, their outfits were almost exactly the same. They had each kicked their shoes off, and when we walked in, they were holding hands along the back of the couch.

"Heeeeeey, you two," Delilah said when we entered the room. She was higher than I'd ever seen her before. I wouldn't say she was stoned out of her mind, but her eyes were red and she had that goofy marijuana-induced smile on her face. Smoking weed doesn't make people nasty or violent the way alcohol can, but it certainly lowers their IQ temporarily.

Teddy walked in then, and Delilah dropped Jacinta's hand.

"Hello, TV staaaar," Delilah said, her voice thick with sarcasm. "How are things?"

Teddy peered at her, then rolled his eyes.

"Well, at least one of us is having fun," he said. Jacinta studied her hands.

Teddy's cell buzzed. He checked the incoming number.

"I need to take this," he said abruptly, and walked outside.

We watched him through the living room windows. He stalked up and down the front lawn in the blistering heat, gesticulating wildly, first barking angrily into the phone and then appearing to become conciliatory, even friendly.

"Could he please make it more obvious?" Delilah said loudly. "He doesn't need to actually talk to her right in front of my face. In front of my *guests*."

She looked at Jacinta, who nodded her agreement. Delilah's expression softened, and she leaned over and planted a big kiss on Jacinta's mouth. Jeff looked at me in surprise. I think the reality of seeing these two girls kiss was less sexy than he'd imagined.

"I just *love* you," Delilah said to Jacinta.

Jacinta blushed. Delilah looked at us expectantly for our reaction, but we gave none. Maybe it was too hot for us to summon any response. Or maybe we were just shocked they were being out in the open like this.

His phone call over, Teddy walked back into the house.

"Dammit," he said when he entered the living room. "It's almost as hot in here as it is outside. This reminds me of being under the studio lights when I was on—"

"Teddy, my sweetest and most precious darling," Delilah said, her voice dripping with sarcasm. "It's so powerfully hot. I don't want to make the cook turn on the oven. He'll sweat to death."

"That's his job," Teddy said. "He's the cook. Kitchens get hot. If you can't take the heat, get your ass out of the kitchen!" He chortled, deeply amused at himself.

"I think we ought to go out to eat," Delilah insisted.

"I thought we were going to have a nice night in," Teddy said. "With old friends and—her." He cast Jacinta a withering glance. She seemed to withdraw into herself like a flower closing its petals at nightfall.

"Don't talk to her that way," Delilah said.

"What way?" Teddy asked. "I was just pointing out that you and I and Jeff and Naomi have known each other for a while, while Jacinta is—new." He said "new" as if he meant to say another, meaner word.

"Let's go to Baxley's," Delilah suggested with a bright, false smile. "There's so much good food, and I know you *love* the service you get there, Teddy." She glared at him, daring him to reply.

"I do," Teddy said. He smiled smugly. "And it's a lot friendlier than what I'm used to getting around here." Delilah narrowed her pretty blue eyes.

I cast a sidelong look at Jeff, who appeared to not be enjoying himself as much as he'd predicted when we were in the car. At any rate, his friend Teddy had won that round by basically openly and shamelessly acknowledging what Delilah was implying.

"You—" Delilah began, and then Jacinta put her hand on her arm gently. The touch seemed to soothe Delilah, who immediately stopped speaking and looked at Jacinta gratefully. Jacinta's smile seemed to warm her and relax her. She smiled back appreciatively.

At this, Teddy's expression darkened considerably. Whatever

ground he'd gained was lost the moment Jacinta's hand touched his girlfriend's forearm. His hulking body tensed. I don't think it was the touch that angered him, per se—it was the clear evidence that theirs was a world from which he was barred entry. It was fine if *other* people couldn't get between his girlfriend and this superfan blogger, but *he* should always be assured his place. I imagined he thought that if he couldn't even get a threesome out of it, clearly their relationship had no purpose other than to irritate him.

"Let's go to Baxley's," he said, turning his back to them. "Right now. I'm hungry."

Thankfully, we were saved the heinous awkwardness of traveling as a group. As we tried not to melt in the heat, Teddy directed the group.

"Jacinta and Delilah, you go in Jacinta's car," he ordered. "Jeff, Naomi, and I will take mine."

"Sounds perfect to me," Delilah said coolly.

"I'm sure it does," Teddy retorted.

We waited while they took off in Jacinta's little white convertible, and then Teddy looked at Jeff and me.

"Do I have a story for you two," he said. "Let's go."

The ride to Baxley's wasn't long, but every second of it was infused with so much tension that it seemed much longer.

"I got in touch with my family's PI," Teddy began. Jeff, in the seat beside him, nodded.

"What's a PI?" I asked, even though I really didn't want to find out.

"Private investigator," Teddy said.

"Your family has its own private investigator?" I asked. "Why?"

"People make threats against our family all the time," he said, and I couldn't tell if he was bragging or just stating the facts. "Extortion, kidnapping, you name it."

"Kidnapping?"

"Yes. The countries in which we do business aren't exactly the safest places for foreigners, at least in some cases. My father travels with an armed guard whenever he goes to the Middle East for Barrington Oil, for example—or hell, even when he goes to Mexico City. But there are problems at home as well."

"Like what?"

Teddy glanced briefly into the rearview mirror, and his eyes met mine for a moment. "Let's just say there are plenty of people who would do anything to get their hands on whatever money they think we've got at our disposal," he said. "They'll come up with every kind of accusation you can imagine. Our PI helps us to know if we can trust the people with whom we've come into close contact."

"You ever investigate me?" Jeff joked, trying to lighten the mood.

"Unnecessary," Teddy said seriously. "You and your family are a known entity with no motivation to harm my family."

"So what'd you talk to your PI about?" Jeff asked, sounding confused.

"That dyke who's obsessed with my girlfriend," Teddy said. "That's what I talked to him about."

Now, there are a few ways you can say "dyke." I'll focus on two: the nice way and the not-nice way. Skags will sometimes refer to herself as a dyke, and she means it in a proud way. She says she's reclaiming a word that has been used against her. Teddy was using it in the not-nice way. Something in the way he spat the word out seemed to imply that Jacinta was disgusting, unwomanly, and fundamentally unworthy of knowing Delilah. Or Teddy, I suppose.

As an ally member of our school's LGTBQ group, I know it's my job to stand up for gays and lesbians when they aren't there to stand up for themselves. I know I'm supposed to be unafraid of criticism from someone so crappy.

But Teddy was driving, and Teddy was in charge, and Teddy was in a mood that kind of scared me. I figured it was better for me to keep my mouth shut than risk getting on his bad side. Who knows, maybe he would've booted me out of the car or something. I certainly knew he wasn't afraid to hurt girls.

"She's not who she says she is," Teddy said. "Her name isn't even Jacinta."

"What do you mean, her name isn't even Jacinta?" Jeff asked. "Is she one of those girls who goes by her middle name or something?"

Teddy laughed sardonically. "Not even, bro," he said. "It goes way deeper than that."

"For real?" Jeff's eyes grew big. "C'mon, man, spill it."

There was an uneasy silence.

"Uh, are you gonna tell us or what?" Jeff asked, sounding impatient.

Teddy smiled cunningly. "Soon enough," he said. "Soon enough."

I made a mental note to get Jacinta alone as soon as possible. Maybe I could do it sometime during dinner. I figured maybe, somehow, I could get her out of there and back to her house before Teddy flipped out on her.

When we got to Baxley's, the girls were waiting in a booth and Misti was nowhere in sight. I saw Teddy's eyes dart around the place, and an expression of consternation briefly passed over his face when he saw Giovanni walking up to take our order.

"You're not a waiter," Teddy blurted out before Giovanni could say anything.

Giovanni nodded. He looked pale beneath his tan, and his eyes were ringed with dark shadows, as if he hadn't slept. Even his gait was different. He walked listlessly, with no spirit. I wondered if he was sick.

"We're short one tonight," he said. His voice was hollow.

"Where's Misti?" Teddy asked. Delilah rolled her eyes and looked at Jacinta, who rubbed her back with one hand.

"She's gone," Giovanni said. His voice caught in his throat, and he coughed a little.

"What do you mean, she's gone?"

"I mean she's gone, man. Fired. We're heading back to

Babylon tomorrow. Gonna work in our parents' bakery for the rest of the summer."

Teddy looked shocked. "Fired for what?"

Giovanni heaved a sigh and looked down at the floor. "Throwing a bottle at a coworker."

You could see Teddy begin to panic. "Who?"

"Me."

"Why?"

Giovanni looked grim. "I found out some stuff," he said.

"What stuff?" Teddy demanded. "What kind of stuff?"

"She was messing around on me," Giovanni said, avoiding Teddy's gaze. "She was up to some stuff. I found out, and I told her, and she flipped. Threw a bottle of beer at me in front of some club members. Manager tossed her out right away. I said I'd take her shift tonight and that we'd both be gone tomorrow."

"Do you know who the guy was?" Delilah asked in an innocent voice. It was a cruel question and we all knew it.

Giovanni looked directly at her.

"I don't," he said. "But if I ever found out, I'd take him apart."

It was clear then to all of us that he was telling the truth. He really didn't know who Misti's other man was. Maybe he didn't even suspect Teddy, poor guy. Teddy's face was a churning mixture of misery, fear, sadness, and anger. Every few seconds, a new emotion seemed to flash across his face. In that moment, I actually felt a little sorry for him. But I felt more strongly than before that I needed to save Jacinta somehow, before . . . well, I didn't know exactly what.

"Jacinta," I asked abruptly. "Do you want to come to the bathroom with me?"

Delilah looked at me from beneath heavy eyelids. "It's only a one-person bathroom," she said. "You two aren't *that* close, are you?" She laughed a little, and Jacinta smiled.

"Where's your girl now, man?" Jeff asked Giovanni.

"Dunno," Giovanni said, shrugging. "She took off on her bike. Hasn't been answering my calls. We stay not too far from here, so maybe she's packing. I'll see her when I see her."

"You're going to stay together?" Delilah asked, raising an eyebrow. "If I found out someone was cheating on me, I just don't know what I'd do." Teddy looked at her sharply, but she ignored him.

"We just need some time," Giovanni said, as if trying to convince himself. "It's different here, away from our friends and our family. She gets caught up in stuff sometimes. It'll be better when we get home."

"Well, I hope things work out for you," Delilah said. "She seems like a *wonderful* girl."

"She is," Giovanni said, smiling a little. "She really is. Anyway, what do you guys want to drink?" He looked around for a moment and lowered his voice. "Anything you want. It's my last night here."

Jeff grinned gleefully. "Then keep the bourbon coming, my good man," he said.

"You care what kind?"

"Surprise me." Jeff elbowed me and smiled. I looked at him

like he had two heads. Delilah had morphed into some kind of evil ice princess, Jacinta looked terrified, and Teddy was falling apart before our very eyes. How could Jeff suddenly be Mister Chipper just because he was getting to drink bourbon in public?

My father told me once that people don't change—they just reveal more of who they really are. If that was true, then I was starting not to like who Jeff Byron really was.

We all ordered drinks then. Well, only four of us ordered alcohol—rum and Coke for Delilah, vodka sodas for Teddy and Jeff, water for Jacinta. I ordered red wine, which my mother will sometimes have "to soothe her nerves." When she's really, really stressed, she does what Skags and I have dubbed a Xanaxtini— a couple of pills with red wine to wash it down. She's not some kind of stereotypical pill popper, but once in a while, I think the stress of being Anne Rye, the brand, gets to her.

Jeff managed to draw Teddy into a discussion about the upcoming football season, while Delilah, Jacinta, and I spoke about Delilah's plans for Fashion Week. I honestly couldn't tell you what they were, because I was acutely aware of the tension hanging in the air. I felt like I was play acting a conversation rather than actually tuning into what Jacinta and Delilah were saying. It was as if I were an extra in some movie about the world's most effed-up love triangle—or maybe, if you added Misti, it was a square?

We were a couple of rounds in when a doleful Giovanni brought us tequila shots and limes.

"On the house," he said.

"Hey, thanks, man," Jeff said.

"No problem," Giovanni said. "You guys are good customers." He reached over to fist-bump Jeff, so then Teddy had to do the same thing, while Delilah mimed throwing up under the table and Jacinta tried not to giggle.

"You do a shot, too, man," Teddy said solemnly. "You deserve it." Delilah snorted, and Teddy glared at her.

So we all did shots together—even Giovanni. I think if his manager had shown up, he would've gotten in a lot of trouble, but it was a busy night and nobody was paying much attention to us.

Giovanni left the table, and Delilah immediately began cracking up. I don't know what usually happens when you combine a ton of marijuana with alcohol, but in Delilah's case, it meant she was suddenly amused by absolutely everything. Jacinta looked at her and smiled fondly, and Delilah held her gaze for a long moment before bursting into another fit of giggles. Jacinta started giggling, too, and that's when Teddy looked right at her and said, "So when do you head back to Florida?"

Jacinta fell silent while Delilah kept giggling.

"It's gotta be pretty humid this time of year," Teddy said.

"Uh-oh," Delilah said, tittering. "He's starting in on something. Everybody get *out* of the *way*."

"Does your grandparents' apartment have air-conditioning?" Teddy continued, never taking his eyes off Jacinta. I peered at her through my wine-and-tequila haze and watched all the blood drain from her face.

"Teddy," Delilah said, her Marilyn Monroe voice even breathier than usual. "Are you trying to start a fight? There's no fighting at Baxley's. Baxley's is for *lovers*." She sent herself off into another fit of giggles. I watched with growing alarm, while Jeff displayed increasing interest as Jacinta and Teddy stared at each other.

"You know she's a fraud, right?" Teddy said to Delilah, finally breaking eye contact with Jacinta. "You know she's a liar."

"Shut *up*, you idiot," Delilah laughed.

"I'm not kidding, Delilah!" Teddy hissed. She quit giggling.

"What are you even *talking* about?" she said, rolling her eyes.

"Your girlfriend here," he said, jerking his thumb at a frozen Jacinta. "I'm talking about this girl. You know her name's not even Jacinta Trimalchio? She made it up."

"So what?" Delilah challenged him. "So what if she made it up? You go by Teddy and your real name is *Alistair Theodore*."

"It's not like that, Delilah," Teddy said. "She's Adriana DeStefano. You remember that girl?"

At this, Jacinta stood up, knocking her glass of ice water into my lap. I jumped, wincing at the coldness.

"I'm so sorry," Jacinta said to me, handing me her cloth napkin. "I didn't mean to—"

"It's fine," I said. "Of course you didn't."

"I don't want to stay here," Jacinta said. I don't think any one of us wanted to stay there. Yet still there we remained, pinned to our booth by some immovable force.

Teddy and Delilah glared daggers at each other from across the table.

"I *know* who she *is*," Delilah spat. "You think I wouldn't know my old best friend?"

Teddy seemed momentarily startled. "You knew?"

"Of course I knew! No—Jacinta, sit down. It's all right." Gingerly, Jacinta sat.

"Of *course* I knew," Delilah continued airily, putting a protective arm around Jacinta. "She *told* me herself. So what?"

"Who is Adriana DeStefano?" I whispered to Jacinta.

For a moment, silence. And then—

"I am, Naomi," Jacinta said quietly, looking down at the table. "That's my real name."

"She's from *Staten Island*," Teddy said, his voice dripping with acid. "Her father was a federal contractor. Bought his way into Trumbo. Into our world."

"Whose world?" I asked, hopelessly confused.

"Ours," Teddy said. "You know. Mine and Delilah's and Jeff's and—ours. People who come to Baxley's. People like us."

He may as well have just come out and said it: *the right kind of people.*

"She's a fraud just like her father," Teddy said. He slammed his hand down on the table. "She's a psycho and a fraud!"

"Teddy!" Delilah hissed. "Do not speak about her father that way. She never did anything to you, and neither did he."

"She never did anything?" Teddy repeated, astonished. "She

never *did anything to me*? Are you out of your *mind*?" He was yelling now.

A manager hurried over and said, "Is everything all right here?"

"Everything's fine," Teddy snapped. "We're fine."

"Please try to keep your voice a little lower," the manager said politely. Then he backed away.

"Yes, Teddy, do shut up," Delilah said.

"You used to go to Trumbo?" I asked Jacinta. "You never told me that. Or your real name." I couldn't help but feel a little—well, maybe "betrayed" isn't quite the word, but you'd think Jacinta would've trusted me enough to tell me this stuff.

"That day when you came to my house," I said to Delilah. "You knew who she was?"

"Not until you left the room," Delilah said without taking her eyes off Jacinta. "Then she told me."

I exhaled slowly. It was starting to make a kind of creepy sense now. All I wanted to do was zap myself home to Chicago and tell Skags everything.

Jacinta opened her mouth and then closed it without saying anything. Her green eyes were big and watery.

"There's plenty she didn't tell you, Naomi," Teddy said. "Like how the feds put her father away for selling busted body armor to the army. Or how her family lost everything but her trust fund—which, as far as I can tell, is how she's been funding this whole summer. Or how she's basically just a freak blogger from Florida."

"Why do you keep talking about Florida?" Delilah demanded. "She's not *from* Florida. She has nothing to *do* with Florida."

Teddy's eyes widened. A slow smirk spread across his face.

"Oh, interesting," he said. "So she *hasn't* told you everything."

"Yes she has!" Delilah said, loudly and fiercely enough for neighboring tables of diners to look over curiously.

"Really," he said. "Tell me all about Jacinta Trimalchio, then."

"Please don't," Jacinta said faintly. "Please, just—please."

"After the trouble with her father, her mother took her to Europe," Delilah said staunchly. "That's where she grew up. Swiss boarding school. She started blogging because she missed it here and she loves fashion. She's *always* loved fashion. We used to dress up together when we were little." She grabbed Jacinta's hand and looked at Teddy defiantly.

"See," she said. "I know everything. And I still love her. I love her more than I've ever loved you. She *understands* me."

Teddy laughed scornfully. "You know nothing," he said. "And you don't love her. You don't even know her. She's been feeding you bullshit and you swallowed it whole. After her dad went to jail, she and her mother moved to a shitty little town in Florida to live with her grandparents. Her mother's been a stripper for years. My PI saw her dance. She gave him a lap dance, in fact."

Jacinta buried her head in her hands.

"Oh, don't do that, *Jacinta*," Teddy said with faux sympathy. "He said she's quite good."

"Th-that's not true," Delilah said. "You're lying."

"This guy has worked for my family since I was a kid," Teddy said. "He doesn't lie about lap dances."

"You pig," Delilah snapped. "You know that's not what I mean. She grew up in Europe, not Florida. Didn't you, Jacinta?"

Jacinta kept her head buried in her hands, not responding.

"Didn't you?" There was a note of desperation in Delilah's voice. Jacinta's answer, when it came, was very small and quite muffled.

"No," Jacinta said.

Delilah sat back in her chair, visibly shocked. I cast a quick, begging look at Jeff, who was watching the scene unfold with rapt attention. I wanted no part of any of this.

"No?" Delilah repeated.

"No," Jacinta said, raising her head up. Her face was stained with tears and with the mascara that was running down her cheeks.

"He's right," Jacinta said. "I didn't go to Swiss boarding school. I haven't been to Europe since my father took us to visit his family in Italy when I was five."

Delilah just looked at her, mouth slightly open.

"Our housekeepers used to bring us to school together. I didn't recognize you at all," Jeff said with fascinated awe.

"Well, the nose job probably threw you off," Teddy said snidely. "That's new. She got it when she got her trust fund. Eighteenth birthday."

"Jesus!" Jacinta burst forth, her eyes fiery with anger. "What are you, some kind of stalker?"

"I think that's your job description," Teddy said. "Along with con artist. So you lied to everybody about your name and where you came from, and even when you told Delilah the 'truth' about where you've been for the past seven years, it was *still* a lie. What else did you make up?"

Jacinta looked at Delilah, who was now staring at her hands. Then she looked at Teddy.

"It's over, *Adriana*," Teddy said, his voice thick with satisfaction.

Jacinta turned back to Delilah in a panic.

"I'm sorry I didn't tell you about where I really grew up," Jacinta said quickly. "I'm really sorry. It was just . . . it was such a bad time. It was so, so awful there. My stepfather . . . it was terrible. I wanted you to think I'd had a nice life. You don't know what it's been like the past seven years. . . ."

Delilah looked confused, which Teddy took as an invitation to speak again.

"We could sue you, you know," he said to Jacinta, his voice rising with each word. "We could sue your ass off for fraud. It's a family tradition, right?"

"Fuck you," Jacinta said, loud enough to invite the attention of nearby diners. One couple scowled at her. Their blond twin little girls stared.

The manager hurried up again, this time accompanied by two valets.

"I think it's time for all of you to go," he said firmly. "I'm not sure what's going on here, but it's affecting the rest of the restaurant."

"Don't worry, man," Teddy said, standing up and stretching lazily. "We're going."

The manager waited to lead us all out, with the valets bringing up the rear. Teddy followed the manager, walking with a jaunty bounce in his step, smiling and saying hi to acquaintances and family friends as if nothing were wrong. Jeff followed. Then came me, and then—whispering frantically back and forth the whole time—Delilah and Jacinta. I couldn't catch what they were saying, and I couldn't even really guess. I wanted to take them both aside and get the real story, but *was* there even a real story? Who exactly was conning who, anyway? My mind was whirling. I wanted to believe Jacinta wasn't a total phony. She was still my friend, and she was obviously hurting.

We passed a dejected-looking Giovanni, who was wiping down the bar.

"Bad night for both of us, man," Teddy said to Giovanni.

"I guess so," he said in a dull voice.

By the time we got outside, other valets had already brought our cars around.

"You girls have a nice ride home," Teddy said pleasantly, waving as they drove off with Jacinta in the driver's seat. The manager stood outside uneasily for a moment before turning around and walking back into the restaurant.

"I'd say this calls for a cigar," Teddy said, pulling two out of his back pocket.

"You had these the whole time, man?" Jeff asked, laughing. He took one from Teddy.

"I knew tonight was gonna be a celebration," Teddy said, smiling. He looked at the valets. "It's cool if we stay a little while, right? I just can't smoke this in my car—my mom would freak out if she smelled smoke in it."

"No problem, man," said one of the valets. "Just, if my manager comes out, you're probably gonna have to go."

"Yeah, you're gonna have a new manager on Monday," Teddy said. "Trust me. I've got a couple of phone calls to make about tonight."

"Fine with me, man," another valet said. "That guy's a dick, anyway."

Teddy laughed and high-fived the valet, then turned to me.

"Sorry I don't have an extra for you, Naomi," he said.

"That's fine," I said, and wandered away while they puffed on their stogies. When would this nightmare of an evening end?

"Man," I heard Jeff say to Teddy, "I knew Jacinta was weird, but I never would've predicted this. What are you gonna do?" Any sympathy he'd previously shown her seemed to have disappeared. Jeff's alliance was clearly with Teddy.

"What am I gonna do?" Teddy repeated with a hard laugh. "Make sure everybody in this town knows exactly who she really is. You remember what it was like when we were kids. Her last name was like a curse word. All those stories in the papers, all those reporters outside Trumbo . . . she'll be gone in no time. Back to the swamp she slithered out of."

"Could you really sue her?" Jeff asked.

"You can sue anybody for anything," Teddy said. "But she's not worth it. As long as she gets out of here, everything's fine."

They went back and forth for a few more minutes about Jacinta the fraud, Jacinta the liar, Jacinta, Jacinta, Jacinta, as if I wasn't even there. I wasn't sure how I was supposed to feel. Jacinta had lied to me and everybody else in town, but she wasn't a monster.

Then the manager reemerged from the restaurant, his face livid.

"I told you all to get out of here," he said.

Teddy chomped on his cigar and chuckled, turning his back to the guy.

"Hey, sir, we're leaving," Jeff said in a conciliatory tone. "Just taking a few minutes to have a cigar. We don't want to cause any trouble."

"You've already caused enough," the manager said. "Now get in your car and leave."

At this, Teddy whipped around, stomped over to the manager, and got right in his face.

"What's your problem, bro?" Teddy shouted as Jeff tried to pull him off. "We're not bothering anybody out here. You already ruined our dinner. Do you know who my father is?"

The manager, who was about five inches shorter than Teddy, drew himself up to his full height.

"I don't care who your father is," he said slowly and loudly. "I care about my customers. And you ruined your own dinner."

Teddy reared back and shoved the man, hard. The manager stumbled backward and landed on his butt on the gravel driveway.

"Whoa, whoa," Jeff said, pulling Teddy away. "C'mon, man. C'mon. We don't need you to get arrested."

"Like this loser would call the cops on me," Teddy said. He spit on the ground.

The valets helped the manager to his feet.

"You're banned from this restaurant, kid," he said, his teeth gritted. "Don't bother coming back to Baxley's. I'll talk to the club board of directors."

"My father has a standing reservation," Teddy shot back. "I'll be back tomorrow if I want."

Jeff looked at me urgently. "C'mon, Naomi," he said. "Let's get in the car. Teddy, let's get in the car. We're all getting in the car. I can drive."

"*I'm* driving!" Teddy roared. "I'm the only one who drives this car!"

"Okay, buddy, okay," Jeff said. "No worries, man. Let's just get back to Delilah's house."

"I'll take a cab, I think," I said. One thing was clear: Teddy was still drunk, and I did *not* want to get in a car with him.

"You'll get out of here immediately," the manager said. "With them."

It didn't seem like I had much of a choice.

"Delilah," Teddy muttered as we all got in the car. "Adriana DeStefano's probably, like, wearing her skin by now. All *Silence of the Lambs* and shit. You seen *Silence of the Lambs*, Naomi?"

"No," I said quietly. I kept thinking about what my dad had taught me: *Never get in the car with a drunk driver. Call me. I'll come pick you up. I won't be mad.* But my dad was far away now, and I wasn't even sure where my mother was.

"You gotta watch *Silence of the Lambs*," Teddy said over the noise of the engine. He gunned it and screeched out of the restaurant's driveway. I fell back against the seat.

"Easy, bro," Jeff said, putting a hand on his shoulder. Teddy shrugged it off.

"You telling me how to drive now, man?" Teddy asked.

"'Course not," Jeff said.

"We all know what a great driver I am." Teddy cackled. "Naomi!" he boomed, suddenly in good spirits again. "This guy ever tell you how many times he failed his road test?"

"No, he sure didn't," I said, gripping my knees. I'd been in a car with a speeding Teddy once before, but this time he was weaving back and forth a little bit as well.

"Three times!" Teddy yelled, laughing. "Three times!"

"Wow," I said. "Three times. Well, I don't even have my driver's license."

"How do you get around?" Teddy asked.

"I walk," I said.

He thought that was the most amusing thing he'd ever heard.

"She walks!" he said to Jeff, laughing. "I love this chick! She's hilarious!"

"She's pretty funny," Jeff said, smiling at me. I ignored him. I just wanted this night to be over already. More than anything else, I wanted to get home, call Skags up, and debrief her about the insane turn things had taken.

"If that psycho bitch is at Delilah's house when we get back, I'm calling the cops," Teddy vowed.

"I hear you, man," Jeff said. "I just don't know what they'd arrest her for."

"Lying!" Teddy boomed. "Misleading honorable citizens!" He drove through a stop sign, and a car swerved to miss hitting him.

After a couple more minutes on Route 27, Dr. Zazzle's billboard came into view. There was a commotion underneath it. In the twilight hour, it was a little hard to see what exactly was happening, but the flashing lights up ahead were unmistakable.

"Slow down, man, slow down!" Jeff said suddenly. "There are cops over there!"

Teddy laid on the brakes, and we were all jolted forward. He slowed to a crawl and turned his head, watching the scene with fascination. A police officer was interviewing a cyclist who was standing beside his bike. A little farther down, emergency workers rushed to load a twisted body onto a stretcher. A second officer watched over them as they worked.

"Looks bad," Teddy said with evident excitement. "Let's ask the cop what happened!"

"Bad idea, man," Jeff said. "Just keep going."

"No, no, we're gonna stop," Teddy said. "It's like these old movies my cousin used to show me. *Faces of Death.* You got to see *real* car crashes on, like, the Autobahn and stuff. Nasty as hell."

"This is sick," I said as Teddy pulled over. "This is seriously sick."

Teddy looked surprised.

"No, it's not," he said. "I just wanna know what happened." With that, he bounded out of the car and over to the officer standing by the emergency workers.

"Let's go after him," Jeff said, sighing. "He does stuff like this when he's drunk."

"You go after him," I said crossly. "I'm staying right here. *He's* the psycho."

"He's just having a rough night," Jeff said defensively. "He's a good guy."

I was about to unleash a few choice words about Jeff's definition of a "good guy" when we heard a sudden wail behind us. We both twisted around and looked through the rear window. Teddy was on his knees, his head in his hands, while the officer bent down.

"Did that noise come from *Teddy?*" Jeff said, aghast. He leapt out of the car. I followed.

We ran up and heard the officer say, "Do you know her, son?" He had a soothing hand on Teddy's back.

That's when I saw the girl on the stretcher, her white

collared shirt splattered with her own blood, half her face sheared off by the road. It was Misti.

Teddy shook his head back and forth, his hands covering his face. I gasped and balled my hands up into fists, as if the pressure of my nails digging into the soft skin of my palms could distract me from what I was seeing. Jeff leaned over and puked.

Then she—or what was left of her—was gone, shut inside the ambulance, which turned on its lights and screeched away from the roadside. The other officer finished up his interview and jogged over to where we stood. The first officer helped Teddy to his feet.

"Sh-she's a server at Baxley's," Teddy said, his face ashen. "Her name is Misti."

"We'll go down the road and tell them," one of the cops said.

"What happened?" Jeff asked weakly, wiping his mouth.

The other cop pointed to a mangled bicycle lying half-hidden by brush. "She was on her bike. Witness was a little far off but said a car came by, plowed into her, kept going."

"She's alive, though," Teddy said shakily. "Right? She's alive?"

"For now," said the cop who'd been interviewing the witness. "Next twenty-four hours will be crucial. You know her family or any people we should contact?"

Teddy was silent.

"Just go tell everybody at Baxley's," Jeff said. "They'll know what to do."

The cops nodded and began to walk toward their squad car.

"What kind of car was it?" Teddy called, suddenly alert and in control again. His voice was steady. "The car that hit her. What kind of car was it?"

"White car," said the cop who'd comforted Teddy. "Witness was too far off to note make or model. Said it was like a flash of white, and then it was gone."

Teddy's face hardened.

"Thank you, Officer," he said tightly.

The other officer glanced back at him. "Hey, aren't you the kid from, what was that show . . . ?"

Teddy smiled his gleaming white smile.

"*Oh, Those Masons!*" he said. "Yes, I am."

The cops looked impressed.

"Great show," said the one who'd recognized him. "Used to love that one."

"Thanks," Teddy said.

The officers waved goodbye and drove off. Teddy turned to us, his expression darkening.

"A white car," he snapped. "Now, who do we know who has a white car?"

I couldn't stand it anymore.

"You think it was *Jacinta*?" I burst out, my voice louder than I'd intended. "So everything's her fault now? Just because she stole one of your girlfriends doesn't mean she tried to kill someone." For about a thousand reasons, I was livid. I wanted to smash in his stupid handsome face.

Teddy glared at me, and for a moment I thought he might hit me. Instinctively, I backed up.

Jeff stepped between us and put his hand on Teddy's shoulder.

"Hey, man," he said softly. "Hey. Just breathe. She didn't know what she was saying. Let's all just breathe for a minute." Wordlessly, Teddy turned around and walked back to his car.

The drive to Delilah's was completely silent. When we parked in the driveway, we all got out of the car. Teddy turned to face us. He was smiling.

"Want to come in for a drink?" he asked, as if nothing had happened. "Jeff? Naomi?"

Creeped out by yet another one of his rapid mood changes, I shook my head no. He looked at me curiously.

"Aww, c'mon," Teddy said, patting me on the back. I shrank from his touch.

"No, thank you," I said stiffly.

Teddy shrugged, waved goodbye, and walked into the house. Jeff looked at me.

"What are you going to do, just sit out here?" he asked.

"No," I said. "I'm going home."

"How? I'm not good to drive yet."

"Well, neither was Teddy, and we got home all right."

"Just wait an hour," Jeff said. "I'll drink a club soda. I just don't want to get a DUI."

"I'm calling a cab," I said, and turned to walk away. Jeff grabbed my arm and spun me back around. I jerked my arm out of his grasp.

"Don't touch me," I said coldly.

"What the hell happened?" he demanded. "Everything was fine and now you're pissed at me? Let's just go have a drink!"

I stared at him and realized he just didn't get it. He didn't understand why it was disgusting and awful to witness what we had witnessed—at the restaurant, and especially after—and just have a drink in some rich girl's mansion as if everything were normal.

Without another word, I walked off, leaving him standing in the driveway, looking frustrated.

Delilah's driveway was a long one, and gated—probably a quarter mile long. I'd gotten halfway down the driveway when I heard a rustling and a whisper from the bushes.

"Naomi! Naomi, over here."

I nearly jumped out of my skin. Jacinta quickly stepped out of the bushes.

"Jesus, Jacinta. You scared the hell out of me." I put my hand over my heart and took a deep breath.

"I'm sorry," she said, shaking the leaves from her dress. "It's just—I can't leave Delilah alone. I have to make sure she's okay."

"So you're hiding in the bushes."

"I need to wait a little while before I drive home."

"So where's your car parked?"

"Not far from here," she said uneasily, digging the toe of her pricey shoe into the ground. "Near the property. We ran into some trouble on the road on the way in, so we put the car someplace safe and walked the rest of the way."

My heart sank.

"Ran into some trouble," I said.

"Yes."

"You mean you hit somebody."

Jacinta looked ashamed. She was quiet for a moment.

"She was scared," she finally said. "She'd been drinking and crying, and it was hard for her to see."

"Who? Misti?" I asked.

She looked at me in confusion.

"No," Jacinta said. "Delilah."

"*Delilah* hit *Misti*?"

"No, Delilah was driving and—"

"But you drove away from Baxley's."

"Delilah said driving would help her calm down. We pulled over and switched seats, and then she went really fast, and then . . ." Jacinta stopped and twisted her hands together.

"It wasn't her fault," she said. "The bike came out of no-where."

"Misti's bike," I said. "Delilah hit Misti."

Jacinta's jaw dropped, and her enormous green eyes grew even bigger. She covered her mouth with her milky white hand.

"We saw them loading her into an ambulance," I said. "Half her face was gone."

"Jesus Christ," Jacinta whispered. "We never saw who it was . . . oh, this is bad for Delilah. Oh God, this is bad for Delilah."

"Bad for *Delilah*?" I wanted to smack her, almost the way I'd wanted to hit Teddy earlier. "Misti might *die*, Jacinta. Adriana. Whatever your name is. Somebody might *die*."

Jacinta's eyes lit up with strange hope. "But she's not dead yet?" she asked feverishly. "She isn't dead?"

I could've strangled her.

"No," I said. "The cop said she's alive. But if you could've seen her face—"

Jacinta exhaled slowly and said, "As long as she's alive. Then it's not as bad."

"It looked pretty bad," I said. "And you need to tell the police."

"The police?" She looked horrified. "Me?"

"Jacinta," I said, speaking slowly, as if to a small child. "It was your car. Everybody saw *you* drive away—me, Teddy, Jeff, the valets. Not Delilah. You."

"You don't believe me?" she asked, sounding crushed.

"Of course *I* believe you! But who do you think they're going to come looking for first?"

Jacinta shook her head vigorously. "Delilah will give herself up," she said. "She'll tell the truth. Her father will get a good lawyer, and she'll tell the truth and no one will get in trouble. It was an accident."

"Jacinta, Delilah was drunk."

"She wasn't *that* drunk," Jacinta said defensively. "No one can prove she was drunk."

"Giovanni knows how much she had to drink," I said. "You really think he's going to lie for the girl who almost killed his girlfriend?"

"I'll say she wasn't drunk," Jacinta said. "I'll say he's lying and she wasn't drunk and the bike came out of nowhere and she was scared and it was an accident and that's all there was to it. That's the truth."

"That's not the truth," I said.

"Yes it is!" she nearly shouted. "That's what I'll tell them and they won't know any different and that makes it the truth!"

I rubbed my temples. I was beginning to develop the kind of headache that usually only happened when I read a book while riding in a car.

"We should both go home," I said. "I'm calling a cab."

"I'm staying here," she said resolutely. "I need to be nearby in case Delilah needs me. I told her to call me if she needs me and I'll be over right away."

"How are you going to get home?"

"I'll wait and see if she calls me. If she doesn't, I'll get a cab."

I was quiet for a long moment, looking at her while she looked at Delilah's hulking, enormous house in the distance.

"Okay," I finally said. "I'm leaving. Just—text me when you get home, okay?" I wasn't sure exactly why I still cared about this girl who had lied to me all summer, but there was something in me that believed in her, that wanted to see her win—whatever that meant.

"Sure," Jacinta said without taking her eyes off the house.

I left her there, in the darkness, my way off the property lit by the late-summer full moon.

# CHAPTER ELEVEN

I managed to sleep, thanks to this stuff my mom has called valerian root. It smells awful, but it works. She wasn't home, so I went into her bathroom and got one of her two medicine kits. She's got an herbal one with hippie-dippie stuff and then a regular one with pills. The valerian root was in the first one. I fell asleep in the living room with a cable news network on. I just needed something to keep me company.

I woke with a start the next morning and saw my mother's face on the morning news. Flanked by her business partners, she was ringing the opening bell at the New York Stock Exchange.

"And just moments ago, cooking and lifestyle guru Anne Rye celebrated the initial public offering of stock in Bake Like Anne Rye!, Inc.," the news anchor said over footage of my mother ringing the bell. "But the Food Network star and frequent morning talk show guest wasn't the only one to benefit from her company's IPO. Everyone on the floor at the NYSE this morning was treated to a cupcake buffet—a first in the Stock Exchange's more than two centuries of existence." And there was a shot of my mother serving cupcakes to an endless line of smiling men in dark suits.

I felt a tiny bit of pride well up within me, and for a moment I was kind of psyched for her. I could say a lot of things about my mother, but I couldn't say she was lazy. The woman worked harder than almost anyone I knew, even my dad—and he was utterly devoted to his students and players.

When the segment on my mom was over, I flipped the channel to the local news, turning it up loud so that I could hear it when I padded into the kitchen. It droned on in the background while I made coffee. It was just white noise until I heard the anchor say, "And in Long Island news, a Babylon girl critically injured last night in a hit-and-run in East Hampton died early this morning." I rushed back into the living room and saw a high school yearbook photo of Misti flash across the screen. "Nineteen-year-old Misti Carretino was riding her bicycle along Route 27 when an unknown driver . . ." I sank into the couch and watched the rest of the report.

"Shit," I whispered. I grabbed my phone and texted Jacinta, *Misti died.* I knew I should feel something for Misti, and I *did*, but the stronger emotion churning inside me was a growing sense of alarm about Jacinta. What was she going to do?

*I know,* came the immediate reply. *Am watching news. Come over.*

I threw on an outfit that would've given my mother

nightmares (ratty T-shirt and drawstring shorts that said "HOT" on the butt—Skags got them for me as a seventeenth-birthday present as a joke). When Jacinta let me into her house, I was surprised to see that she was basically wearing the same thing—a frayed Seminoles T-shirt and what looked like a pair of old gym shorts. They hung so loosely on her lean frame that I wouldn't have been surprised if they'd fallen off in front of me. Jacinta's hair was messy, and she wore no makeup. She looked like the world's tallest, palest eleven-year-old.

"Hi," she said, sounding tired. "I made breakfast."

"Oh, thanks," I said. "I didn't eat yet." We walked through various rooms, their glamorous luster dimmed somewhat in the daytime, and reached her magnificent kitchen. On the table, she'd laid out two bowls, two spoons, two glasses of orange juice, a carton of milk, and three boxes of cereal.

"Oh," I said. "How nice." I realized that I sounded the way my mother sounds when she wants to make the best of a less-than-ideal situation.

"I love cereal," Jacinta said, dropping into a chair and motioning for me to do the same. "It's basically all I ate growing up. I mean, not in New York but—after. And microwaveable dinners. But mostly cereal." She poured herself a bowl of Froot Loops, and I poured myself a bowl of Kix. I couldn't remember the last time I'd had plain old cereal for breakfast (or orange juice that wasn't fresh). Even back home in Chicago, I liked to at least have a home-baked muffin in the morning. I'd make a batch each week and put in all kinds of nuts and grains and good healthy things. My dad called them "fiber bombs," which I guess they were, but they were still delicious. And I always cooked at sleepovers—huevos rancheros, French toast, real easy stuff.

Kix tasted better than I remembered, though I kept thinking we should add a protein and a fruit to round out the meal. I guess that's just my weird programming.

"So what happened last night?" I finally asked. "I mean, after I left you." I didn't really know what else to say to her, so I figured I'd start with that.

Jacinta stirred her Froot Loops with her spoon. "I stayed in the bushes and texted Delilah, but she didn't text back. So I sneaked up to the house and looked in one of the windows, and she and Teddy were sitting down and talking."

"How did they look?"

"They looked calm. No fighting. I don't think he did anything to her. So I figured I should leave before they saw me, and I did."

"How'd you get home?"

"I walked."

"You *walked*?" I asked in disbelief. "From the *other side* of the pond? That'd take, like, an hour."

"It did," she said. "But I didn't mind. It was nice to walk. Helped clear my head."

We ate in silence for a couple more minutes, our spoons clinking against the bowls. It occurred to me then, for the first time, that I might get in all kinds of trouble if the police ever found out that I knew what I knew. Awkward silences sometimes give rise to uncomfortable realizations, I guess—especially when you're maybe in danger of being an accessory to a hit-and-run. My heart started beating faster, and my palms began to sweat. I felt a little surge of fear rise within me.

"Jacinta," I said, putting my spoon down and looking right at her. "When are you going to tell the police about the accident?"

She looked startled.

"It's been over twelve hours," I said, my voice rising a little bit. "She's dead. They're going to start asking questions."

"You know I can't go to the police," Jacinta said. "They'd put Delilah in jail. I can't let them do that. She'll do the right thing when she's ready. She's been through a lot."

"Been through a lot," I said. "Like drunk driving over some girl on a bicycle and just going home?"

"It wasn't like that," she said. "It was more confusing than that. And then after she broke up with Teddy . . . it must've been a difficult night."

"Wait, what? When did she break up with Teddy?"

"Well, last night. Remember I said she was going to?"

"Yeah, but—I mean, did she call you or something?" I was confused.

"No," Jacinta said. "But I assume that's what they were discussing when I saw them through the window."

I just looked down and resumed eating my Kix. She was living in a dream world.

Then again, what did I know? I'd never taken Delilah

Fairweather for the type of person who could run a girl over and just keep going. Maybe she was also the type of person who could break up with her longtime boyfriend immediately after committing vehicular manslaughter. I just couldn't imagine any breakup conversation with Teddy ever being a calm one.

I poured another bowl of Kix, at a loss for words. Jacinta had lied to me, but for some reason I couldn't identify, I still cared about her. I was still rooting for her, somehow, to make it out of this thing unscathed.

The doorbell rang then, and Jacinta looked at me, her eyes wide with fear. My heart jumped.

"Do you think it's the police?" she whispered.

"I don't know," I said. "But if it is, you have to tell them the truth."

She got up without a word and walked through the maze of rooms. I followed her.

When she opened the door, it was a maintenance guy dressed in work clothes, carrying some equipment.

"Pool man," he said by way of greeting. "I'm here to close it down for the season. You the renter?"

"No one told me you were coming," Jacinta said.

He shrugged. "Owners sent me. I do it every year. Okay if I head on back?" Without waiting for a reply, he started around the side of the house. Jacinta turned around and rushed through the house, going out on the back deck. I got to the deck in time to hear her plead, "Won't you please wait another day?

Everyone's gotten to use it, but I've never had it all to myself."

"I heard about the everyone part," the guy called up to her. "Heard you had a couple of real ragers out here."

"You heard that from the owners?" Jacinta asked, sounding alarmed.

"Naw," he said, chuckling. "Word around town. Owners barely check in except with the broker and with me, twice a year. You ever met 'em?"

"No," Jacinta said.

"Me neither," the guy said.

"Anyway, could you wait a day?" she asked again. "Please? I want to go swimming."

He paused for a moment and looked her over.

"Why the hell not," he said, relenting. "I got another job to get to this morning, anyway."

"Oh, thank you!" Jacinta exclaimed, jumping up and down and clapping with girlish glee.

My cell rang then, and I stepped away to answer it. It was my mother.

"Hello, Madame IPO," I said. "Is that what I should call you now?"

"I need you to bring me my bag," she said. She sounded frantic and out of breath, as if she'd been running.

"Well, hello to you, too," I said.

"I'm not screwing around, Naomi. I need you to bring my bag." Her voice cracked on the word "bag." Quickly, I walked into the first-floor bathroom and shut the door behind me.

"What the hell is going on?" I asked. "You sound like you're losing it."

"Dammit, Naomi! I just need you to bring my bag."

"Which bag?"

"My bag with my two medicine kits," she whispered.

"Bring them where?"

"To New York."

"*Now?*"

"Yes, now! Call a cab. A helicopter will be waiting for you in thirty minutes."

I was bewildered. "Are you sick? Don't you have anything up at the apartment you can take?"

"Why would I call you out on the island if I had my pills with me in Manhattan?" she snapped. "I am in the midst of a severe frosting crisis, and I don't need your *stupid* attitude. Don't question me. Just do as I say."

"Well, you don't need to be a bitch about it," I said.

Silence. I figured I'd get in trouble for that one.

But then she surprised me.

"Naomi," she said quietly. "Please. I need you."

It got me, the way she said "I need you." I'd never heard her speak to me that way before. I'd never heard her speak to anyone that way before.

"Okay, Mom," I said. "I'm coming. Don't worry."

"Thank you," she said, and I could tell that she really meant it.

I paused before I got off the phone.

"Hey," I said. "I love you." I felt completely weird saying it to her, but something told me she needed to hear it.

"Oh," she said, her voice catching. "Oh, me too. Me too." Then she hung up.

When I left the bathroom, Jacinta was clearing off the table.

"He's not coming back until tomorrow, love," she said brightly. "Isn't that lovely?"

As soon as I opened my mouth to speak, I felt uneasy.

"I need to go," I said, my stomach beginning to turn over. "My mom needs me in the city."

"Oh," Jacinta said, looking disappointed. "Well, I hope she's all right."

"I'm sure she'll be fine. She always is." Something inside me, that same voice that said I ought to tell my mother I loved her—well, that something told me I shouldn't leave Jacinta there all alone.

"Maybe you should come with me," I said, even though it didn't make any sense, even though my mother would've absolutely freaked out if I'd brought anyone with me.

"Oh, that's sweet of you," Jacinta said over her shoulder as she resumed cleaning up our breakfast. "But I've got to stay here and wait for Delilah to call. She'll probably want to spend the day here." She began washing the dishes in the sink.

"Delilah's not coming over," I said, but the rush of water was too loud and she didn't hear me.

"Delilah's not coming over," I said louder. She turned off the water and looked at me quizzically.

"What's that?" she asked. "I didn't catch that."

I hesitated.

"Nothing," I said. "It was nothing. I better go."

She dried her hands on a dish towel and came over to hug me tight. She smelled like roses.

"If you're back tonight, let's go for a swim," she said.

"All right," I said. "See you later." I left her there, in the kitchen, looking like a kid playing dress-up in a grown-up's gym clothes. She fairly exuded hope, that most unreasonable thing.

I changed before I went to the city, of course. If my mother's "severe frosting crisis" had nearly put her in hysterics, then my raggedy outfit might actually cause her to go completely and utterly mad. I picked out the only one of the Marc Jacobs dresses she'd bought me that I had yet to wear. It was her favorite and, of course, it was the one I liked the least—it was pink, with lacy, girly frippery and frills around the neck, short sleeves, and hemline. It looked as if it were made out of candy. I even put on the kind of subtle makeup of which my mother approves—lip gloss, neutral shadow, mascara. I thought that if I looked pretty for her, *her* kind of pretty, I might make her feel better. As I ran a brush through my hair, I remembered the last time I'd tried to please her with my appearance. I was ten, and she was fighting with my father all the time. I found her crying in her room one day, and even though I was already a little too old for it, I asked her if she wanted to have a dress-up tea party. She wiped away her tears and said that she did. So we got dressed up in these matching Laura Ashley dresses she'd bought us, and we put on hats and had tea in the living room. It was the first time I realized I could change her mood if I tried.

As the cab rolled away from the house, I looked back to see if I could catch a glimpse of Jacinta. But she was somewhere inside the house, waiting for Delilah.

My second helicopter ride was actually a lot more anxiety-filled than my first. It wasn't the height or the loudness that bothered me. No, what I found was that I couldn't focus on anything but Jacinta—not on the beauty of the changing landscape below me, not on the dumb magazine I'd brought with me, not even on texting back and forth with Skags, who was trying to tell me some story Jenny Carpenter had told her about how the other Beasts were all really into doing cocaine and how she'd never been comfortable with it and how they always made fun of her for it. I really wasn't in the mood to think about the Beasts.

When the helicopter landed, I walked away from the heliport for a few minutes to clear my head. I decided I just ought to call Skags, since the texting thing clearly wasn't helping me out.

"Wow, another phone call!" was how Skags answered the phone. "I must be really special."

"Look, Skags, I'm sorry I haven't been in touch that much this summer," I said all in a rush. "But I have to tell you what happened, and I need you to listen and to promise not to tell *anybody*, okay?"

"Okay," Skags said, immediately getting serious. "Go."

I wandered around the neighborhood, walking past fancy

office buildings and fancier residential palaces, spilling my guts to my best friend. She listened for something like ten minutes, and when I paused to take a breath, she said, "Naomi."

"Yes?"

"You know how serious this is. And you're involved. If you don't tell the police what you know, you could be an accessory to the crime somehow."

"I know," I said.

"You need to call the police and tell them exactly what you told me," Skags said firmly. "This isn't just some dumb drama. A girl died. She had a family. They need to know the truth."

I was quiet for a little while.

"You're not actually thinking about keeping this a secret, are you, Naomi?" Skags asked incredulously.

"No, of course not," I said slowly. "I'm just thinking. Maybe I should give the others a chance to tell before I tell."

"You really think Delilah is going to confess?" Skags said skeptically. "I mean, if Jacinta or Adriana or whoever was even telling the truth about who was driving."

"Maybe she will," I said. "I don't know what she's thinking. I haven't even heard from her since we were at dinner last night."

"And why do you think that is?" Skags asked pointedly. "She's going to distance herself from you and Jacinta and anybody who might know the truth about what happened. Because even if she was just a passenger in that car—and I kind of think she *wasn't*—it's going to look bad for her family."

"What if I gave them a day?" I said. "Another twenty-four hours. And if no one has said anything by then, I promise I'll go to the cops myself."

"I think you should do it right now, but I guess another day won't hurt," Skags said. "But you know, if this were last summer, you wouldn't have even gotten in that car with Jeff and Teddy at the restaurant. You would've *walked* home if you had to."

"I know." She was right. She's usually right about everything.

After we said our goodbyes, I took a cab from the Financial District to my mother's apartment on the Upper East Side. We raced up the FDR and past the Brooklyn, Manhattan, Williamsburg, and 59th Street bridges. It was a really gorgeous day, and Brooklyn looked like a postcard from across the river. Queens looked like, well, Queens.

I rode the elevator up to my mother's apartment and knocked on her door. Her assistant, Lilly, opened it. Lilly had an identical twin sister named Tilly, who was Rachael Ray's assistant. Their family had cornered the business on making coffee and dental appointments for cooking show stars.

"Is it bad?" I asked Lilly in a low voice. Lilly and I have a kind of understanding. She stays in the city, so I don't see her often during the summer. But when I visit at Thanksgiving or call the apartment because my father forces me to, Lilly gives me a heads-up on my mother's mood.

"It's awful," she whispered, and led me into the living room. I recognized my mother's lawyer and one of her business partners, but I hardly recognized my mother, who had been crying for what looked like hours. She wasn't wearing any makeup, and I could see the fine lines and wrinkles she had yet to Botox away. I had never seen her looking this ragged.

"Hello, Naomi," said the lawyer, who looked gravely concerned.

"Hi, Naomi," said the business partner, who looked to be on the verge of exploding.

"Oh, thank God you're here," said my mother.

"Hi . . . everybody," I said. My mother rushed to me, grabbed my hand, and led me into her immaculately appointed bedroom. I handed her the bag, and she quickly unzipped it and took out some lavender oil, rubbing it on her wrists. Then she threw down two Xanax without water.

"What's going on?" I asked. "What happened?"

She looked at me, tearstained and worn. "They just—the story just broke on CNN—there's a problem with the manufacturing facility," she said through gulps of air as she fought back sobs.

"What manufacturing facility?"

"The one"—gulp—"in Ch-Ch-China"—gulp—"with the fr-frosting."

"The Secret Special Whatever Frosting?"

"Yes," said my mother, and she began crying again in earnest.

"Anne!" her lawyer called. "You'd better come look at this."

I put my arm around my mother, something I couldn't ever remember doing, and walked her back into the living room.

CNN was showing the footage I'd seen earlier that morning, but with a different narration.

". . . Bake Like Anne Rye!, Inc. is under federal investigation for knowingly allowing a banned carcinogenic chemical additive to be used in the production of its frosting at a plant outside Beijing. . . ."

I looked at my mother, then at her lawyer, then at her business partner, then at Lilly, then at my mother again.

Everyone avoided my gaze.

". . . CNN has obtained copies of phone recordings that clearly indicate Anne Rye knew the chemical would be included in the first shipment, which is already being removed from the shelves at Target stores across the country. Target issued a statement, saying . . ."

"Why are they saying that?" I asked, looking around at everyone once again.

No one said anything.

"What's going on?" I asked again.

Nothing. Not a word, not a glance.

"Mom?" I looked at her.

"Anne," her lawyer said in a warning tone, but it didn't work.

"Well, it's not illegal in China!" she burst out. "They told me there was one study—one *little* study—that said it was dangerous. There are studies that say *Tylenol* is dangerous. Everyone said not to worry, so I didn't worry!"

I felt this freeze go through me, from my gut down to my

toes and then up to the top of my head. Like all the liquid inside me suddenly solidified into one cold block of Naomi.

"It's not illegal in China," she repeated, this time in a whisper.

I took my arm off her back and let it hang limply by my side.

"Those bastards sat on this till today," the business partner muttered, slamming his fist into his hand. "They sat on this so they could ruin our big day. Goddammit!"

My mother sank down into an overstuffed chair and buried her head in her hands. "This is going to *destroy* the magazine launch," she moaned. "And forget my next cookbook. I'm surprised they haven't called to cancel it already." As if on cue, Lilly's cell rang.

"I'm sure it's not them," Lilly said reassuringly before picking up the call. "Hello? You're with whom? *Us Weekly?* No, Ms. Rye is not interested in making a statement at this time." She hung up the phone.

"Oh, just say 'no comment!'" my mother snapped, stamping her foot like a child.

"Okay," Lilly said quickly. "I'll do that next time." The phone rang again, and she headed into the kitchen to pick it up. But we could all still hear her say, "Hello? With the *Times?* No comment. Goodbye."

"It'll be like this all day," the lawyer said evenly.

"I got a buddy, worked at BP during the spill," said the business partner. "He knows the guys who did PR for them. They're specialists at this kind of thing. We should look into it."

"All right," my mother said faintly. "I don't care how much they cost—let's get them."

I was almost out the door before she noticed me leaving.

"Naomi?" she called after me. "Naomi, where are you going? Naomi, I need you!"

I didn't say anything. I just let the door slam behind me. I got into the elevator and rode it down.

There's a bus that runs to the Hamptons. It's called the Jitney, and you can catch it at a few places in Manhattan. I looked up the schedule on my phone and found the nearest pickup location, about twenty blocks away. It would depart in forty minutes. I started walking.

My mind was kind of numb. It was full, I guess, with the equivalent of white noise. I systematically deleted each of my mother's texts as they came in—they were plaintive, then angry, then cold, then angry again, and finally whiny. I didn't pick up when she called. I deleted all four voice mails before listening to them.

Maybe it was coldhearted of me to leave her in her time of distress, even if the distress was of her own making. But I couldn't take it. I couldn't stand there and be supportive when I knew, just as well as I knew my own name, that she absolutely didn't give a damn about the people who might've eaten the frosting and gotten sick from it. What she cared about was her reputation, and her income, and whether this would affect her getting invited to Alec Baldwin's wife's charity auction.

I went into a corner bodega and grabbed some napkins from

the coffee counter. When I was back on the street, I wiped off the mascara and lip gloss and threw the napkins in the trash. I had to spit in the napkin to really get the mascara off, and I didn't care how gross I must've looked to passersby. I just wanted that stuff off my face.

I got to the Jitney stop early and sat down on a bench and called Skags.

"You okay?" she asked as soon as she picked up.

"So you heard."

"Of course I heard. It's all anyone's talking about on the cable news shows." Skags loved cable news shows so much, especially Chris Matthews, whose animated freak-outs always cracked her up. Not until Skags told me she knew about my mother's scandal did it hit me that everybody would soon know—my other friends at school, my teachers, and even people I didn't know. As if hearing my thoughts, Skags said, "This'll all die down soon. It's the twenty-four-hour news cycle. They *have* to find stuff to talk about. Tomorrow it'll be some hot blond chick who got kidnapped, or some celebrity in rehab, or something goofy the vice president said."

"I don't know, Skags," I said. "It's a federal investigation. This could, like, affect everything she does."

"Not to be a bitch," Skags said, which is exactly what someone says before they're about to be a bitch, "but your mom isn't Madonna. She's Anne Rye. You think anybody cares that Martha Stewart went to prison for a little while?"

"Oh my God," I said, so loudly that two little girls walking down the street turned and stared at me. "Do you think they'll send her to prison?"

"No idea," Skags said. "I'll ask Diana at dinner tonight."

"Who is Diana?"

"Jenny's mother. She's a lawyer."

"You're on a first-name basis with Jenny's *mother*?"

"She asked me to call her Diana," Skags said. "I'm amazing with parents. It's really quite impressive."

"I feel like nothing is normal anymore," I said.

"Normal is overrated," Skags said.

"Well, I could use more of it in my life," I said. "I'm coming home."

"When?"

"Tomorrow. The day after. I don't know. As soon as I can get a flight."

"You need to go to the cops before you leave," Skags said sternly. "Your mom will handle whatever she has to handle. You've got your own stuff to worry about. You have to tell the police."

"I know," I said. "I will. Tomorrow. I just—I can't handle it today. And Delilah might do the right thing."

"Yeah, right," Skags said. "This one's all on you, Naomi."

After we got off the phone, I tried to do some people watching from that bench on Fifth Avenue. Skags loves people watching. She can go to the park, sit down under a tree, and people-watch all day without getting bored. I'm not like that. I try to imagine what different strangers are like at work, at home, in the bedroom, but I just get distracted by my own thoughts. And my thoughts kept wandering back to Jacinta Trimalchio, or Adriana Whatever. It was like I didn't have room to think about my mom. Maybe I actually respected Jacinta more than my mother.

Just as I knew I "should" be on my mother's side no matter what, I knew I "should" despise Jacinta, or at least look down on her. But I didn't. I still liked her and I still respected her. Why?

I was noodling on this idea when my phone buzzed with an incoming text. It was from Jeff Byron.

*Please pick up,* it read. And then the phone rang.

I considered letting it go to voice mail, but instead I picked up.

"Thank you," Jeff said as soon as he heard the din of city noise.

"What's up?" I asked.

"I thought you would want to know that Delilah told her parents what happened," he said. "They're going down to the police station today to talk."

I was shocked.

"Are you serious?" I asked. "She told the truth?"

"Absolutely," he said. "So don't be surprised if you see squad cars next door tonight."

"At Jacinta's house? Why?"

"Why? Because she murdered someone with her car and kept driving, is why. She even hid the car in the woods near Delilah's house and made Delilah promise not to tell anybody.

She said she'd be sorry if she did. Can you believe that psycho?"

"But that's not true," I said with a trace of indignation that surprised even me. "That's not true. Delilah was driving. She and Jacinta switched places on the way home."

"Who told you that?"

"Jacinta!"

Jeff gave a dry, bitter little laugh. "Jesus, Naomi, she really got to you, didn't she? You're going to believe some crazy grifter over Delilah? You saw them leave. We all did. Jacinta was driving."

For a moment my head spun. Could Jeff be right? Maybe Jacinta had made up this story, too. It would make sense— she was already a liar about big and small things alike. Why wouldn't she lie about something this huge, something that could put her in prison for decades or even the rest of her life?

And then I thought about that morning, about the childlike hope in her eyes when she said that Delilah would probably want to spend the day at her house, and I knew she'd told me the truth. Maybe she'd lied about where she was from, where she went to school, and even her own name, but Jacinta Trimalchio had been honest about what happened last night. And that meant Delilah Fairweather was a liar—and a criminal.

I realized then that Jeff was still talking.

"I have to go," I said hurriedly, and hung up on him. Then I dialed Jacinta. She picked up on the first ring.

"Hello, love," she said, as if everything were perfectly normal.

"Listen to me," I said in a low voice. "Jeff just called and told me Delilah is going to the police with her parents. She's going to tell them you drove the car last night."

Jacinta was silent.

"I know you must be upset," I said. "I know this is hard. But you have to get a lawyer, and you have to go to the police yourself. You have to show them you're not guilty."

Jacinta's voice, when it came, was faint and exhausted.

"I can't afford a lawyer, Naomi."

"Sure you can," I said, even though I realized I didn't know what I was talking about. "You've got your trust fund, right?"

"It's done. Gone. I spent it all this year."

"You spent *all* of it?"

"My nose job in April. The house June through August. The parties. The car. The Birkins. Everything. It's gone."

I racked my brain desperately for an answer. "Well, they'll get you a public defender, then. If they even charge you! Which they might not, if you go to them before Delilah does. Tell your side of the story. Tell the truth. Show them you're not afraid."

Jacinta was silent again. I plunged onward.

"You can't give up!" I whispered, turning away from the older woman who had just sat down beside me on the bench. "You can't! I know you're sad. I know you're scared. I know you lied about a lot of stuff. You *can't* let her lie about this. They could put you away for life!"

"I know," Jacinta said, her voice so quiet I could barely make it out. "I know they could. I have to go now. Thank you for everything."

"No, just listen—" I pleaded, but she hung up.

Then it was my turn to call with no answer and text with no response.

I felt the dread and fear pool in the pit of my stomach. This was bad. This was very, very bad. Maybe I should go back to my mother's apartment and apologize—even if I didn't mean it—and try to get her to charter me a helicopter back to East Hampton so I could sit with Jacinta. She needed a friend right now. Well, she needed a lawyer, but if that wasn't possible, maybe a friend could help. Or maybe I could get her a lawyer! My mother's lawyer was undoubtedly still at the house—he might know somebody who would take Jacinta's case for free, or let her work out a payment plan or something. Anything. I just knew I needed to get to her as soon as I could, and the Jitney would take at least three hours if the traffic were all right.

Then the Jitney arrived, and I had to get on it. At this point, there was no way to tell if my mother would help me get back to the Hamptons. I couldn't risk *not* getting back there that day. If a slow bus was what I had to take, a slow bus was what I would take. So I got on the Jitney, and I found a seat by the window by myself, and I watched the sights and sounds of Manhattan blend into the sights and sounds of Queens, and then Long Island. I had my iPod on me, and I listened to a bunch of episodes of my favorite podcast, "Stuff You Missed in History Class." The hosts' voices provided the background noise I needed to keep some part of my brain busy.

By the time we reached East Hampton proper, I was utterly

nauseous. At first I blamed it on the bus ride, but I knew that the bus wasn't the problem. Because it wasn't just nausea that had me in its grip; it was fear.

I've spent a lot of my life, at least since I was about eleven or twelve, trying as hard as I could to be nothing like my mother. But when the Jitney dropped us off and I took one of the cabs waiting at the stop, I felt a kind of panic I'd never experienced before. My heart was beating very fast, and I was sweating buckets. My teeth were chattering, but I wasn't cold. I actually felt as if I were overheating. It was the most uncomfortable feeling in the world, and all I could think was, *I have to get to Jacinta's house. I have to get to Jacinta's house. Everything will be fine if I just get to Jacinta's house.*

I did what my mother's expensive, superstar private yoga teacher taught her to do: deep breathing. You breathe in for four, hold for seven, and then out for eight. You've got to get the breath down into your belly for it to work—at least, that's what the yoga teacher said. So I did it, and it helped. But it didn't stop the panic—it just made it more bearable.

The cab driver looked at me with concern.

"You okay?" he asked. I must've been as pale as Jacinta was on a normal day.

"I'm fine," I said, gritting my teeth. "Just a little tired."

When we drove down the street, I expected to see police cars parked in the driveway and Jacinta being led off in handcuffs, but that wasn't the case. In the late-afternoon sun, everything looked perfect. Not a blade of grass out of place. And the street was utterly quiet—no sound of lawn mowers buzzing or hedge clippers swishing, no groan of the weed whacker, no little kids out playing. Nothing. Perfect and complete quiet. And yet, I still couldn't fully relax. I rang Jacinta's bell several times, but I couldn't detect any movement inside the house. Maybe the police had already taken her in?

I walked into my house and kicked off my sandals. Upstairs, I ripped off my Marc Jacobs dress and threw it on the floor. I changed back into the outfit I'd worn on my trip from Chicago: the Cure T-shirt with a belt, the old Docs. It felt like slipping back into my real skin instead of the plastic facsimile I'd been wearing all summer long. I yanked my two suitcases out of the closet and started throwing clothes in as fast as I could. I left the Marc Jacobs dresses hanging in the closet, except for the one I'd tossed on the floor. All the while, my nerves jittered.

Immediately after I finished packing, I began to feel a little dizzy. I realized I hadn't eaten anything since Kix with Jacinta hours ago. It was five o'clock now. I went downstairs and made myself a BLT. I walked out onto the back deck to eat it, and that's when I saw something floating along the gentle current in Jacinta's river pool.

I couldn't have said what it was from where I stood, just that it was something that wasn't a raft or a pool toy. I could've just let it be, but my gut told me to investigate. I was about thirty yards from the pool when I dropped my sandwich and began to run.

And then I was there at the poolside, staring down at Jacinta's naked body floating facedown like a waterlogged angel.

I knew she was dead. I knew it the way I'd known I shouldn't leave her that morning. But I had to do something. Anything. I had to act.

And so I pulled her out of the water, her long, lean body topped by a soaking mess of white-blond hair. She was cold and limp, and even as I lay her down to begin CPR—something I'd learned in health class the previous year—I knew it wasn't going to work. There's the kind of dead from which you can bring someone back, when a heart stops for a brief collection of moments because of trauma or sickness, and you can shock it or pound it back to life. And then there's the kind of dead that's just final, from which there is no return, when the spirit or soul or whatever you want to call it has completely left the body. When you're alone with the body, you can feel the absence of something, some intangible presence that indicates person-hood. I was alone with Jacinta's body, breathing into her mouth, pumping her chest, but Jacinta wasn't there with me. Jacinta was gone.

And then I did something that still doesn't make sense to me.

I sat down next to her, cross-legged, and put her head in my lap. I stroked her hair and rocked back and forth gently, and I said, "It's okay. It's okay. It's okay." I didn't weep. I didn't scream. Over and over again, I told myself and the shell of my friend that it was okay. It was okay. It was okay.

That's when I saw the pink envelope lying in the grass.

It was addressed to me.

# CHAPTER TWELVE

They ask a lot of questions, police officers. Sometimes they ask questions that make sense, like how well did you know the deceased. And sometimes they ask questions that seem completely random, like what kind of sandwich were you eating, and where did you get it. I guess some of it is just them trying to make small talk, and some of it is them trying to figure out if you're telling the truth.

They showed up pretty quickly after I called them—three squad cars and an ambulance. The emergency workers ran over to Jacinta and tried to revive her, even though I'd said she was dead when I called 911. Maybe they were just following protocol. It seemed a little silly to me. But they didn't keep at it long. Pretty soon they stopped and got out a body bag, started doing paperwork. You could tell they'd seen this sort of thing before.

I didn't cry, not then. I was numb. The thought crossed my

mind that I ought to tell them about Delilah Fairweather, that she was the girl driving the car last night, not Jacinta. But I didn't say it. I don't know why.

I told them what they wanted to hear. I did not tell them about the pink envelope. I'd hidden that in my boot even before I called 911. It was for me, anyway, not for them. If Jacinta had wanted to say anything to them before she killed herself, she would have called them. But she hadn't, of course, and instead waited for Delilah to do the right thing.

The cops said I could go home, and that's when Jeff Byron pulled up. He got out of the car and ran toward me, and he tried to say something to me, but I wouldn't listen. I felt nothing but revulsion when he grabbed my arm. I shook off his hand like it was burning hot. I think he was going to follow me across the lawn, but one of the cops said something to him quietly, and Jeff just stood there and watched me go. I could feel his eyes boring into my back as I opened the sliding glass door to the kitchen and shut it behind me. It was nearly dark outside now.

I stood in the front room, looking through the window and watching as the ambulance pulled away, Jacinta's body stowed in the back. The cops followed. Jeff stood by his car for a long moment, staring at the house, before getting in and driving off. That's when my cell phone rang.

It was my mother.

I picked up. I picked up because I'd forgotten I wasn't talking to her, and because it seemed like the normal and proper response to one's phone ringing. It rings, you answer. That's how it works. I went through the motions as if I were a machine set to automatic mode.

"Hello?" I said. It sounded to me as if my voice were coming from very far away.

"Darling!" my mother chirped. Her voice betrayed not a hint of sadness or remorse.

"Mom?"

"Yes, it's Mom, sweetie. You have been so tough to reach today!"

"Oh," I said. I had the feeling that if I were up to having normal emotions, I'd be confused. Instead I just listened.

"You know, about earlier today—I don't want you to worry one bit. It's not going to affect anything. We've already got my lawyer working on it, and today I met with the most amazing PR man who is going to fix this mess. I may have to sue a few parties in the process, but that's all right. What's important to me is that *you* know *I'm* fine." She was jabbering away at a mile a minute.

"I'm going home, Mom." My voice sounded faint in my own ears.

She missed a beat then.

"You're w-what?" she asked.

"I'm going home. To Chicago. Tomorrow. I'm going to buy a ticket online. I'll have a shuttle service bring me to the airport." I said it all mechanically.

"But, darling, you're still here for another two weeks!" she said. "Surely you want to spend more time with your friends."

I was silent for so long that she finally said, "Well—I'm not coming back tonight, so I won't get to say goodbye to you. I want to say goodbye. Don't you?"

"Goodbye, Mom," I said, and hung up.

She didn't call or text back.

I called my dad, even though I knew he was probably at a game with his summer league team. He didn't pick up his cell, but the sound of his voice on his outgoing message made me tear up. I still didn't feel anything, exactly, but my eyes got wet all the same.

"I'm coming home, Daddy," I said hoarsely, after the beep. "Tomorrow. I'll see you soon." And that was it.

I ran a bath and poured some bubbles in. I stripped off all my clothes and stepped into it. It felt like I imagine a womb would, warm and safe. My shoulders dropped a little, and I let out a ragged sigh, and opened Jacinta's envelope.

The note had a URL and a password. It also contained other things—passwords and certain instructions—but she'd drawn big arrows pointing to the URL and password, so I figured that was the most important part. I got out of the bath just as soon as I'd gotten in, wrapped my wet body in a towel, and went to my laptop. The URL led to a website, Vimeo, with a password-protected video. My fingers shaking, I typed in the password and hit enter.

The video was nothing fancy. Jacinta had clearly shot it on her Web cam earlier that day. She'd put on one of her fabulously weird outfits, pinned her hair up at odd angles, and done her makeup to perfection. She looked, as always, like a stunning alien visitor to Earth. And she told her story, straight to the camera.

"I want you to know that while I've lied about plenty of things in the past couple of months, everything I'm about to tell you is a hundred percent true.

"I'm Jacinta Trimalchio, but my real name is Adriana DeStefano. I was born on Staten Island. My father was a weapons contractor; my mother was a housewife. When I was little, my father got a big contract to provide body armor to the US government. We made a lot of money. We moved to the Upper East Side, and they enrolled me in Little Trumbo, Trumbo Academy's elementary school. That's where I met Delilah Fairweather.

"We loved each other right away. We were best friends, but we were always something more, something bigger than friendship. When I couldn't see her for a day, I cried. When she couldn't see me, she threw tantrums so bad her mother would call my mother in desperation and ask when our next playdate could be. We were a part of each other, Delilah and me. We were intertwined. She was a year younger, but we used to tell people we were twins. We said we were going to marry brothers and live in the same house.

"When I was eleven and Delilah was ten, my father was indicted on federal charges. The court found that he had knowingly and deliberately sold faulty body armor to the government, and that it had been used in the wars in Iraq and Afghanistan and had resulted in injuries and deaths. My father had blood on his hands, the papers said. The news cameras camped outside our building all day and all night. They followed my mother when she brought me to school. We couldn't go anywhere. We couldn't do anything. And nobody would talk to us. In school, Delilah would look at me with these big, sad blue eyes, but she wouldn't speak. I knew it wasn't her fault. I knew her mother had told her not to talk to me. But it cut my heart.

"They took everything—the apartment in the city, the cars, the beach house in East Hampton, and all the money, everything but my trust fund. They sent my father to prison for a long, long time. He killed himself there, right away—hung himself with his bed sheets. We had nothing left. His family came to the funeral, but none of my mother's family, none of my friends. Nobody even called.

"We moved to Florida. It was supposed to be temporary. My grandparents gave my mom some starter money, and she rented a one-bedroom apartment. I slept on the couch. She got a job as a cocktail waitress. She met a guy there. Soon he was my stepdad. He hit me when he was drunk. I told her, and she hit me, too. She said I was trying to ruin the only good thing in her life. She sent me to live with my grandparents in their retirement village. About a year later, her husband was arrested and put in prison for assaulting a man at a bar. My mother didn't apologize, but she asked me to come back home. I went.

"Divorced and down to one income again, my mother quit the restaurant and started dancing at a place up the road. She'd done ballet in high school. But then she'd married my father and had never worked a job until we'd moved to Florida. Anyway, she was a good dancer and got a lot of feature spots and made a lot of money. She would come home with big, fat rolls of cash. Sometimes she'd come home with customers, too. Once she brought two of them home at two in the morning, and I left the house so I couldn't hear the noises they made.

"Ever since we'd moved to Florida, I'd kept track of what my old friends were doing. They were all on Facebook, and none of them locked down their profiles, so it was easy. I knew they wouldn't accept a friend request from Adriana DeStefano, so I made up a name and made a fake profile. Except eventually it became my real profile, because I liked the fake name so much that I started using it on the fashion blog I made to distract me from everything else in my life.

"I didn't have many friends at school except for this one kid, Alexander. Alexander was the only out gay kid in eighth grade. We used to dress each other up like we were dolls, with makeup and hairstyles and everything. The rule was that you couldn't peek at what was being done to you until the look was totally complete. We always took before and after photos. Alexander and I read fashion magazines like they were our bibles, and I spent all my free time on style blogs, so that meant I could identify practically anybody's clothes and say who designed them.

"And that's pretty much what led to me starting *The Wanted*. At first it was just a daily record of what I was wearing from the neck down. But then it turned into a way for me to keep in touch with people from Trumbo, even though they didn't know they were keeping in touch with me. I started copying and pasting their photos from their parties. And then they'd come to the page and see it and share it with their friends and their friends' friends, and pretty soon kids from other schools started sending me photos from their parties, and at some point newspaper and magazine writers took notice, and the serious fashion world, too. It was the first time in my life anyone noticed me for something I did on my own. It changed my life.

"The whole time, I followed Delilah Fairweather's life. She grew up to be just as beautiful and as wonderful as I knew she would when we were little. I always knew she would be a star. And I always knew what I would do when I turned eighteen and got my trust fund: Find a way back to her. Find a way back to us.

"As soon as I got my money, I left Florida behind and rented my house and my car and my new life. I went shopping for everything I should've had, everything I could've had if my father hadn't been a criminal.

"It was the best summer I could've asked for. We were everything I wished we could've been, and more. We were in love. Real love. And when the accident happened, I thought Delilah would do the right thing and tell the police the truth: that she was the one who drove the car that killed Misti. It was partly my fault, too—I shouldn't have let her drive. She said it would calm her down, so we pulled over by the side of Route 27 and we switched.

"I want everybody to know I don't think it was her fault. She was scared and sad and yeah, she'd been drinking, but she wasn't *super*-drunk. She was maybe a little tipsy. If anyone is still looking for the car, it's in the woods near the Fairweathers' house. Delilah knew where to hide it. I know now that she told the police I was driving. She's not a bad person. She's the best person I know. She really is. I wish you could know her the way I know her.

"Anyway. That's the story. That's all of it. And I want you to know that I'm sorry for everybody I hurt, for everybody I deceived. It's not what I wanted. It's not what I meant to do.

"I'm sorry. I'm sorry. I'm so, so sorry."

And that was the end of the video.

I looked down at Jacinta's note and saw that it was spotted with something wet. Then I touched my face. I'd been crying. I'd been crying and I hadn't even noticed.

I read the rest of the note. And now I knew exactly what I had to do.

# CHAPTER THIRTEEN

Very early the next morning, I waited at the end of the driveway for the passenger van to pick me up. It wasn't as fancy as a chartered helicopter or as private as a town car, but it was cheap and would get me to JFK.

A black BMW convertible with the top up rolled down the wrong side of our street. It had tinted windows, and if it belonged to any of the neighbors, I'd never noticed it before. It came to a stop right in front of me. Slowly, the driver's side window rolled down, and I found myself face-to-face with Teddy Barrington.

"Hey, Naomi," he said.

I stared into the distance, not saying a word.

"Naomi, I'm sorry about what's happening with your mother," he said, just as if this were a normal conversation under completely normal circumstances, just as if I weren't making a studious effort to ignore him.

He paused to see if his offer of sympathy would elicit any response from me. I gave him none.

"Years ago," he continued, "my father almost got nailed with some insider trading bullshit. Some asshole prosecutor was trying to punish successful people so he could win points in the press. Dad beat it, though. So will your mother."

I sighed loudly and turned my back to him. It was probably the rudest thing I'd ever done. And it really threw him for a loop, too. I don't think Teddy Barrington, ex–child star and scion of one of America's wealthiest families, was particularly used to being ignored.

"Naomi," he said in a pleading tone. "You can't still be upset about the other night."

I whirled on him then.

"You mean the night your girlfriend murdered your other girlfriend? The night you're helping her lie about? That night?"

Teddy's eyes flashed with anger. "It was an accident," he said. "If you didn't listen to that psycho so much, you wouldn't—"

"Her name was Adriana DeStefano," I said. "And you can go to hell."

Something truly unexpected happened then. Teddy's handsome brown eyes filled with tears. They were angry tears, but they were tears nonetheless. He looked like the world's tallest toddler. I stared at him in disgust until he rolled the window back up and screeched off.

The passenger van came not long after. I'm not a fan of being in close proximity to strangers, but it couldn't be helped. I muttered an unenthusiastic hello to the other people in the van and squished in between the window and a woman with skin pulled so tight across her face you could practically see every single contour of her skull. She had a companion, a friend with similarly bad plastic surgery.

"That's the suicide house," murmured Skull #1 to Skull #2.

I glared at both of them with such undisguised hatred I'm surprised their fake skin didn't melt.

I put my earbuds in and listened to my iPod on shuffle. When we got to the Shinnecock Canal, the only point on the trip with a momentary view of the ocean, Bill Withers's "Ain't No Sunshine" started playing. I stared at the distant waves and thought of Jacinta and Adriana. I'd barely known them, but somehow, I missed them both.

# CHAPTER FOURTEEN

Holed up in a corner of Alan's Coffee Shop, I hit refresh on the site over and over again. It was only 11:58, and I hadn't set it to update until noon, but I was growing impatient. It had been a day since I'd arrived home in Chicago, and I'd done everything Jacinta had wanted. But I wanted to *see* it to know it was real.

I drank my double espresso and felt increasingly irritated. I guess caffeine doesn't really help you stay cool, calm, and collected in situations like that, but Alan's makes the best espresso in the world. And since I hadn't gotten much sleep the night before, I needed it.

11:59. God, this was taking *forever.* I drummed my fingers on the communal tabletop, earning myself a sneer from the girl sitting across from me. I shot her a tight, insincere smile, which is how Midwesterners say "I hate you" to strangers.

And then finally—*finally*—finally it was noon, and I could see the results of my handiwork.

I hit refresh again, and this time the front page of TheWanted.com updated with a post labeled "THE TRUTH." In the post, I'd embedded the video Jacinta had made—only this time it was public and accessible to everyone, just as she'd wanted. And that meant it was also automatically on *The Wanted*'s Twitter page (200,000 followers) and Facebook page (250,000 fans).

I hit refresh again and looked at the Twitter and Facebook widgets on the post. At first it had been tweeted and liked zero times. Within five minutes, the tweet count went up to 10, 20, 35, 50. The Facebook likes climbed similarly from nothing to dozens. As the minutes passed, both counts got higher and higher, reaching the triple digits within the hour. And the comments rolled in, one after another, also numbering in the hundreds within sixty minutes. I sat in that coffee shop all day, hitting refresh, reading the comments, the tweets, the Facebook posts. Other blogs picked it up, big ones—major gossip blogs, even a few big news sites. There was no question about it: Jacinta Trimalchio's final act had gone viral almost as soon as it had appeared online.

As for what happened now—well, it was out of my hands. I'd done my job. I'd done right by Jacinta, something so few people had done in her short life.

I think I sat there for five hours before a breathless Skags banged into the place. She always did make a noisy entrance.

She was holding hands with Jenny Carpenter, who looked at me with shy eyes.

"Naomi!" Skags shouted, earning her the ire of nearly every other customer of the coffee shop (including my across-the-table neighbor). "Where the hell have you been? I've been trying to get a hold of you all day!"

I turned around and said, "Well, hello to you, too."

"It's discount day at the record shop!" Skags said. "They've got a mint-condition bootleg of Liz Phair's Girly-Sound songs. They said they'd only hold it for us for an hour. C'mon, we'll split it!"

"Hi, Jenny," I said.

She looked at me timidly.

"Hi, Naomi," she said.

"You know she gets like this every single Monday, right?" I said. "Every Monday is discount day at the record shop."

"I know," Jenny said, and we shared a smile. Skags rolled her eyes.

"Enough with the femme bonding," she said. "If we don't get there within ten minutes, they're gonna sell it to somebody else and my life will be freaking *over*. Naomi, get off your dumb computer and live in the real world."

I took one last look at *The Wanted*. The hit counter on the post was through the roof.

"Okay," I said, and shut my laptop. Then I shoved it in my shoulder bag and followed my best friend and her girlfriend out into the late-summer sunshine.